THE WHITE JAGUAR

"A riveting read."

— Alex Shoumatoff *The New Yorker*

"Comprehensive plot . . . highly atmospheric thriller."

— *Publishers Weekly*

"Vividness in the evocation of the Amazon milieu . . . lively . . . atmospheric."

— *Kirkus Reviews*

"Take this novel to the beach and settle into the Amazon jungle with a German coke tyrant."

— *Playboy*

"Exotic . . . exciting . . . surprising and well-paced read. Its characters have appeal and the theme is exciting. If you are a fan of Graham Green, you will probably enjoy this adventure immensely."

—*South Bend (IN.) Tribune*

"An exciting story — exotic setting, beautiful women, diabolical villain."

— *Baton Rouge (LA.) Advocate*

"THE WHITE JAGUAR is a novel worthy of its namesake — exotic, exciting, extraordinary!"

— Robert Bloch, author *Psycho*

THE WHITE JAGUAR

William Appel

PaperJacks LTD.

TORONTO   NEW YORK

PaperJacks

THE WHITE JAGUAR

PaperJacks LTD.

330 STEELCASE RD. E., MARKHAM, ONT. L3R 2M1
210 FIFTH AVE., NEW YORK, N.Y. 10010

Richardson & Steirman edition published 1985

PaperJacks edition published November 1986

This is a work of fiction in its entirety. Any resemblance to actual people, places or events is purely coincidental.

CDN ISBN 0-7701-0571-8
US ISBN 0-7701-0493-2

Printed in the U.S.A.

THE WHITE JAGUAR

Also by William Appel:

**WATER WORLD
THE WATCHER WITHIN**

Acknowledgements

A special thanks to Richard Brill of Amazon Explorers whose invaluable contribution of research was omitted from the hardcover edition. And to my special friend and colleague Sandra Berkley for her help with this edition. Also many thanks to Tony Seidl, Chris Kingsley, Nancy Parent, Jim Connor, Colleen Dimson and Nancy Ehrman for their terrific support and enthusiasm.

Dedication

To my mother and father, Rose and Jack Appel. And to my best friend, Michelle.

On the road to vengeance . . .
one discovers life

André Malraux
Man's Fate

Part I

Chapter One

The woman the natives called Little Bird slowed her Land Rover as she passed the open-air market of Puerto Porqueño. Ava was a blonde in her late thirties. Her features held an underlayer of melancholy, of life lived to its depths. When she listened she excluded everything else; her expression was beguiling by virtue of some deep, indestructible optimism and decency.

To her right a group of tourists moved toward a cruise ship moored at the dock a hundred yards away. Scandinavians or Germans, she thought, from the look of them. Many were boldly carrying jaguar skins over their arms.

The obviously smuggled skins reminded her of what she had just found out about the snake farm where she worked. She had known for some time that something strange was going on. Many more snakes were moved in and out to the airport than any venom business required. And too many of the reptiles were anacondas, which had no venom. She had discovered that the farm was owned by Karl Buchreiser — the cocaine king called the White Jaguar — and now she knew they were smuggling cocaine out with the snakes.

Despite being bathed in the sweat that refused to evaporate in the humidity of Western Amazonia, she was suddenly seized by a chill. She looked quickly around her, as though someone might be reading her mind.

For an instant she thought she saw, in the wave of shimmering heat rising from the road, the savage face of a man. She had seen him yesterday too, and believed he might know what she had discovered about the snakes. He smelled of smoke and earth; his huge hands were gnarled as the roots of a *samauma* tree. His strange eyes were the color of rain. Sweat dripped down between her breasts. *Easy now*, she thought.

The clay road was bordered by leaves and ferns as tall as men. Buried deep in the underbrush on moss-covered logs grew red and yellow mushrooms so delicate they disintegrated when touched. How she longed to stop the Rover and admire them.

Once again she considered telling the police what she had discovered about the snake farm and her boss, Gus Coufos. But how could she know which of them was not on Gus's payroll? Gus had been in Puerto Porqueño thirteen years, and she, barely two and a half. He had contacts in high places, whereas she had always been drawn to the common people. He was a successful businessman who employed a lot of locals; she was just a poor ex-Peace Corps worker. Ava had turned her attention back to the road when she was startled by a loud metallic sound behind her. She heard herself screech in alarm as her right foot slammed on the brake. She turned around. An empty aluminum box had fallen with a clatter from the back seat onto the metal floor. She began to breathe normally again.

Jumpy, Ava turned off the engine. She took a few deep breaths, and let them out slowly. She sat there, listening. In the canopy of trees overhead, she saw howler monkeys that had become paralyzed from terror by her screeching. Screeching, she knew, was a method hunters used to make them easy targets. She turned the ignition back on and sped away in the Rover.

In moments, Ava was parked at the Colonial, one of the first hotels built in Puerto Porqueño. She knew there was a phone booth in the women's room. As she walked, her body had the jerky, lightweight uncertainty of a sparrow on the ground.

In the Colonial's outdoor café, prosperous-looking, well-dressed men in razor-creased pants, silk shirts, and straw Stetsons kept leather bags clutched tightly to their sides. Most of them, she knew, were smugglers. They sat drinking and talking while boys shined their shoes.

Once inside, she waited until the single telephone booth was free, and dialed the overseas operator. She checked her watch: 2:45 P.M. Colombia time and New York time were the same. Her older brother Mike, who managed investment portfolios from an office in his brownstone, would probably still be working, because the stock exchanges hadn't closed yet. It was dangerous to speak about what she had discovered over the phone, so she would simply ask him if he'd received the tapes yet.

He was not at home.

"Thanks," she said to the operator. She would try later, but she wanted to leave a message with his answering service. It was the second message today.

The sun was still high when she left the hotel. As she climbed into the Land Rover, she thought she saw the man with rain-colored eyes drive his jeep out from behind the hotel. When the driver turned his head, she saw that it was someone else, and breathed deeply with relief.

Putting the Rover in gear, she resolved to go deeper into the jungle. No one would look for her there. She could think. And she could plan her next move.

When Ava reached the tall trees, she parked the Rover out of sight of the road. Climbing out, she spotted a lizard crawling over a stone. For an instant the little creature stared at her with lidless eyes, then scampered away. Ava remembered how the warmth of a stone could fill her with a soft laziness that would melt away her anger or fear or weariness. She realized how much she loved this place.

While monkeys howled overhead, she wondered how long it had taken her to be able to distinguish, amid all the other shades of green, the lighter, almost translucent green of the plantain fronds in front of her. She sat under a giant yellow flowered *berruco* tree whose branches were as thick as the trunks of beech trees. The troop of howlers had passed, and in the windless silence she imagined she could even hear beetles sucking sap from the nearby tender shoots.

Tall tree trunks stood like columns of smoke in the surrounding humid mist, pierced by sparkling shafts of sunlight searing through the leafy canopy.

She strolled toward the river, where turtles basked on mired logs. Her clothes clung to her like slime,and as she continued, she plucked layers of spiderwebs that smelled of decay from her face. Still, physical discomfort could not dispel the magic of this place. Vast interwoven roots emerged from the earth like sculptures of wood and mud. The late afternoon sun tinted the river till it shone like a golden flame reflecting infinite shades of green. Ava lost herself in an immensity which seemed on the edge of time and space. She knew, then, why she hadn't been able to leave this place, despite the heat and the mud and the insects and the disease and the darkness so black that it felt furry and damp against her face. The Indians often said of whites who could not leave: *They have lost their souls in the forest.* The Indians were wrong, at least in her case. She had found her soul here. It had been like choosing to stay shipwrecked.

The river, which had been glowing like melted butter, was suddenly dark. Ava lifted her head and saw that the sun had already begun to edge below the trees. In an instant it was night. Glowworms lit up the darkness like circles of fire. Monkeys with phosphorescent eyes darted from behind ferns, peering at her.

When she returned to her Rover, a white fog seemed to be rising from the ground, and she didn't see the man who darted behind the tree. Suddenly she heard the howlers fleeing overhead. She had an almost overpowering urge to empty her bladder. Instead, she pushed her fist into the pit of her stomach. Starting to breathe again, she slowly pulled a dagger from her waistband.

Chapter Two

As Michael Rush went through his daily exercises, thoughts of Ava kept flitting into his mind. He hadn't spoken to her in two weeks, and every time he had tried to telephone her at work or at home she was not there, despite the fact that she had left him messages.

Had the natives of Puerto Porqueño seen Michael Rush, not one of them would have guessed that he was Ava's brother. His hair and moustache were brown and wavy. Ava's hair was straight and blonde. His dark complexion came from their father. Ava's fair skin came from their mother. Compared with his birdlike, slight, and uncertain-looking sister, Michael occupied his six-foot-two-inch frame with ease and confidence. Yet in Michael's fortyish, craggy face, especially in his heavy-lidded brown eyes, was the same undertone of melancholy, of life lived intensely. He shared her indestructible decency also, but not her innate optimism. In its place was neither pessimism nor cynicism, but an uncomplicated acceptance of reality. Curiously, his expression and his manner suggested a man who was unfinished.

He arranged himself on all fours and raised his knee in the classic position of a male dog urinating. He felt a tightening in his hamstring as he accidentally kicked the rosewood Ming coffee table. He needed to empty his mind of Ava and relax. Trying to do so, Michael stared out through the French doors that opened to a terrace where he could see snowflakes drifting like goosedown in the late afternoon air currents. The snow had already whitened the garden.

When snow came to Greenwich Village, it gave Michael the feeling that he was in the Manhattan of the nineteenth century. He could imagine horses' hooves in the snow. He felt sure the sight would have delighted him, that life would have been simpler in those olden days. He loved the view in the spring when a small waterfall trickled over the stones in his rock garden.

He looked at the room with its thirteen-foot-high coffered ceiling and original moldings. The patina of the walnut paneling gleamed rosily. Firelight reflected on crystal decanters on a sterling tray. A spotlight shone on the leaves of the six-foot-high Rafus palm planted in a 2,100-year-old Chinese porcelain pot. It was the kind of room that could cure a headache. He remembered a comforting feeling he'd had one morning months ago while running his hand over the glazed mahogany baluster of the main staircase, heavy as a bedpost. This same setting that predated him by a century would outlast the brief diversion called his life.

Despite all the strong, elegant, masculine tones of the house, there remained something elusive about it. More accurately, something of the owner was left out of its rooms. The house was as impersonal as a stage setting.

His head between his knees now, Michael thought of the way his sister had always held her head high. Without warning his thoughts reeled back to their last telephone conversation.

"Call me collect, once a week," he had said.

"There's nothing to worry about."

"You're right," he said. "I'm just paranoid. Never mind that you handle lethal snakes all day long in a place filled with malaria, hepatitis, TB, leprosy — not to mention hostile Indians. Why the hell couldn't you pick a safer place?"

"Because, Mikey, as I've told you twenty times, I'm needed by the Indians. Besides, every day I'm closer to finding a cure for arthritic pain, using the venom of a snake found only in the Amazon. Remember, I'm a herpetologist, not an adventurer. So stop playing big brother."

During her last visit, Ava, leaning against the black marble of the fireplace, had glanced up at his favorite Turner oil, *The Lighthouse*. Then she turned back to him, playfully and teasingly calling the house Tara of the West Village.

Michael's extensive collection of hand-carved antique pipes was displayed on an English hunting table. He remembered an article Ava has sent him months ago after he had written her that he enjoyed antiquing. In the article, the author theorized that the increased popularity of antique collecting in America was a yearning for a time when values meant something and people's roles were more secure in their world. Michael replied that Freudian approaches were overused, adding that the practice of amateur analysis was dangerous.

Looking at the room, he saw it through Ava's eyes: the desk, the Persian rug, the French grandfather clock. This wasn't the relationship he thought they would end up with. He was supposed to be the guy in the white hat, Ava the village schoolmarm. Instead, he dealt with wealthy cattle barons, and she was helping the poor homesteaders.

As he continued his workout, the snow turned to hail. He could hear it striking the French doors. Thoughts of Ava crept into his consciousness again.

He remembered one snowy day three years ago when she had been in New York. They had gone to visit his partner, Ben Aliza, at his new ski lodge in Stratton, Vermont. One the way home the hail had come down so hard that Michael had to pull off to the side of the road.

"Do you," Ava began, "think a lot . . ."

"— talk louder, the hail . . ."

"Do you think a lot about Mom and Papa?"

"Sometimes."

"Every time I end a relationship with a man, I think of them."

The yellow rain slicker and matching hat she wore and her shiny face reminded him of the girl she had once been.

"How do you mean?" he said.

"I mean sometimes after an affair, even if I'm glad it's over, there's this terrible void. You know?"

"I know."

"Well, sometimes when the pain is awful, I think maybe Mom and Papa were right."

"You mean right to have the kind of marriage where you stay together no matter what?"

"Not no matter what, but with fewer expectations than people have today — even than I have. Fulfilling one's roles gives a relationship a plan and meaning so that you don't need intimacy. I know they loved each other; I don't mean they didn't."

"I know what you mean. I also think that when

Mom nearly died of pneumonia, Papa got really scared. I think he appreciated her more after that."

"Appreciated what a slave he had. I'm sorry, Mikey, I know he got that from growing up in a peasant European background." Her expression grew mischievous. "Do you think she ever had an orgasm?"

"I'm not so sure *he* did."

They both laughed.

"Wouldn't it be hysterical if Mom really had multiple orgasms and Papa was a stud?" she said.

They laughed again.

"Would you believe that I'm a grown woman and I still can't picture them making love?"

"Neither can I."

The very next afternoon, the mailman delivered a small, square package containing several audio tapes from Ava.

Chapter Three

Ava felt the blade wrenched from her grip by hands so inhumanly powerful they seemed mechanical. A man's fleshy, callused hand tightened around her neck. It smelled of tobacco and sweat, and his sour breath scalded her ear.

The sudden movement had startled the birds. Thousands of them, big and small, shook the branches overhead and alerted roosting turkey vultures, who flew from the treetops.

She kicked and fought and bit his arm till the handkerchief, reeking with chloroform, pressed against her face.

When she woke moments later, her hands and feet were tied with lianas. One of her sandals was gone, the right shoulder of her peasant blouse was torn. What she saw next made her scream and then bite a piece of flesh out of the inside of her cheek. The man was filling a hypodermic.

He gagged her with a ball of plantain fronds. She screamed into the fronds. When he lifted the needle, she didn't even feel the sudden gush of urine that streamed down her leg. At first she waited, praying that it was only a placebo to frighten her into succumbing to rape. Then she prayed he was only going to rape her. Finally, when she felt the great rush of fullness in her head and chest, she prayed that the injection had been diluted enough so she might live.

Her heart accelerated, then slowed, then seemed to stop completely. Her lungs were incapable of supplying her need for more air. The starlight intensified, as did the sounds of the jungle. Great waves of heat were replaced by sudden drafts of glacial cold. Her fingertips and toes and lips grew numb. Both ears popped simultaneously, and her head felt as if it were exploding. A tremor shook her lips. A slight twinge at the back of her neck swelled into a general, diffused headache. She felt icy, and tremors shook her body.

I'm flying all apart, she thought. At the same time, her chest constricted even more tightly.

She closed her eyes, and the colors dazzled her. She soared. When she opened her eyes, the man had shrunk till he was no bigger than a rat.

Where the moon shone, leaves on the trees had turned as bright as fresh green paint. The sky fell on her, and the earth rose from below, and she was sent soaring to meet them. Then the river turned green; it stopped and flowed backward.

She sat, desolate, under the risen sky.

Ooogn! Ooogn! Ooogn! Her whole body trembled with the howling from above. The monkeys' music was multi-colored and solid; she could break off bits of the notes like pieces of glass.

A crack appeared in the earth beneath where she sat, growing larger and larger. Soon she knew, she would fall into the chasm.

The eyes of a glowworm pinned her in a spotlight so brilliant it hurt. Suddenly she was sucked into the yawning crack — whirling rapidly down through bursting vaults of color and sound. Her body, loose as a dead snake, seemed to drift. Once, twice, the abyss closed and she was propelled back into air and onto firm ground. But the *Ooogn! Ooogn! Ooogn!* broke into pieces of glass again as she repeated her head-long descent. Taking a breath hurt horribly.

Then she found herself laughing at a preposterous parade of peccaries, macaws, sloths, and manatees, playing flutes, tubas, and drums. Even as she laughed, the musical medley surrounded and swallowed her. If only she could stop laughing, she knew she'd have a chance. But she couldn't. Her mouth filled, and then she was swallowing the entire parade of creatures and then the glowworms, and finally, the night itself rushed into the void within her.

A great wind flicked her up like a grain of pollen, and whirled her inert body into oblivion. Finally there was nothing to hang on to, no feeling, no thought.

Ava's murderer picked up the gag that had fallen from her mouth, untied the lianas, and stuffed them into his pockets. He wiped his prints from the syringe and placed it in her dead fingers.

From across the river came the vibrating metal clang of a bellbird sounding as if the creature were appalled at what had just happened. Its peals echoed through the ancient trees, then vanished as the lizard on the stone had.

The next day, the mist did not lift till quite late, as if the sun was reluctant to divulge what had happened in the forest.

Chapter Four

When Michael saw the package the mailman had set on the black lacquered Chinese dining room table, he let out a great sigh of relief. He would chastise Ava for not having gotten in touch sooner. He hoped she hadn't spent too much of her meager salary on what was obviously his Christmas gift.

"Mike, are you busy? I want you to read your interview in the new *Financial World!*"

The booming voice belonged to Ben Aliza, Michael Rush's business partner, who had come out of the office they shared on the ground floor of the house. Michael spotted the copy of the magazine under Ben's arm and saw the excitement in his bright blue eyes. They were blue in a way which — unless you knew him — made it impossible for you to tell whether it was a blueness of surface or blueness of depth. Ben still looked like an offensive end: six foot two, wide shoulders funneling down to a narrow waist, and big spatulate hands. His haircut made him seem like a gray-haired boy in a magazine ad for a football camp. Ben had been on vacation in Mexico. His skin was leathery brown. He smelled of expensive aftershave. Except for the tiny pouches under his eyes, his expression was as youthful as it had been in high school before time had etched on his face the lines that made him original. It was a comfort to Michael that in a world with so much change, Ben stayed the same. He kept Michael grounded. He often wished he could be more like Ben, who rarely permitted life to make him melancholy.

Michael smiled, and with his hand on Ben's big shoulder, he followed his partner into the office off the foyer. He preferred to open Ava's gifts in private, anyway.

Ben gently pushed Michael into a chair and raised his feet onto his desk. Michael felt touched because his old friend found it so hard to express intimacy of any kind.

"I let Kathy go home a little early and put the answering service on," Ben said. Kathy was their secretary. "Now you and I can have a little celebration."

Ben reached into the liquor cabinet behind his desk. Built into the wall behind his and Michael's desks was a television set running the New York

Stock Exchange tape. Ben picked up a crystal decanter and began fixing their drinks.

The walls were lined with bookshelves filled with gilt-edged leather volumes with silk bookmarks. In black frames hung testimonial plaques commemorating Michael's civic and charitable achievements. Photographs showed Ben shaking hands with Joe Namath, Johnny Carson, Paul Newman, and other celebrities. The place had the pleasant smell of the reading room of an English club: furniture polish, leather, and books. Firelight glimmered on the brass pulls of the massive Tudor desks.

"To the Dow at two thousand," Ben said, handing him a Baccarat tumbler. "And to the best analyst on the whole fucking Street."

"To friendship," Michael said and drank deeply. They had first become friends on the football squad at Roosevelt High in Brooklyn twenty-five years ago. They had joined the SDS together in college and had taken a training course given by the Weathermen in urban guerrilla warfare.

Michael, expelled from college for his political activism, went back to school nights and worked days to support himself and his wife. Then he joined Bache as a research analyst. It allowed him independence. He was immune from corporate politics. He soon became the *wunderkind* of the Street. When Michael suggested to Ben that he would do well selling stocks and bonds, Ben had joined Bache as a trainee in the

institutional department. He was soon a top sales-
man.

One night over dinner eight years ago, they decided
to merge their complementary talents into a business
of their own.

Now Ben excused himself to use the john.

What joy, Michael thought, *if my parents could have
seen my name in* Financial World. He also wished
they could have seen his office, and shared in the joy
of his success.

Financial World *is not the* Post, he said to himself.
His mind went back to the Corner Shop on Avenue M.

Four-thirty A.M., the sound of snow falling upon
snow, and his mother was shivering and bent from
having dragged in the heavy snow-covered cases of
milk bottles. She knelt to light the coffee urns, and
her varicosed legs struck him as fresh wounds would
have. His father, panting and grunting, dragged in
the wet shovel. Even the hairs in his nose were white
with snow.

"Careful with those magazines, Mikey," his father
said. "The *Financial World* is not the *Post*. Rip it and
you rip their Bible."

Their Bible. Even at twelve, he knew *They* were
people his parents could never be, and that they were
gambling all their strength each day so that their two
children could be like *Them*. *They* — the very rich,

whose lives were like movies starring Cary Grant and Carole Lombard.

Could he ever banish seeing his success darkened by shadows from the past? Often his memories were more real than the present.

Michael sat watching the light on the bonsai tree on the bookshelf. A client had given it to him. It was an exquisitely symmetrical tree over two hundred years old, the color of a forest moss. Ava had said she disliked bonsai because they reminded her of what life did to some people.

Michael's eyes settled on a sterling-framed photograph of Ava on his desk. Even his secretary's reaction to his success was more exuberant than his own sister's! There were thousands of men working in the Street. Men with much better education, background, and contacts. Men who fought like gladiators to get a seat on the subway, and more fiercely to win a partnership in Rush and Aliza. But if Ava were to walk in this minute and read the *Financial World* article, she would make him feel he was a black knight from some corrupt royal court, rewarded for his cruelty to the populace.

He looked at the framed photograph of the Stock Exchange floor on that famous Black Tuesday, 1929. He looked at the terror in the faces of the stockbrokers and then at a quote from the *Wall Street Journal* that hung framed over his desk. He kept it to remind him to be cautious in every detail, never to take anything for granted.

> There are not likely to be any large inventory problems. Credit is plentiful. We advise the accumulation of select quality securities.
>
> May 14, 1929

Ben returned, saying, "I'm off. Late for a date. You never asked about the market."

"Okay, how was the market?"

"One of those days, huh? That package from Ava — is she getting to you again?"

"Again?"

"No big deal for me to cancel, it's only Alison. Everything improves if we hoist a few drinks."

"Thanks, Benny. I'm okay. Have a good time. Say hello to Allie."

"And you," Ben said, pulling on a blue cashmere coat. "Ava is okay, you know."

What was in the package from Ava?

"Mike?"

"Oh, sorry, my mind was wandering. Good night, Ben."

It was an ordinary brown paper package tied with cheap cord. As he opened and examined it, sweat broke out on Michael's palms. Ava's handwriting was small and cramped, unlike her usual expansive style. The package contained cassette tapes. It was obviously not a Christmas present. For a moment, he felt a terrible reluctance. His fingers trembled as he placed a cassette into the living room tape deck.

Hi, number-one brother.

The sound of her voice brought a smile to his lips.

I hope you're fine, and Ben, too.

He sipped his drink.

Mikey, I'm scared.

Fear began creeping up into his consciousness.

For a while now, I've been suspicious about what's been happening at the snake farm. Too many snakes are being shipped out from the airport to zoos. There's just not that much zoo business. Besides, the farm is in the business of selling venom, and most of the snakes being shipped have been anacondas, which have no venom.

Michael was so still he could feel his heart beating.

Recently I found out from my friend Nicole that the farm isn't really owned by my boss, Gus Coufos. It belongs to a guy named Buchreiser, who just happens to be one of the biggest cocaine dealers in the world.

His heartbeat was throbbing in his side, at his temple, under his jaw. Ava had been an addict when she was a teen-ager. She spent close to a year in a halfway house before being released.

I thought of going to the police, but they're too corrupt. I don't know what to do, except I know I've got to do something. This bastard Buchreiser uses the Indians to farm coca and poses as their friend. But he's really responsible for a policy of genocide against them. He's killing off my Indian friends, and I don't know what to do. What can I do?

Michael slammed his fist down on the rosewood coffee table so hard that his bones seemed to ring. "Get the hell out of that godforsaken place is what you can do, damn it!" He was on his feet and pacing.

On the other tapes you'll find valuable information on my work about deriving medicine from snake venom. This tape is just a precaution in case something happens to me. I'd like you to get my research to the right people in New York. If you're still planning to visit me this year as you said, and you're not too busy, now would be a good time.

He listened to the rest of the tape, but Ava only spoke more of the Indians.

He stamped over to the tape deck and punched off the power button. Then he ran his fingers through his hair from forehead to the back of his neck as if in an attempt to organize his thoughts.

His hand was shaking slightly when he dialed the overseas operator, and it began to tremble visibly when he discovered Ava was neither at home nor at the snake farm. In the section of the bookcase where he kept some of Ava's books for safekeeping, he ran his hand over the spines of *The Wretched of the Earth* and *Social Welfare — Charity to Justice*. Next to the books was a button with a laminated picture of Dr. Martin Luther King, which Ava had kept as a souvenir from the March on Washington. Touching her objects was like reaching out and touching his sister.

Absentmindedly, he looked out the window. There was snow in the air one day three years ago, too, when Ava was last in Manhattan. His eyes lost their focus now, and he saw her just coming in from the street. They had kissed and hugged in the doorway, and then he had carried her luggage inside. Snowflakes sugared the shoulders of her camelhair coat and a six-foot plaid scarf crisscrossed her neck. From under the green snow-spattered wool cap with the red tassel, her green eyes glittered like those of a child who just had a nice surprise. Mike knew the surprise was himself. Her cheeks were rosy from the cold, and she was smiling as she saw his house for the first time. That smile he had known all his life told him how happy she was to see him. She had smelled of cold fresh air and almond soap.

"Well, this house certainly disproves the theory that one can't find a decent place to live in Manhattan."

For a long time, Michael sat in silence. Then he tried again to reach Ava. He continued to call unsuccessfully all through the cold night.

The following day, still unable to contact Ava, Michael boarded an Avianca 747 at JFK for Bogotá on the first leg of a flight to the Amazon — and Puerto Porqueño.

Chapter Five

Eduardo, the man with rain-colored eyes, was afraid of snakes; in self-defense, he had studied them. Now he stamped his feet to warn off the reptiles as he walked under the shade trees toward Gus Coufos's bungalow. The Greek had been very pleased to hear how cleanly Eduardo had done away with the blonde and had promised him a surprise. Maybe, the man thought, he was finally going to get promoted in the organization. Perhaps even to meet Buchreiser, the boss of Coufos and everyone else who lived in the palace in the jungle.

This last thought was exciting. It almost made Eduardo forget about the snakes. There were dark sweat patches all over his body, moons under the arms of his jacket, and a wet band at his waist. He hiked up his pants and imagined what life would be like as a lieutenant in Buchreiser's organization, living in the palace. He had heard about Buchreiser's chefs brought in from all over the world. And women of every shape, color, and sexual skill.

Suddenly the man with rain-colored eyes felt something weighty drop onto the back of his neck from above. He screamed and danced away madly. But by the time Eduardo pulled out his .44, he saw that it wasn't a snake at all, but only a monkey-ladder vine. What a terrifying place! Vines looking like snakes, and snakes looking like vines! He examined the large scar on his right forearm, where he had been bitten by a twenty-two-foot anaconda. It always made him queasy. Gun still in hand, the man continued in a careful walk toward the bunga-low.

Disgusting creatures. They ate rats. One day, in a trap, Eduardo had watched a snake devour another snake — half of it down his throat. Both serpents were thrashing their tails. The swallower could neither slide away nor stop consuming the other snake.

Cautiously, the man lifted his gaze from the path and surveyed the farm. It consisted of broad paths between big grass ovals. Scattered among the ovals were cement shelters for the reptiles. He knew he had nothing to fear from them. It was impossible for the snakes to escape; the ovals were surrounded by water moats with straight and steep cement sides. Still, he was wary.

In the palace, he was told, there were no snakes, no lizards, and no mosquitoes.

When he knocked on the door, one of Coufos's women appeared. She was a young brown girl with round, full arms and high breasts.

"Gus is in the milking area, Eduardo," she told him.

The thought of the fangs dripping their deadly milk made Eduardo sick to his stomach. The girl brought him a cup of water. He gulped it down.

"There is no snake you cannot outrun," she said.

"Yes," he said. "If one knows where he is." He knew that a strike from one of the *Bothrops* (which were most common on the farm) was followed by blindness and suffocation, and paralyzed the victim's neck regardless of the part of the body the snake bit. The venom was selective. But Eduardo did not want to think of such things, ever.

"Your gun, please," the young girl said.

Eduardo handed over his weapon reluctantly. He would tell Gus that he'd like an exception made for him.

When Eduardo reached the rooms where the snakes were milked, his eyes were rimmed with red. Without warning, something grasped his shoulder. His heart emptied. His throat gave out a strange sound. He had to reach down into the deepest part of himself for the strength to open his eyes and turn around.

It was Gus.

"Please," Eduardo said, leaning against the wall for support. "You know how this place scares me."

"Very sorry," Coufos said. He was six inches shorter than Eduardo's six feet. Coufos's skin was the color of dark tree bark. There was sweat on his upper lip, like water beads on butter. Coufos extended an inordinately large hand for a man his size.

Eduardo's bloodshot eyes now were as wary as those of a dog who had just been kicked. Behind Gus, he could see into a room where some horses were being inspected by a man in a lab coat. He knew this was where the horses were injected with venom so their blood would produce the antibodies for use as human serum.

"Gus, I got to get away from here."

"Sure, sure. Come." Coufos led him into a room where the already immunized blood of horses was going through processes to separate the antivenim. Coufos dismissed a technician and offered Eduardo a seat on a black couch. Coufos settled behind a bamboo desk.

"Drink?" Coufos asked.

"Beer."

Coufos went to a small refrigerator, took out two bottles, and gave one to Eduardo. The iced beer soothed him. Then he noticed a photograph on the wall of a snake hanging in six bracelets from a low branch. He concentrated on Gus's eyes so he wouldn't think of the snake. But Gus's eyes had no depth, like a goat's.

"You handled the white girl well," Coufos said. "The Boss is happy."

Buchreiser, Eduardo thought excitedly. His eyes still strayed to the picture of the snake.

"It bothers you, my friend?" Coufos said, pointing to the picture. "Why did you not say so?" Coufos stood, took down the picture, and slid it into a drawer in his desk. "You are safe as in a church. Look around you. No windows. Only the single door, with no room at the bottom for any snake to come through."

"It does not make sense, I know. But I fear snakes."

"Yes, people are happy that you did well. Soon you will have a reward." *Eduardo is dependable. But what if someone makes the connection between him and Ava and me? He has to go.*

"Now please excuse me. I have something to get you from the next room."

"A surprise?"

"Yes."

"Thanks, Gus."

"You take a beer." He switched on a radio to top volume. "Listen to music. Take it easy. I will be right back."

When Coufos had gone, Eduardo poured himself the rest of the beer and then went to the refrigerator for another bottle.

Because of the music, he didn't hear Coufos outside, removing a part of the air conditioner. But when he turned his head, he saw the dozen fer-de-lance Gus had let loose through the opening.

He watched, unbelieving, as the snakes began to surround him. Their maroon tongues tasted the air for his scent. They had slithered to within a foot of him now. And two had already begun arching their backs to strike when he screamed and tried to run.

Chapter Six

"I know my sister did not kill herself," Michael said. Realizing he was towering over Puerto Porqueño's Chief of Police Marquez, he pulled up a highly polished chair and sat down.

In a floor stand behind Marquez's desk was his country's striped yellow, red, and blue flag. As he spoke, he toyed with a miniature of the flag on his desk. Marquez was small and weather-beaten. Michael thought of him as an ancient-looking peasant child. His ears were large. They were set nearly at right angles to his head, like those on the mongrel dogs of Puerto Porqueño.

"It is a difficult thing to accept: that someone you love can take her own life." In contrast to his appearance, Marquez's speech was crisp and powerful. His mobile face had a great range of expressions. "But did your sister not have a history of drugs?"

"Yes, but that was a long time ago, when she was under twenty. She even worked in halfway houses since then, helping others to be cured of the habit."

"Unfortunately, the percentage of addicts who return to drugs is high."

Despite the air conditioning, Michael was sweating. He was slightly nauseous. The image of Ava's bloated and decomposed remains haunted him: someone or something that was once Ava. Animals had ravaged her body. Ants had scavenged her flesh. That wasn't his sister. His whole body was a clenched fist and he tried not to dwell on Ava's fate.

"Ava would never use a needle. She's been afraid of them ever since she was a little girl. She passed out once in a doctor's office just from seeing a hypodermic."

"If enough pleasure is promised, one can overcome incredible fears," Marquez said.

Michael was unaware that he was on his feet again. "True, but there were no other needle marks on her body, and no signs in her nose that she had been snorting the stuff."

Before he spoke, the Colombian stared at the painting of Simón Bolivar on the wall to the right of his desk. To Michael it seemed the little man was deriving inspiration from the Great Liberator.

"Who can guess when and why someone returns to using drugs or whiskey, or any habit?"

"If my sister was a suicide, why is her Land Rover missing?"

"We are not so civilized here that we don't have car thieves. The Rover was found just a few hours ago."

"Do you know who took it?"

The policeman nodded.

"Who is he? Have you questioned him? What does he say?" Michael could feel the hairs on his arm tingle as he waited for Marquez to answer.

"His name was Eduardo Estevez. We found his wallet in the Rover. He is dead."

Michael slumped into his chair as Marquez went on.

"He died accidentally. He was visiting someone at the snake farm. One of the snakes got loose and bit him."

"I think he sounds connected to Ava's death. First he steals her car, then he's found dead on the farm where Ava worked."

"When people here find things in the jungle, they think they belong to them. Because Eduardo Estevez was a car thief does not mean he was also a murderer. And the snake farm has many workers. Probably he was visiting a friend or relative."

Michael recalled Ava telling him how high up corruption ran in Colombia. He decided not to tell the policeman about Ava's tapes detailing the cocaine smuggling going on at the snake farm. If the wrong people had found out about her suspicions, she would have been in the greatest danger. "How do you explain that Ava tried to reach me twice on the day she was killed?"

"And what is so unusual, Mr. Rush, about a sister trying to phone her brother?" Marquez made the gesture of putting his hands behind his protruding ears.

"Nothing. But I hadn't heard from her in weeks. She sounded very frightened on my answering machine." The rich and wonderful smell of coffee brewing in an outer office clashed with the bitter taste of grief in his mouth, a grief mixed with rage.

Marquez removed his hands from his ears and they sprang back. "If you will permit me, Mr. Rush, I think perhaps your sorrow originates in your belief that your sister did not kill herself."

"But—"

"Please." Marquez held up a hand the color of cured leather. "I see your distress. I truly sympathize with you. Yet, you have seen the official police report and the autopsy report. They contain no signs of attempted rape or robbery. We all agree here that it is an obvious case of suicide. Why do you think otherwise? Did she have enemies?"

"She was loved by everyone."

"Exactly. Have you asked yourself why someone would go to all the trouble of making her 'murder' look like a suicide?"

"That's all I've been asking myself since I saw her."

"And?"

"And I'm going to keep asking myself that till I find out who killed Ava. If it takes the rest of my life."

Marquez stood. The interview was over. "There is an old Spanish saying, Señor Rush. 'To know what one cannot change is to believe in God.'"

Outside, Michael hailed a taxi. As he stepped into it with his head down, he thought of the way Ava had always held her head high. Suddenly his thoughts reeled back to their last argument.

"Where were we?" he had asked.

"Far apart, as usual," Ava had said.

He examined her. Her long, delicate hands and the fine structuring of her face suggested something too fragile and finely made for all the hazards of her radicalism.

"Look," he said, "I help people make money. Honestly. Fairly. With the money they pay me, I travel. Experience. I live well. Okay, very well. What's wrong with that?"

"Nothing. Except the people you ought to be helping are paying for it."

"Poor people don't pay money managers' commissions," he said sarcastically.

"They pay in different ways. You've forgotten. Just because you got hurt once trying to change the system, you don't even vote anymore or read a news story that doesn't have a direct effect on the stock market. Don't expect me to approve."

"You want to make me out to be a heavy, go ahead. Did I say a word when you wanted to help *them*? The *people*?"

"No, you didn't. You figured I'd take a few black and Spanish kids to the zoo. Maybe get their parents to register to vote. Sell UNICEF cards. Oh, Mike, whatever happened to my idealistic brother?"

"He grew up."

Michael frowned. He no longer wanted to think of their arguments. They had always been able to draw on their love for each other. Now that possibility was gone forever. He felt cheated and threatened, as though a part of him, a part that agreed with her activism, had died with her. He shivered, despite the Colombian heat.

Chapter Seven

Medical Examiner Ortega's office overlooked a courtyard with a dry fountain. A few rows of token red flowers surrounded it. The overhead fluorescent lights were so bright that his secretary's red lipstick looked mauve.

Michael followed her to the examiner's office.

Ortega did not rise. Looking up from the papers on his desk, he shook Michael's hand briefly. Dr. Ortega wore wraparound sunglasses, a silk suit, and a diamond pinky ring. His grim mouth made him look dangerous. Michael's eyes surveyed the room. In the left corner was the Colombian flag, spattered with gray stains. Above the flag Michael saw rain-spattered cracks in the leaking wall.

"How can I be of help to you, Señor Rush?"

"I wish to see your report on the cause of death of Eduardo Estevez."

Ortega rose. "Come, please."

Michael was led down a corridor to a room jammed with filing cabinets. There was the raw smell of old, damp paper.

Ortega handed Michael a folder. Michael stared at the Spanish print.

"I can't read Spanish."

"What do you want to know?"

"How did he die?"

Ortega lifted his sunglasses and looked back at Michael with an expression Michael had seen in the eyes of countless civil servants. They were always annoyed by any increase in their workload. Ortega repossessed the folder and began to translate aloud.

After a few moments, Michael said, "Excuse me, how many times did you say Estevez was bitten?"

"Seven."

"Are you sure?"

Ortega looked up and put his hand on his hip challengingly. "I examined the body myself."

"Thank you, Dr. Ortega. I really appreciate your help."

Michael went directly to the Colonial Hotel and phoned Ben Aliza.

After explaining what he had learned about Ava's death, he said, "Estevez had seven snake bites on him, Ben. Who waits around to be bitten seven times? I'll bet he was murdered. And I'll bet he killed Ava."

"I'll come down and help you, Mike. Marquez is definitely not kosher. And the fact that Estevez worked for Coufos, who Ava thought was a front for Buchreiser. . . . These cocaine guys don't play touch football."

"If you want to be a party to murder, come. If not, stay."

"Are you all right, Mike?"

"I'm just angry. Thanks, Ben."

"Okay, I understand. Jesus, I—I'm so sorry. Anything I can do?"

"I'm bringing Ava back to New York. Will you help me arrange her burial in the family plot? You'll find everything you need in the office safe."

"It's done."

"Two fucking grams. . . ."

"All I can say, Mike, is that I don't know what to say."

"You're always there for me, Ben. That's enough. I'll be on the next plane."

The Isla Verde Guest House was a stuccoed one-level structure the color of baby aspirin, which failed in its attempt to look Spanish. There was a statue of the Virgin Mary at the front door. Under the aluminum shelter was a shiny Volkswagen minibus.

What Michael saw as he slammed the taxi door made his scalp freeze. By the entrance of the guest house he saw a slim woman about five feet four with

short-cropped blonde hair. She looked like Ava! Then
he realized the blonde hair was flecked with gray.
The woman was about fifty.

As he approached, he saw that the woman's complexion was as pale as Ava's, except for a ruddy spot
high on each cheekbone. From Ava's description, she
would be Mrs. Hoffman, her landlady.

"I'm Michael Rush, Ava's brother, Mrs. Hoffman.
I spoke to you on the telephone."

"I am so sorry," she said with a German accent.

Her watery blue eyes revealed her sympathy. "My
husband shops in the town," she said. "Come inside."
She held out an outstretched hand.

Mrs. Hoffman opened the door to Ava's rooms as
one might the lid of a coffin. Michael felt a tic in his
right eyelid.

She had lived in a single room. The lingering scent
of Ava's perfume assaulted his nose. Books were
everywhere: in a large handmade bookcase, on her
nightstand, and stacked on the floor.

Plants spilled over from hanging pots on the
windowsill and, it seemed, on every flat surface. On
top of a rosewood highboy was a collection of sou-
venirs she had told him about in her letters. They had
been collected from the countries in which she had
served in the Peace Corps. He picked up a hand-
carved mahogany giraffe he remembered. She had
brought it back from the Congo.

A mosquito net hung like a cloud over her single
bed. There was no air conditioner.

On one of the walls, he saw some framed photographs. One depicted a manatee eating flowering water hyacinth. Another showed an Indian boy in front of violets the size of apple trees, feeding a scarlet parrot a seed he clutched in his teeth. Still another was of a huge snake with a spear-shaped head and geometric designs on its body. The snake was surrounded by snakelings each about twelve inches long.

Atop an antique wicker table was a terrarium and a small aquarium. In the terrarium were a half-dozen frogs. Michael marveled at their colors: pink, bright yellow, strawberry. Some could sit on a quarter, others on a dime. The aquarium contained four turtles which climbed over one another continually. He imagined they sought comfort in each other during the absence of their owner.

Michael's heart jumped when he came upon a framed photograph of himself and Ava with their parents. It sat on her nightstand. He looked through the rattan desk and bureau, examined every piece of clothing in the closet.

He discovered Mrs. Hoffman in the kitchen. She was sitting under a cuckoo clock with her chin on her crossed fingers and her eyes closed. Could she be praying?

Mrs. Hoffman rose and took his hands in her bony fingers. They stood for a moment, silent.

When he got in the taxi, the door handle was too hot to touch.

Less than a week later Michael had returned to

Puerto Porqueño. He had shaved off his moustache and had had his hair straightened and dyed black. In the inside pocket of his sports jacket he carried two passports. One was genuine. The other Ben Aliza had obtained with much difficulty and at great expense. It bore the name Miles Rudd.

Chapter Eight

"What is that delicious smell?" Mary Mahoney asked as a slight, animated man in a lime jumpsuit applied her makeup outside Nicole de la Houssaye's hut. A camera was standing a few feet away, looking as out of place as an astronaut in the Carrijura Indian village 175 miles upstream from Puerto Porqueño.

"*Arepas*," Nicole answered as the makeup man left the interviewer and came over to study her face. "They're corn dumplings."

The sun made tiny droplets of moisture visible on the wisps of russet hair at Nicole's temples. Nicole grinned at the makeup man, showing a pair of smile lines that, at thirty-three, had formed around her full mouth. She sat with one foot resting on the opposite knee, her back as straight as that of a sphinx.

"My God, I love your eyes!" the makeup man said to Nicole.

"Thank you."

They were brown, but the outer fringe of her left iris, about two to three millimeters wide, was bluish gray.

"I hope nothing's wrong," the makeup man said as he worked.

"It's not harmful. Usually it happens to older people and to both eyes. It's called *arcus senilis*."

"Whatever it's called, it's gorgeous." He wielded his eyebrow pencil.

"Hello, sweetheart!" Mary Mahoney said as an Indian boy approached her from one of the fifteen small thatched huts perched on piles. The child—embarrassed by her enthusiasm—ran off to join some boys, mingling with chickens, ducks, and pigs amidst a regatta of white butterflies. Close by, a bare-breasted woman was planting cassava.

The village lay on the shore of a lagoon of chocolate water where lush trees submerged and sent up aerial roots. The surface of the water was crowded with flowering lilies and Victoria Regia—a lotus with pods up to five feet in diameter. In contrast to Puerto Porqueño's riverine milieu, the village had a lake-country atmosphere.

Nicole picked up a gourd filled with passionflower juice and sipped slowly. She wore a white cotton blouse and pale blue jeans.

"How many people live in this village?" Mary asked.

"Sixty or so, but there are thousands more Carri-jura living deep in the jungle, and many other tribes."

"Ready!" the makeup man said, finished with Nicole.

"Ready to shoot, Mary?" the director asked.

The camera dollied forward.

"Two years ago, Nicole de la Houssaye, former gymnastic-gold-medal winner for the United States, and coach to many Olympic hopefuls, disappeared. Despite a worldwide search, unequaled since the one for Amelia Earhart, America's—to quote Ronald Reagan—prettiest ambassador, unquote, was no-where to be found. And we didn't find her. She found us. I'm honored that Nicole chose me to let the world know where she is and to help bring her thrilling story to all of us. I'm proud to introduce the legendary Olympic athlete, Nicole de la Houssaye."

The excitement seemed like a weight in Nicole's chest. Somewhere in the afternoon, she heard a macaw mocking her as she said, "Thank you, Mary." She heard her voice straining, felt the hot roll of excitement building in her. She was on the parallel bars and had lost points for a bad dismount. Now she was behind. Her last routine was coming up. She felt something taking over her—a meshing of her mind and her body. Simultaneously, her muscles went loose and springy. She knew nothing was impossible with trust and concentration.

"Two and a half years ago, I started to get a lot of

lower back pain. Soon the pain went up to my spine and it became impossible to turn my head. I felt as if I'd been run over by a truck. A doctor told me I had a crippling form of ankylosing spondylitis, a kind of arthritis, and soon my whole spine would be fused. I went to many doctors in the States, then all over the world. The prognoses were identical."

Nicole shifted slightly in her wicker chair, remembering the stunning blow of the doctors' words. When she spoke again, there was a new quietness in her tone that only hinted at that terror.

"I was so healthy, in the usual sense of the word. I didn't smoke or drink, ate only the healthiest foods, and got plenty of sleep and exercise. But the year before, I had had a failed love affair, and I now know that the suppressed rage I had suffered at that time, plus the pressure of world-class competition, had to find an outlet."

"Do you believe that your rage and the pressure actually caused your arthritis?" Mary asked, eyes flickering at her watch afterward for a time check.

"Yes. My emotional tension had kept my adrenaline pumping till I got adrenal exhaustion, which I think led to my arthritis."

"You're actually saying, Nicole, that we can get arthritis when we're run-down emotionally, the same way we get colds when our resistance is low?"

Nicole nodded. "It can be physical or emotional, or both. In my case, it was emotional."

"And are you cured today?"

"Yes."

Mary slapped at a mosquito, and Nicole became acutely aware of the film crew surrounding them—cameraman, director, makeup artist, hairdresser, technicians. She was struck by the incongruity of these people in her jungle.

"Maybe all this would be clearer if you explained how you found a cure here in the jungle," Mary said. A flock of horned screamers flew overhead, their loud braying resounding through the trees.

Nicole nodded, thinking of her dead friend Ava. "I met a woman herpetologist here, Ava Rush, who was working on a cure for arthritis and terminal cancer pain, which used snake venom. There had already been some small success with painkillers derived from cobra venom. Ava figured that the fer-de-lance venom—it's a local snake whose venom is similar to the cobra's—might also be effective."

"And did she succeed?" Mary was skeptical.

Nicole nodded and went on. "Yes, but not dramatically. Then she decided to combine the pain-relieving properties of the coca leaf with the venom. She fed rats coca leaves and then fed the rats to the snakes. After a few weeks' treatment with this combination, I could turn my head. Five months later, I had hardly an ache."

Mary frowned thoughtfully. "That's an amazing story, Nicole. The AMA, though, believes that all the alternative arthritis treatments are ineffective, and potentially dangerous. Over the years, there have been a lot of questionable treatments, from pectin and grape juice to copper wristbands. Why are you so sure that venom and cocaine cured you? Perhaps you would have gotten well in any event."

Nicole knew what Ava would have been up against—convincing the medical world that she wasn't dispensing snake oil. "It's coca, not cocaine. I wasn't the only one cured in this way. I've seen dozens and dozens of people cured. Some were so crippled that they were standing with their heads pointing to the ground."

Mary Mahoney looking interested now, leaned forward, "Yes. Is this a new disease? A symptom of our time and our type of civilization?"

Nicole remembered asking Ava almost the same question and recalled her answer almost verbatim: "Egyptian mummies in the Valley of the Kings were found with skeletons whose spines were typical of ankylosing spondylitis. In the eighteenth century, the Bishop of Cork described a man who was rigid from his head to his ankles. He could work only as a watchman in a sentry box where he could look only in one direction, unable to desert."

"Fascinating. How did you happen to be in the Amazon?"

"My mother was an entomologist. I used to come here when I was a girl. I was always drawn to it.

When I got tired of the nausea from taking anti-inflammatory pills and dizziness from taking cortisone, I decided I'd try some of the Indian cures for pain."

"Such as?"

"Such as poultices of coca leaves laid on my joints."

"Did that help?"

"Absolutely. So did the heat and the moisture here. They helped me so much that I could do the exercises to prevent the stiffening of my spine."

"So it wasn't just the snake venom and coca."

"It was mostly the snake venom from snakes that had eaten rats that had eaten coca leaves. Yes."

Nicole didn't like this conversation. Sharing her cure with the world was not as she had envisioned it. Perhaps the book she had helped Ava with would be more effective. This interview was missionary work. The press would call her cure "alleged," at the very best. Still, as Ava had often said, if only *one* person can be helped—but Nicole was losing her original excitement. She had mentioned the Carrijura Indians of this village and others to Mary and the genocide that was destroying them. And Chochobo, their chief, who had led them here into the jungle to farm the coca that was refined into cocaine, so they could buy guns and defend themselves. Mary had promised to discuss the murder of the Indians if there was time.

Nicole did not hear Mary's next question. She was

thinking of her trip upstream the next day, and how she might convince Chochobo, her friend, that now—with all his coca money—there were other ways besides killing to save his people.

Chapter Nine

From the ladder of a 727 jet, Michael stepped into the steamy afternoon air of Puerto Porqueño for the second time. He had arrived in Bogotá the day before at 5:15 P.M. Because there were never any feeder airline flights to Puerto Porqueño until 10:45 A.M., he had to spend the night in a small hotel. He had slept only five hours in two nights. He scratched his lip, as he often did since he had shaved off his moustache.

Despite his dark glasses, the sun was bright. It was unmerciful, making his tired eyes water. He grasped the handrail and made his way down the hot aluminum steps. His right buttock was still sore from the gamma globulin shot his doctor gave him to prevent hepatitis. The tetanus and typhoid shots given last year when he had vacationed in Egypt were still effective. He had a vial of chloroquine pills for malaria stored in his luggage.

As he waited for his bags, tired and sleepy, the frantic activity of the ground crew made him feel that he was watching from another dimension.

Now, in the dazzling street, he stepped over a colony of red ants on the march and wondered how many times Ava has passed through this airport. *What was the strange smell of this place? Heat? Soil? Vegetation? Decay? Smoke? Dung? The smell of Amazonian skin?* The air was incredibly humid. Michael felt it break on his skin like tiny beads of rain.

"Taxi, señor?"

Startled, Michael spun around to confront a slight and gaunt man leaning against a cab. His features, except for the animated eyes of the mestizo, would not have looked out of place on a totem pole.

"I'm going to town," Michael said.

As he rode in the taxi he concentrated on each tree they passed, as if it held some cryptic message to explain Ava's end. He remembered little from his recent trip here to identify her remains; he had been so shocked and grief-stricken. His hand made a gesture at his throat as if to monitor the passage of air.

They passed a huge tree with roots like the ribs of a whale's skelton. Other trees had roots like tunnels. A hundred yards or so from the road lay the jungle, in every imaginable shade of green.

The never-ending river smoked with mist. Michael

rolled down his window. There was a smell he had
thought he'd forgotten. It was like the smell of the
monkey house at the Bronx Zoo. He had taken Ava
there when she was a child. Now he half expected to
see a brontosaurus emerge from the green forest.
Instead, a skein of white herons, like patches of snow,
flew over the burnt-sugar-colored river, filled with
flowing islands of grass. He closed the window, but
the smell of the monkey house seeped in nevertheless.

The taxi lurched round a turn; Michael braced
himself.

A wave of drowsiness swept over him. He rubbed
his eyes. Then he rolled down the window and thrust
his face into the foul-smelling wind.

"Damn!" Michael exclaimed and struck his hand as
a mosquito drew blood. The insects, which must have
arrived through the open window, whirred steadily
around him with whining little motors. Suddenly
rain came in gray sheets. Then, except for the sound
of the rain—on the roof, on the road—there was
absolute silence. He shouted at the driver, "How can
you see through the windshield?" But he could not
make himself heard over the rain. Then the driver
parked on the side of the muddy road with the motor
running. Michael felt an unreality that went beyond
fatigue. There are places you never forget. The smell
of the monkey house, the sound of the rain—they
would be with him as long as he lived.

Suddenly the rain stopped. The world became

silent. The trees steamed and the air smelled of perfumed flowers, wet wood, and grass.

The engine stalled abruptly. It took three agonizing attempts to turn it over. After some protracted chugging, the engine ran smoothly.

"Is this the rainy season?" Michael asked.

"We have only two seasons," the driver said, laughing, "the rainy and the wet."

Michael liked the cheerful man.

"I am Raimondo," said the driver. "You need anything, you come to me. I take care of it. I am honest. You get a good deal. You need a woman, something to smoke, you call it by name. *Esmeraldas*, coca, I take care of it."

Grass, emeralds, cocaine—Ava could have been killed for any one of these. Without responding, he took the business card the driver offered over his shoulder.

"Raimondo can get you anything. You no like women, I get boys. Maybe you like fishing or you like to take pictures of the animals, the jungle, Indians, Monkey Island, the snake farm. I am guide."

"I love fishing," Michael lied. "And I do want to take a lot of pictures."

"Here we are."

They had reached the center of town. There were a few, three- or four-story buildings, right-angle streets, and, most prevalent, low houses surrounded by gardens. The town tumbled toward the river only yards away where an open-air fish market thrived on its bank. The air was torpid, and the slight breeze carried the stench of rotting fish. All around, glued to the outermost houses, was the jungle.

There was a row of shops whose windows displayed kitsch souvenir jewelry and what looked like expensive leather bags. At several currency stores, men sat with large briefcases on their laps.

As they drove past the main square surrounded by some trees and flowers, Michael could see three rusty steamboats and two six-passenger hydroplanes. Seaplanes were everywhere.

As Michael stepped out of the taxi, he got many stares but no smiles. The Hotel Macaw was painted yellow and looked out over the Amazon, which was about two miles wide here and the color of pewter.

The sidewalk café was crowded with military men, civilians, and what he guessed were tourists, all sitting at cast-iron tables, sipping fruit juices, beer, or whiskey. Everyone inspected him brazenly.

In the lobby were flashily dressed pimp types and men in work shirts, three-piece suits, and polo shirts and shorts and sultry women with painted faces.

The toothless woman at the desk kept wiping sweat from her neck with a grayish handkerchief.

"No more rooms," she said.

"I telegrammed. Rudd, Miles Rudd."

"All out. But if you pay me something, I can find a room."

He slammed his reservation down on the desk.

A younger woman emerged from the office in back and said that only a double room was available at fifty dollars a night.

"Okay," he said. He was soon being led to his room by a young man with the high cheekbones and delicate features of a fashion model.

"Woman? Coca?" the boy asked.

"*Cerveza fría.*"

The room contained two short, narrow beds, a cracked linoleum floor, a single low-wattage overhead light bulb, and a toilet with a discolored bowl. A peephole was drilled into the door. Below a broken air conditioner was a huge stain in the shape of Italy on the stucco wall. Even if the fifty dollars included the price of a bribe, this was the best hotel in town.

The room seemed unusually empty, the way a living room does the day a Christmas tree is thrown out. For an instant he felt as if he were still married to Ruth, and recalled the sad, vague stirrings of failure. He could see Ruth hovering over him, a helpless, anxious look in her eyes on many long-ago mornings—*Mickey, do you think the holiday was okay?*—and felt the same hopelessness, the same sorrow in not being able to provide her with all the answers to all of her often hidden, needy questions.

To fight his mood, he unpacked his bag, some books, and Ava's tapes. He'd brought a Spanish-English dictionary, *Snakes of the World*, a book about cocaine, a battery-powered tape recorder and player, and a copy of *Barron's*. He hid the books about snakes and cocaine in his underwear.

Gus Coufos left the hotel's outdoor café and walked across the street to the bar called Coppola's. The Greek's quick, darting eyes and languid movements resembled those of the snakes he had loved since he was a boy and had come to admire above all other creatures. The cabby Raimondo sat waiting for him at a table in the rear.

"Well?" Gus said.

"You said to report any *norteamericano* strangers who are—how you say?"

"Suspicious." Gus laughed. "Look who helps with English."

"Suspicious. Yes."

Gus remembered his orders to Raimondo and others in the organization to look out for a North American who might have come to investigate Ava's death.

"And?"

"And this one says he comes for what the *turistas* come: fishing, pictures."

"So?"

"So he looks sad for a *turista*. And he is nervous. He tries so hard to be nice."

"You did well, Raimondo. I will check more into this North American." He slapped the cabby's back good-naturedly, and with his other hand slipped a bill into his shirt pocket.

"Thank you, Gus."

"Thank you. And keep the eyes in your head."

"What?"

"Keep watching."

"This I will do."

The bellboy returned with a bottle of Heineken's and a note.

Dear Mr. Rudd,

My name is Gus Coufos. I am American Greek who comes one time from Miami and am sick for home. I would like it very much if you would have drink with me tonight in the hotel. We meet at bar. Eight, please.

Gus Coufos

Michael felt a tug of excitement. He could hardly contain it. Coufos was seeking him out because of Ava. He wrote a note accepting the invitation.

Chapter Ten

From the Hotel Macaw terrace Michael watched
the sunset, a kaleidoscope of stained glass. Dusk came
quickly. He would have to meet the Greek soon.
Wondering what the man wanted, he stared at the
courtyard with its clogged fountain and palm trees.

The hotel reminded Michael vaguely of the one
he and his first wife, Ruth, had stayed in once in
New Orleans. *No*, he though, *it wasn't a hotel*. It was
a garden apartment called Linda's Court. Some of the
letters had worn off the sign. It had read *L nd s C urt*.
It had been seventeen years ago.

He remembered coming home one evening to discover that their apartment was bare. No tables,
chairs, rugs, curtains, paintings, lamps, records,
record player, china, glasses, or flatware. The bookshelves and all the books were gone. Ruth had made a

complete sweep. He had been in shock. Three years of marriage gone wrong.

Michael often mourned their lost years. Ruth was once full of hopes and needs, hopes Michael had shattered unwittingly and needs he'd been unable to fill. "I don't know what I want!" she would shout in frustration. "I just know it was dumb, dumb, dumb for you to get kicked out of college for your stupid SDS. And now the Weathermen! I can't stand it anymore. The FBI coming here to question me like I'm a criminal. I'll be an old woman before you finish going to night school and paying for dear baby sister Ava's college—which we certainly can't afford. Oh, whatever my plans, I just know you're not in them." In the end, she had stripped him not only of all the household goods, of furniture, but of the courage to try again. Why was he thinking of Ruth now?

It began to rain. It was not the rain he was accustomed to in New York, where the sky got dark and a cold rain fell on the dirty city streets. This downpour was like the bottom bursting out of a water-filled paper bag. Big, heavy, independent drops pounded the fronds of the palms. The smell of clay and steamy stones, rose to his nostrils.

The rain reminded him of days in Wall Street. On his way to lunch in the rain, he often passed through bank lobbies and outside entrances and lower levels, avoiding getting a single drop of rain on his face. How well he knew the Street! The bronze statue of

Washington at Federal Hall. The shoeshine boys and fruit vendors lining the iron fence outside Trinity churchyard. His favorite restaurant had an antique ticker-tape machine next to the cash register. His favorite bartender served outsized cocktails known as "John's Dividends."

In the bathroom, he killed a silver-dollar-sized centipede near the toilet, with his shoe. Then he tried to draw a bath. There was only a trickle of water. He sat on the bed and read *Barron's*. In the stock market, people were buying natural-resource companies: oil, lumber, paper—end-of-the-world stocks. Fools! He bought his clients the best growth issues he could find.

At least he could brush his teeth. Michael lay on the bed. The pillowcase smelled of cornstarch.

Just before eight Michael took the elevator to the lobby. He found Coufos at the bar.

"Nice you come, Mr. Rudd."

"Call me Miles, please."

The Greek's extended hand was broad and powerful, like his body. It was also dry and fibrous. He seemed to be all gristle and bone.

Michael drank what Coufos was having—*aguardiente*, an anise-flavored Colombian aperitif. Up close, Coufos's upper lip appeared rubbery, camel-like.

"What brings you to Amazon, Miles?"

"I understand there is a lot of opportunity here."

"For what?" The Greek's eyes were cool and flat.

"As an opportunist I don't much care for the specifics."

Coufos guffawed, slapped his back, and ordered another round.

"I am—how you say—an opportunist also, Miles."

"Really? And what kind of opportunities are you dealing in lately?" He immediately regretted the word "dealing"—too close to drugs. But Coufos's face showed no alarm. Could it be possible he was getting away so well with what he was doing?

"Now I have biggest snake-venom farm in Colombia."

Michael's scalp froze. *Ava*, he thought. *Ava*. He wanted to down the refilled pony glass. Instead, he forced a smile and put on a fascinated expression.

"I've found opportunities in snakes also. I have, uh . . . certain acquaintances who collect for Butantan."

He watched Coufos's face light up at the mention of the São Paolo Institute of Butantan, which he had read about on the airplane. It was the largest venom farm in Latin America. Because of the Greek's conspiratorial look, Michael decided to try and open him up even more.

"Some people have a knack for obtaining permits to export reptiles for zoos and museums. That can bring great opportunities, with good connections in the United States."

"I hear some snakes get to be in big underground

trade of collectors," Coufos said in a near whisper, obviously enjoying himself.

"There are trades in which it is impossible for a man to remain virtuous," Michael said playfully.

"Why do you not eat with me. Dinner? Maybe we can find opportunity, both you and me."

"Delighted."

"So, you travel much, Miles?" Coufos said, raising a glass of Vino Moriles, a local wine resembling Chianti.

"Yes, I'm a passionate traveler also," Michael said, lifting a forkful of fish stew.

"Also?"

"In addition to looking for opportunity. You never know where it will knock."

The Greek laughed, a bit too boisterously.

"What is this stuff? It doesn't taste like any kind of fish I've ever had."

"*Vido de pescado*. It is catfish from here that grows six hundred pounds. Cooked in hole in ground, covered with hot rocks."

"Delicious."

Michael kept up a steady stream of touristy questions all through dinner, till Coufos seemed empty of suspicion and filled with boredom. There was no more mention of snakes, of deals. Coufos was playing it safe, though he did ask Michael to visit the snake farm.

The meal finished, Michael suddenly felt he had

had his fill of the Greek. He needed to get away from him. He would learn more at the snake farm. But how could he bow out gracefully? .

As if in answer, a woman came in out of the rain. At the sight of her, Michael's skin grew clammy from a rush of adrenaline, and his heart seemed to swell.

She was a tall, big-boned woman, perhaps five feet eight or more, and her bottle-green dress was so dappled with raindrops that where it clung to her body, it appeared almost transparent. He was certain she was naked underneath the dress. She had the kind of woman's body he considered ideal when he was in his twenties and early thirties. Although his taste had changed since then—now he preferred the slimmer, more athletic type—he was stirred by her high, full breasts, generous hips, obvious mound of belly, long legs.

"I see," Coufos said, "you also like more than travel."

"What? Oh, yes, she's quite a beauty."

"Why not buy drink for her? Listen, I know how the heat here can boil a man's balls. I must go, it is late. Tomorrow you come visit my farm, yes?" The Greek stood.

Michael agreed and shook Coufos's hand good night.

After the Greek had left, Michael turned his attention to the woman to try to rid himself of the unpleasant effect of the snake man. She was no less than twenty-eight, no more than thirty-five. Her unparted hair, so black it was almost purple, fell in loose, damp curls to below her shoulders. There was a peculiar, limpid nakedness to her flesh. With the faint violet shadows under her eyes, this gave her a debauched look.

Michael watched her. She carried herself with sinuous grace, and her infrequent gestures were grand and uncontrolled. She came over and sat right next to him and ordered a martini. She had the gift of poise—no twisting or squirming, no fiddling with jewelry, no primping. She sat quietly, composed, pulled back deep within herself. An earthy warm scent emanated from her. He longed suddenly to be where she had pulled back into, if only for a moment —to escape from the place he was in.

He watched her reach down into a supple leather handbag and take out a cigarette. In the glow of her lighter's butane flame there was a solid enameled quality of her skin. He felt it would squeak if he rubbed his fingers across it.

She inhaled generously and raised her eyes as she blew out smoke. In her gaze, he had the sense of being momentarily illuminated, and the air around him grew warm. There was a hard aggression in her manner, yet a coolness. Suddenly he felt sure this woman was a hooker. And . . . Coufos had left soon after she entered.

She smiled at him seductively and crossed her perfect legs. Her dress hiked up; the flesh of her thighs was perfectly white, smooth, glistening. *Did Coufos set me up?* he wondered.

"How long are you here for?" she asked. Her voice was deeply pitched and slightly raspy, with no trace of a Spanish accent.

"Don't know yet," Michael replied.

He realized she wore no makeup at all—no lipstick, no eye shadow, no blush. The expression in her gray eyes was almost totally empty.

"What are you here for?" she asked.

"A little pleasure, a little business."

"What kind of business is that?"

"Investments. And you?" he asked, in a tone to let her know his true meaning. "What kind of business are you in?"

"I'm in the jewelry business. Colombia is famous for its emeralds, you know, and, of course, its gold."

"That must be lucrative," he said, smiling, still curious. "Are you ready for another drink?"

"Please."

The *aguardiente* was suffusing him with warmth. He felt strangely free, falling away from gravity. Enough booze, though. If she wasn't a hooker, maybe she was working for Coufos anyway. And in that case, he would fill her nearly lobeless ears with what he wanted to get back to the snake farmer.

"Miles Rudd," he said.

"Jackie. Do you have any good blow?"

"Sorry, I don't."

"No matter, I've got some in my room upstairs."

In her bedroom she took a small silver box from under the pillow and a tiny gold spoon out of her purse and offered it to him.

Remembering his recent experiments with coke— with a knowledgeable friend back in New York— he wetted his fingers and tasted the powder.

"Mannitol," he guessed. "Not the worst thing to cut with. Although I could do without a laxative just now."

Her eyes widened.

"You're quite an expert."

That would sound good to Coufos.

"Just careful."

He lifted the tiny spoon of white powder to one nostril, holding the other closed with a finger. He snorted. Almost at once came the burning sensation in his nose, followed by a faint numbness. Soon after came the explosive effect on his brain.

A surge of heat seethed through him, making his blood pound and his nerves quiver.

"Not bad," he said, unsteadily handing her the spoon.

He watched as she dipped the spoon into the silver box of coke and inhaled it.

Soon she was staring back at him with glistening eyes.

"Not bad, you say?" she gloated, unaware of the new stridency in her tone. "You must be used to dynamite."

"No, not used to it. I don't overuse anything."

"You're sure it's not the cost?" she said, unbuttoning his shirt and slipping her hot hand inside onto his skin. "You know what they say—coke is nature's way of telling you you're not earning enough money."

He wanted Coufos to believe he had plenty of money, so he forced a laugh.

She laughed along with him and led him to the bed.

"I'm sure it's not the cost," he said. Her hands began to tease and pull. Jesus, even her nails were hot.

"Where are you from?" she asked, sliding his zipper down with practiced fingers.

"San Francisco," he lied, as he had planned in case the questions got specific. He had lived in Marin County for a few months. "And you?"

"New York. You never said what kind of investments you're here for," she said as she ran her dark hair slowly over his naked groin.

"It certainly wasn't because you haven't asked." She looked up abruptly. He decided to act more like a seduced man before she grew suspicious. "Just teasing. I'm a businessman. I don't care what the investment is, so long as it's very profitable."

Suddenly he felt her tongue, and after a moment she got up and lowered herself down on him.

"There . . . we . . . are," she murmured huskily.

With her above, her hair covered both their faces, a waterfall that swayed as he rose.

He ran his palms over her nipples and was surprised to find them hard. Maybe she wasn't a hooker. Or maybe it was just the coke.

Suddenly he felt her inner muscles tense once, twice. He felt himself balancing on the brink. She rammed her belly against him, and he filled with fire all the way to his throat, then exploded, sending pieces of himself everywhere.

Afterward, he lay smoking a cigarette and Jackie dressed.

When they said good-bye, Jackie had brushed her hair and was wearing tortoiseshell glasses. She looked cool, pretty, scholarly.

Michael returned to his room, took a scalding shower, and ordered another cold beer, trying not to think of syphilis. Then he phoned the desk.

"This is Mr. Rudd in six-twenty-three. Could you please connect me with"—damn! he didn't know her last name—"the lady in two-fourteen?"

"Sorry, señor, she has already checked out."

He hung up and checked his watch. Who checks out of a hotel room at two-thirty in the morning in a town like Puerto Porqueño with only one afternoon flight a day? A hooker who probably works for a creep like Coufos. So he had been right.

Hours later he stood on his terrace, looking out into

the utter blackness of the Amazon night. He was too upset and anxious to sleep. His thoughts were on the substance still in his body, the substance that had killed Ava, and on having made love—having had sex, he corrected himself—with a person who could be connected with her murder.

Chapter Eleven

Nicole awoke at dawn, when the darkness of the forest was no longer black but the bluish green of a cavern illuminated by light filtered through the upper canopy. As luxuriously as a cat, she stretched in the still cool air and allowed herself to wake at her own pace. Her eyes drifted into focus. She saw the roof of the hut, where several overlapping layers of palm fronds shed rain but let smoke escape. The fronds had been layered horizontally across pole rafters, doubled over, and lashed in place with strips of bark and enormous wishbone-shaped tree roots which straddled the roof to hold it down. The Y-shaped roots were favorite perches of a half-dozen or so of her pet macaws and, when the birds were away, blue morpho butterflies appeared.

Nicole rubbed her eyes gently, reopened them, and

studied the rafters where she had hung earthen pots, mortars and pestles, gourds and packets, palm-leaf baskets, a flute, drying herbs and spices, medicinal vines, and a manioc-root sieve of wickerwork. Then she rose from her bed, which she had had imported from Bogotá by air. She would have preferred to use a hammock, as the Indians did, but instead used a hard mattress with a wooden board underneath to help keep her spine straight. She always slept on her back, without a pillow. Now she slipped on her moccasins, and made breakfast of fruit and cassava bread.

Then she sat quietly and concentrated on her breathing till her eyes seemed to float in her head. Deep breathing helped to insure that her chest and rib cage remained flexible. She exercised in this way three times a day for fifteen minutes. First there were deep bending exercises. Then, to stretch her pectoral muscles and straighten her upper torso, she locked her hands behind her head and pulled her elbows as far back as possible. She began to perspire.

Later, when she left her hivelike dwelling and went into the glare of the sun, she felt the humid, airless heat even more. The atmosphere was thick with wood smoke and the scent of cornmeal dumplings. She heard a flute, saw the old man who played it. She remembered what she had said to Mary Mahoney about the Indians. At the edge of the rain forest, a boy was practicing with a blowgun. A barebreasted woman passed her and waved her hand. Nicole smiled, remembering how the village women had once wrapped their arms around their chests self-consciously in front of her.

An old Carrijura man approached. His face was lean, yellow-bronzed by sunburn and malaria. He had a hawklike nose and a broad mouth. He wore strips of jaguar fur around his loins, and anklets and necklaces of viper fangs. He was her friend and mentor, Xingu. He had taught Nicole which berries and nuts and mushrooms could be eaten, and how to fold a green-leaf cup to drink the clear water of the creek. He thought her habit of lapping water from her hands was extremely rude. Xingu taught Nicole the names of plants and animals—which were edible and which were not, and which were inhabited by spirits. He showed her how to make a fire with a hand drill and how to move without sound.

She had asked Xingu to get word to Chochobo, chief of the Carrijura, and tell him that she wanted to come to speak to him.

"Chochobo says you may come," Xingu said.

Nicole had expected Chochobo to agree. Still, she was very pleased. Some of the pleasure went out of her when she saw how shrunken and bent Xingu had become since his wife had died a few months before. Liverish spots had appeared under his eyes. His bones could now be seen through his parchment skin. Nicole had the impulse to try to make Xingu laugh, to cheer him up. She decided not to try. *White people can force themselves to smile*, she thought. *Indians have to feel happy to smile.*

"When do we go?" she asked.

"Now," Xingu said.

She heard a cloud of mosquitoes whine around her. She knew there was no point in waving them away. She had trained herself to submit.

Soon she was following Xingu to his dugout canoe. As was the custom when she went to visit Chochobo, the entire village came to say good-bye. One of the local headman's three wives brought food for the trip. There was a splendid-tasting fish called *pacu* that had been smoked and stuffed with rice. It was wrapped in plantain leaves. There was also a bunch of fat claret bananas, a huge calabash of *masato*—maize beer—and, for Nicole, a gourdful of sour murky wine made from the *maracuia*, a jungle passionfruit.

Suddenly a woman who had been sitting nearby fell to the ground, writhing.

"What's wrong with Genta?" Nicole asked Xingu.

"Last night she heard that her brother, who was with Chochobo in the forest, was dead."

"Is she ill, too?"

"I do not think so," he said.

Then Nicole nodded. She knew that suppressed negative feelings become powerful and are stored in the body. And she knew well the Indians understood the value of releasing the stress throughout the whole body. Perhaps that was why so few Indians ever got cancer.

Finally the woman sat quietly on the ground again, with everyone surrounding her. The men and boys came silently, one at a time, to touch her shoulder or her cheek, while the women and girls picked lice from her hair with their fingers, and mites from her feet with bone needles. Some of the children had piranha scars on their thighs. Nicole, her eyes stinging with tears for the gentle humanity of these people she loved, brushed the woman's hair with a densely thistled pod.

Soon, though, Xingu announced that they must be on their way to Chochobo.

Nicole carried the bag containing their lunch while Xingu carried the canoe through the jungle to what the Indians called the River Sea—the Amazon. Nicole had learned the quick, fluid Indian way of walking. She felt safe with Xingu, whom she knew could save her life a hundred times over without her realizing it. He knew how to avoid trees laden with poisonous tarantulas; where hidden and camouflaged snakes lay; how to recognize quicksand that looked as solid as cement.

The forest floor was a jumble of rotted wood and decaying leaves. Liana vines hung, looped, and intertwined everywhere. Bougainvillea dripped heavy with blossoms, and startling flame vines intermingled with black-velvet gloxinia and frangipani.

There were crimson passionflowers and orchids of every hue. The scent of flowers mingled with the rank, humid soil and the rotting vegetation.

"Rains will come soon," Xingu announced. "I have seen the size of the young turtles. I have been listening to the rain frogs."

Nicole regretted that Mary Mahoney had not been interested in how much the Indians taught her.

Without warning, Xingu stopped and turned completely around. Nicole stood frozen as she watched the Indian put the canoe down silently and take a knife from inside his jaguar fur. He brought his hand up to his mouth in the universal signal for silence. He plunged the blade deep into the earth and bent over to clench his teeth around the shaft. It was the old Indian technique for amplifying the vibrations of distant footsteps.

Suddenly the old guide leaped up from the ground and was at her side, one hand clasped over her mouth, the other gripped around the knife. Nicole felt her heart in her throat. She looked into the bush where the Indian's eyes were staring intently. Three brown men, with red dots painted on their faces, naked except for their penis sheaths, stared at them down the shafts of their drawn arrows. Their lavender gums were drawn back in anger, exposing yellow teeth filed to sharp points.

Stealthily, Nicole reached into the pocket that held her switchblade. It was so quiet that a bird could be heard hopping on one of the leaves of the canopy above. Xingu and the others said nothing. Nicole felt her scalp tighten.

"*Moina ga teng?*" one of the strangers asked finally. *Where are you going?* At least their language was one they could understand.

Xingu answered that they were going to visit friends in the forest on the other side of the river.

"Who?" the same man asked.

Nicole knew that Xingu would guard Chochobo's hiding place with his life. But she also knew he would not lie.

"Chochobo," Xingu answered.

The man who had asked the question lowered his bow, which acted as a cue to the others to lower theirs. The bowmen smiled. Nicole began to breathe again.

The strangers said they were from a tribe deep in the rain forest. Game was sparse in their area, so they were on their way to hunt tapir at the nearby salt licks. They had collected a lot of wriggling grubs, some as big as Ping-Pong balls, and invited Nicole and Xingu to join them for lunch. Xingu said they would be honoured, but they must attend to important business. The men left quickly and quietly. Nicole and Xingu continued their journey.

The jungle became a maelstrom of thick, fleshy leaves, shiny and rubbery, and fruited shapes. All at once, the scent of flowers, the odors of the soil, the fecundity and rankness of growth crowding in from

all sides unnerved Nicole. She felt a sense of un-
bridled sexuality.

They passed an ancient village overgrown with
purple-flowered tonka bean. Nicole had a sudden
image of Chochobo. His face was framed by two
broad lines of black fruit stains which accentuated
his dark, bright eyes and bold, clear face: the fierce
and beautiful aspect of a falcon. The skin on his lean,
muscular body was the color of golden tobacco leaves,
and shone from rubbings of palm oil. She blinked her
eyes to dispel the image, but when she opened them,
she imagined she saw the bright sun gleaming on his
forearm sinews.

"You breathe hard, Nicole," Xingu said. And she
saw that he had stopped and set down the canoe. He
stood before her with an outstretched palm filled with
coca leaves.

"No, thank you," she said regretfully.

Chochobo had taught her that the drug would
interfere with her body's natural rhythms and might
bring back her arthritis. She watched Xingu take his
coca with a little lime, which extracted the cocaine
from the leaf. He sucked on the leaves as one might
suck a peach pit. Nicole knew many Indians who had
chewed coca three times a day since boyhood and still
enjoyed perfect health. Many lived to be very, very
old. Besides its medicinal use, coca was part of the
Indians' religion, work, and tradition. She believed
that the white man's attempt to control the Indians'

use of coca was ignorant interference, similar to an attempt to outlaw beer in Germany, coffee in the Near East, or betel chewing in India.

Nevertheless, Nicole disapproved of the use of cocaine by her Western friends. She knew that the drug caused many deaths even of people like Ava, who had been her friend for a brief, happy time. Ava, whose caring about others had inspired her to respond to the Indians and who had enriched her life.

Nicole thought of Buchreiser. She became so angry that her hands began to shake.

"We rest and eat now," Xingu said. "The river is only a little walking away."

She ate ravenously. As always, Xingu was right. They soon reached the Urapu tributary of the Amazon. Xingu tasted its water to be sure it was the right branch of the river to lead them to Chochobo. The sight of the coca-colored water which led to the colossal Amazon River evoked emotions of mystery. It contained, she knew, one-fifth of the world's fresh-water supply. White people forced to travel over this incredible expanse of water by boat—day after day, week after week—had been known to go mad.

Nicole had become accustomed to the constant chatter of the jungle. Yet it ceased on the river. It was like having her pulse stop.

Eighteen-foot-long alligators followed them, sur-facing occasionally, looking curiously at Xingu's paddles. Once or twice she heard the cough of a prowling jaguar. Along the riverbanks, flowering walls of tea vines with their yellow flowers competed with garcinias and spiny palms, pineapple and plantains. From the shore a lesser kiskadee erupted in its low, wheezy call. Dragonflies hovered over the water, quivering silently.

Suddenly Nicole ducked a low-hanging branch.

A moment later, Xingu shouted from behind her: "Why did you not tell me?"

She turned around and was relieved that the Indian had seen the branch. "I was going to, but I remembered that you never tell people. You let them find out for themselves."

"You will be a Carrijura yet!" he laughed.

As they went downriver, Xingu brought strange new plants and birds to her attention.

"I wish I knew what you know," she said.

"What I know is only a drop of water to what my father knew, and his father before him. They trusted their own eyes, their own senses. When I was a boy, I was once so sick that everyone in the village believed I would die. My parents did not ask others to help me. They studied *me*." Xingu looked up quickly. "Rain."

At times, Nicole found the Indian's language as hard to understand as Xingu must find hers. Whenever she said, "It is raining," he would say, "What is 'it'?"

Xingu always sensed the rain long before Nicole

did. Within minutes a torrent descended upon them with such force that it caromed off her head and body and even the river itself. It was not like rain at all, but like tiny pebbles of water. It lashed her back, twisted branches from the trees, and turned the day into twilight. The noise was so loud that they couldn't hear one another.

When the rain stopped, Nicole squeezed the water from her hair. Soon the sun would bake her skin and clothes dry.

At last they reached the place. The sun was now high in the sky.

Nicole placed a hand over her eyes to shade the blistering sun. Suddenly she saw Chochobo sitting on an albino jaguar skin in front of an A-shaped hut just five yards away.

Chapter Twelve

"Okay, Jackie, what you find out about Rudd?" Gus asked as the whore entered his bungalow. The chocolate points of her breasts showed through the sheer T-shirt she wore over tight beige trousers.

Jackie lit a cigarette and blew the smoke from her dilated nostrils. "He's definitely not DEA or any other heat," she said. Lowering herself onto the Naugahyde couch, she avoided looking at Gus's blubbery upper lip.

"Because he tells you that?"

"Because I can always tell when they're faking, honey."

"Something else?"

"He's not an addict. His nose is clean, and there's not a track mark on him."

"And?"

"He knows a lot about blow, knew mine had been stepped on with mannitol and that it was just okay. He doesn't talk much about himself. He says he's from San Francisco. A businessman."

"No more?"

"I'm telling you he didn't say shit."

"Okay, okay. I send you to Marita's place in Rio so Rudd does not see you hanging here." He glanced at his watch. "You go. He be here in half hour."

"Drink, Miles?" asked Gus.

"Thanks, I don't drink when I'm doing business." Knowing Ava had worked on the grounds outside and had been in this office-den of a room—had probably sat on the same plastic couch where he now sat—was unnerving. He could use a drink, but he wanted to keep up the impression of soberness, dependability.

"I no say yet we do business," Gus said.

"I also drink coffee when I'm doing possibilities," he said, lifting the cup Gus had handed him.

Gus's smile was slow in coming.

"I like you, Miles."

"Thank you." He looked about the windowless room, at the picture of the braceleted snake hanging from a low branch above Gus's desk. "Snake farms always fascinate me."

"Would you like to see?"

"The whole twenty-five-cent tour, if you don't mind."

"What?"

"Just an expression."

Gus led him to a room wallpapered with snake-skins. It contained wall-to-wall cages that were waterless aquariums with chicken-wire lids.

It was so hot Michael had to take off his sports jacket. He remembered Ava telling him that snakes, being cold-blooded, can't retain heat, and in captivity must live in a temperature-controlled environment. Up close he could see that the cages contained wood logs and hiding boxes. The wallpaper was beautiful —and frightening. It made him imagine a snake the size of the room. There were instruments for catching and handling snakes, both in the field and in captivity, including the most common clamp stick with rubber-covered prongs and the small hook essential in lifting very small venomous snakes.

"What a setup!" Michael said. He was reminded of how Ava had always liked animals, even insects and reptiles that repelled most people. He decided to ingratiate himself even more with Gus by para-phrasing George Bernard Shaw, from a book he had read in New York about wild-animal trafficking: "When a man wants to murder a snake, he calls it sport; when the snake wants to murder him, he calls it ferocity."

Gus turned quickly and looked back at him. The snake man had allowed his eyes to show depth. "How you are right, my friend. If not for snakes, rats, and mice, you would not have room to walk. And of all the ones that kill, he is the last to attack." Then the Greek's eyes became flat and guarded again.

Gus opened a cabinet and took out a forceps. Then he swiftly reached into one of the cages and held the head of an eight-foot-long bushmaster. "A beauty, no?"

"I'll say."

Gus set the snake down again in its cage. Michael hoped the question of sexing the serpent wouldn't arise. He hadn't gotten that far in his reading.

Gus opened a rectangular aluminum can below the cabinet, then picked up a dead rat with the forceps and flicked the rodent into the cage containing the bushmaster. The serpent—pinkish, with black blotches extending along its body—remained still for a moment, then began to edge toward the rat, bringing the lateral, S-shaped striking loop to nearer and better advantage. The reptile showed its forked yellow tongue, while its vibrating tail, hidden among the leaves of its cage, produced a loud buzzing sound. Michael didn't want to watch what would follow, but he knew Gus was testing him. He tasted bile as the snake struck the rat and then swallowed it, the shape of the rodent visible as it moved down the reptile's body.

"Fast, huh!" Gus exclaimed. "If it was a baseball player, think how fast he can throw."

"But not nearly as exciting as your curve ball."

Gus turned quickly.

"What do you mean?"

"You know too much about snakes to pick one up with a forceps. You just want to see how much I know about snakes. I don't blame you. One can't be too careful of businessmen nowadays when looking for opportunity."

Reminded of Buchreiser's caution, Gus's smile came faster this time. "I do like you, Rudd, even if you no trust me. I cannot trust nobody either."

"Good. At least you're not prejudiced against North Americans."

Coufos beamed. "Do you know how can tell male from female?"

Michael dug the nail of his index finger into his palm. "Turn them over?" he tried.

Coufos didn't laugh.

"Look," Michael said. "I told you I had some business with snakes. I did. I made some money. I didn't make them my life's work."

"Forgive. I am a careful man."

"Careful is good business. But too much distrust can destroy opportunities before they have a chance to yield dollars."

"This is true. Let us have no more distrust." He patted Michael on the back and then pointed to one of the cages. "One-day-old litter fer-de-lance," he said as they bent closer to a cage containing over fifty snakelings, each about twelve inches long. "They have fangs and poison when born. Here is Melina, their mother."

Michael looked into the adjoining cage and saw the distinctively lance-shaped head and beautiful geometric design of the five-foot serpent. This was probably the same family of snakes shown in the photograph on Ava's wall. Michael caught his breath.

"I knew a man," Coufos said, "who got bit by one of these. Vomits blood for eighteen hours before he shoots himself in the head. And once, I was in Honduras, I hear story about how strong is fer-de-lance poison. A doctor at the serpentarium at Tela told me.

"In Honduras, is custom of people of small towns where is the railroad to meet all trains and to sell fruits, tortillas, madehome candies. One woman, her special was coconut candy. She cut up coconuts on old-fashion nutmeg grater, so her finger ends have small scratches—hundreds—from touching grater. Her husband, who worked on plantation close to her, is brought home hurting from bite of a *barba amarilla*—fer-de-lance. The husband is put to care of native doctor, so wife can only help to wash place where fangs cut. The man he dies in two hours. And wife dies the next morning. The venom goes through her scratches."

Michael shivered. "Incredible."

"How about you join me in little drink now?" Coufos said.

Michael's stomach gurgled. "I might be persuaded to break a rule and have just one brandy."

"Good!"

As Michael and Coufos sat sipping brandy, the smaller man spoke.

"Okay, no more children games. Why do you come to me? For business?"

"Because I figured anyone who welcomed me the way you did might have good connections, and maybe something to hide."

"Aha!" Coufos exclaimed, and slapped Michael on the shoulder. "A man like you I want never to have for enemy. What kind of business you have in your head, Miles?"

"Money. That's the big incentive. The product doesn't matter."

"I no deal in wild animals no more."

"Neither do I, at the moment."

Coufos raised the snifter to his lips and looked out over the rim. "So. Any ideas?"

"I'm told there are many valuable things in Colombia. Spanish gold, the world's finest emeralds, marijuana . . . cocaine."

Coufos's face showed no expression. "Which you like best?"

"Whichever is the most profitable."

"Okay. So make believe I do business with these things you speak of. How do you fit?"

"Maybe you can use an intelligent executive type

who can keep his mouth shut, with contacts in stocks, bonds, commodities all around the world. You know, legitimate investments are more than just good ways to launder money. They're a safety valve. A man can deal only in cash without people becoming suspicious."

"What you did before, in such high-class businesses?"

"I worked as a stockbroker on Wall Street for five years. For the last ten I've been in the business of managing people's money. Very rich people."

"If you do so good, why you want to change?"

"Simple. I want to be in the position where others manage my money."

Coufos set down his glass and stared at the amber liquid, then deep into Michael's eyes. When he spoke it was in the tone of a man who was still undecided.

"If I was the German—I mean the big boss—I would need to think more before I try what you want."

Michael nodded, tensing at the thought of working with "the German." "I would, too. Caution is a valuable thing."

There was still something about Rudd that bothered Coufos. Maybe because he made himself too easy to get. He would go to the palace and ask what was to be done with him.

"Whenever you're ready," Michael said flatly. But he could hardly conceal his excitement. He was sure he had drawn the first bead on the string that would lead him to Ava's murderer or—for the first time a new possibility emerged—murderers.

Chapter Thirteen

"I go now to visit my people," Xingu said to Nicole.
She didn't have to thank him. The Carrijura felt no
need for thanks. There was no such expression in
their language. There was also no need to arrange
a meeting for the journey back. Xingu would appear
when she needed him.

Nicole surveyed the collection of dwellings constructed of wattles and thatch. The air was redolent
with the smell of roasting meat. Men, women,
children, most of them naked, quickly surrounded
her. She recognized Chochobo's twelve-year-old son.

Then Chochobo's favorite wife, Liara, a young
woman of perhaps nineteen, came out of his hut and
sat with him on the jaguar skin. They both had the
short otter haircut of the Carrijura. They looked more
like brother and sister than husband and wife. The
beautiful Liara clutched her young, luminous knees
in her arms.

As Nicole approached the hut, Liara stood and went inside. She did not seem pleased to accept her husband's meeting alone with the white woman. While Nicole was compassionate toward Liara, she wanted to be alone with Chochobo.

One day, months before, Nicole had come across the young woman with Chochobo in the forest. They had been swimming in the river and were drying themselves on the bank. Sparkling droplets on the tips of their straight hair reflected the sun with the intensity of shards of glass. Nicole decided to leave, preserving their privacy, but she did not. Instead, embarrassed, she sat and watched them as they made love.

After making love, Chochobo had blown his breath into a strip of dried hyacinth, tied the strip into a ring, and placed the ring around the neck of his wife, saying, "Guard well my breath."

Their childlike tenderness had made her so want to be made love to that she had caressed herself to orgasm later that evening.

Now Chochobo stood as Nicole drew near.

Chochobo was a strong man. She guessed he was in his late thirties. His tribe's numbering system had only three numbers: one, two, and more than two, so the Carrijura knew ages only approximately.

Pride without arrogance shone in Chochobo's dark eyes. He wore a headdress of toucan feathers, fer-de-lance-skin armbands, ankle thongs, and a necklace of caiman teeth. Twin serpents were painted on his legs. His face was black with genipa juice, and he wore a macaw feather—a symbol of war. A small gourd tied around his muscular waist had been polished smooth and white with a brace of leaves; it hung from his jaguar-hide loincloth like a giant penis.

He had an angular, bony face. The nose, uncharacteristically small for an Indian, and a full lower lip, gave him an appearance of unexpected vulnerability. It contrasted sharply with the fierce, falconlike aspect of Chochobo's black, fruit-stained face, with the sharply defined muscles of his body, and with the veins in his large hands and thick skin. He was beautiful, like an untamed animal unaware of its grace.

"Welcome," he said. He possessed two voices. This one, coming from his belly, was deep and soothing; the other, coming from his throat, was high-pitched and wrathful.

"It's fine to see you, Chochobo."

"Come," he said, and beckoned her inside his hut. Suddenly a jet plane broke the sound barrier. The incongruous sound caught in the surrounding ancient trees, echoing and receding slowly to sound and resound far, far away. It lasted several minutes, and Nicole saw a curious sight. None of the older Indians seemed affected, only the young—the children were running about excitedly. Chochobo turned and she looked into his eyes. Beneath his pride she saw a sadness so deep that it seemed to stretch back into a time so far that Nicole could not imagine it. Not only were his people overwhelmingly outnumbered, but their enemies might annihilate them even from the sky.

Chochobo turned abruptly and entered the hut. His five wives greeted Nicole politely but distantly. A single animal hide dried to the hardness of wood leaned against one of the walls; against another was a sharpened piece of bamboo for cutting hair. An infant lay in a hammock, above which rattling frog skulls, threaded on a liana, hung from the ceiling. The baby reached out to them.

Presently the wives departed with the baby, leaving in their wake a palpable mistrust and jealousy of Nicole.

The women had prepared a feast: a caldron of turtle soup, fried tapir and yams, cakes of manioc, palm fruit, several varieties of honey, and skinned frogs, wrapped in pishani leaves, and cooked over the fire, served with manioc gruel and herb tea. Nicole liked the taste of the yams, palm fruit, and honey. Chochobo was not hungry; he picked at some of the food, though, out of respect for his wives.

They did not speak as they ate. At first she felt uncomfortable with Chochobo's uninhibited gaze, but then, as always, she grew accustomed to it. Soon she was gazing back, absorbing his quiet intensity, reminded of how he led his people by example, not threats and coercion. As he had established his reputation for being brave long ago, he could afford to. Nicole believed he would have been a leader at any time of his life.

"You are a fine *cacique*." Nicole almost didn't know if she had thought this or said it.

"I will not be a *cacique* for a long time. A person comes as a leader for a special time and need, then moves down whenever that time is over. This is a tribal involvement."

Nicole smiled, feeling a little more confident for what she was about to broach. "Why must you sell the coca to the white man now?"

"To buy these," He went to a chest made of palm, opened it, and took out a rifle. "We have many men joining us, even from tribes we have been at war with for many rises of the river. Some of them come from so far away. To travel to them would take time for a new moon to grow full."

"There are too many white men with weapons that make even your new rifles seem like toys," Nicole said. "Besides, the money you get from selling coca to the white man cannot save your people. An evil trail cannot lead to good."

"Coca is a good thing."

"Yes, but the white man uses it to make cocaine, which is evil."

"If the white man makes evil of yams, shall we call yams evil?"

"Of course not. If only I could explain it to you."

She thought of all the atrocities on which Buchreiser's palace in the jungle must be built. Of Ava's death.

Chochobo poured more tea into her cup.

"Be careful, Chochobo! The tea will overflow!"

"Like this gourd, you are full of opinions. How can you take in what I say unless you first empty your cup?"

About to defend herself, she looked into his wise face and smiled instead.

"I'm sorry. Please speak."

Chochobo rose without warning, went to the entrance of the hut, and called a woman's name. While he stood waiting, Nicole had time to appreciate how big and powerful he was. His days of hunting and fighting had made him strong. The V-shape of his broad shoulders funneled down to his narrow waist, and the muscle and sinew of his forearms and thighs and calves flexed pneumatically as he moved.

Soon a young girl of perhaps twelve or thirteen appeared at the entrance. Chochobo took the child's hand in his and brought her to Nicole.

"Please tell this woman, who is our friend, how it was for you in the white school."

The girl looked at her feet as she spoke. "The white teacher taught me how to cheat in football, how to stumble so that it would throw off another player and seem to be an accident, so to win. Now I have to work hard to forget it."

"Thank you," Chochobo said. He cupped her small

face so gently with his huge hand that Nicole was touched by his tenderness. Then he led the girl outside.

"I never said—" Nicole began when he returned.

"I am not finished. We Indians get bad treatment because we tell the truth. If an Indian says, 'I don't know,' the whites are often sure the Indian is lying because he *must* know. We do not want them to change us. We will die in our true world if we have to, but we will not live in their false one."

Chochobo rose and stood again at the entrance to the hut. The dark red evening sky reflecting on his chest and thighs enhanced his commanding appearance. Nicole became aware of his abundance of blue-black hair. A helmet of hair. The word "free" did not exist in Chochobo's language. *In actuality*, she thought, *there is nothing for a Carrijura to free himself from. His spirit is not seeking truth, but holding on to it.*

"And what," Chochobo began in a tone that seemed to come from across the widest part of the river, "do you think is the answer for my people now—to be still so we can be killed?"

Waiting for her reply, he left the entrance and went to light torches from a pilot torch. Soon dancing shadows silhouetted against the darkness were reflected on the golden patina of gourds hanging from the rafters and the palm oil on Chochobo's shoulders and chest.

"There are many more plants in the Amazon valley than there are hairs on both our heads," she said. "And still many more to be discovered. Only a few have been used by the white man to make medicine. Your tribe has the pukatire plant. If a woman takes it, she doesn't get pregnant for two years. It would take years of research to learn what your people already know."

"I am listening."

She thought of Ava, of her dead friend's dream. "The venom of the fer-de-lance snake is used by the whites to cure snakebites and make the blood stop flowing. In the white world, it sells for twenty-eight thousand dollars an ounce."

"I do not understand such worth."

"I'm sorry. The venom sells for more than the cocaine the white man makes from your coca."

"But many more need coca than the snakebite medicine. Do not worry so, my sister and friend. We are relatives to all who swim or fly or walk. We will survive because we are Indian, and we are of the spirit. The spirit cannot be destroyed."

How could she argue against the age-old beliefs of this man? Why were environmentalists more concerned about snail darters and whales than they were about the loss of Chochobo's people?

Chochobo came over and sat next to her.

"Now, my sister, I would like to know what *you*

plan to do now that you are well. Will you go back to your people?"

"I . . . I don't know what to do right now."

"Why?" he asked softly. He placed his hand on her shoulder. His touch was gentle.

"Well, because I feel safe here. It is the only place in which I know myself. I like it here, where only important things matter."

"What is that?"

"The joy of life. And to face death unafraid." Here, where death waited in every tree and under each rock, she had learned to make friends with her arthritis and to transform loneliness to aloneness. Finally, she had learned to face her own death.

"You have learned well," Chochobo said.

"Yet I still miss a lot from back home. . . ."

"A sick Wauru chief named Taxupuh was once taken from his village, flown to São Paulo for a great white doctor to cut him. 'How could a man go back to this place after seeing how our people live?' he asked the doctor when he had seen the city. 'How can you breathe the foul air there, and sleep with the noises? How can you eat food with false tastes?' Now I ask you, my sister, how?"

"It is not simple, Chochobo."

As soon as the words left her mouth, she looked up into Chochobo's eyes. They both knew she had not answered his questions.

Chapter Fourteen

After making sure that everyone on the snake farm had gone home, Gus Coufos locked his office from the inside, switched off the light, and turned on his penlight. He went to the closet and pushed aside the suits and sports coats. Then he reached into his back pants pocket and took out a wallet-sized calendar from a calfskin case. He measured off an outstretched palm and a half from the top of the ceiling and from the farthest point to the right. Then he held the card up against the designated spot.

A mechanical clicking sound followed. Coufos started counting as the wall behind the closet opened in the center and its two halves began receding. When he reached ten, the wall had vanished.

Coufos stepped inside. As usual, it was dark and dank. He had thought about expanding the room to

provide for more ventilation. This worried Buchreiser, the only other person who knew of its exis-
tence. He said that workmen would be witnesses.
For this reason, Buchreiser made Gus Coufos do the
carpentry and wiring himself, to Buchreiser's speci-
fications. The snake keeper thought of what
Buchreiser had ordered him to do with Rudd, and
checked his watch. The American was due in little
more than an hour.

Coufos came to a great glass cage half filled with
water and pointed his flashlight on a yellow anaconda. The reptile shone like a glowworm from the
luminous parasites that lived on its scales. The
effect was startling because of the animal's great
size: the snake was over thirty feet and had the girth
of a small oak tree.

The anaconda hissed and showed its scalpel-
sharp teeth, some of which were more than two
inches long. Although not poisonous, its teeth gave
the snake an almost inescapable grip, and the great
constrictor's hundreds of powerfully joined muscles
were able to crush a man into bloody pulp in
moments.

Coufos was sad as he thought of what Buchreiser
had ordered him to do to his beautiful friend. How
many times had he done it? He removed the syringe
from his shirt pocket and examined it carefully to
see that it was filled properly. It was.

Attracted by Coufos's body heat, the anaconda

came toward him. Coufos, suppressing his regret, raised the lid carefully, reached in, and, holding the yellow anaconda by the tail, inserted the syringe under a scale and drove it into its flesh.

The tranquilizing fluid entered the snake's log-thick body where his tail began. It started thrashing violently. Coufos looked away.

Moments later, the cage was quiet. The Greek turned his gaze on the snake. It lay on its side, inert. The snake keeper climbed into the cage. Opening the empty stainless-steel food box, he beamed his flash with his left hand and set his calendar card in the upper-right-hand corner with his free hand. Then he waited for Buchreiser's electrical genius to show itself again. In seconds, the false bottom of the box opened. Coufos moved aside the produce scale. Then he carefully removed the Ohaus, the precision laboratory scale with a three-posted equal arm, pharmaceutical balance, and stainless-steel trays, capable of measuring thousandths of a gram.

The Greek reached down and removed the treasure: forty-five condoms filled with ninety-eight-percent-pure cocaine, each weighing fifteen ounces, with a total weight of just over nineteen kilos. When he had removed the great nylon sack and the stretch forceps from the food container, and replaced the scales and the lid, he sat contemplating the fortune before him and thinking about the coke trade—from South American soil to the New York market. The South American farmer sold a kilo of his coca leaves for five dollars. That was made into a paste selling for seven hundred dollars a kilo. After reaching the States, the kilo went through many middlemen, each cutting it yet again. The nineteen kilos would soon be worth about twenty-three million dollars! It was no wonder that Buchreiser lived in a palace. He was as rich as the richest king. Coufos shook his head. He must stop this idle dreaming. Buchreiser gave Coufos orders he hated, but orders that must be carried out.

Coufos lifted the stretch forceps in one hand and a handful of condoms in another and walked over to the anaconda.

He inserted the first condom down the throat of the beast. He hated to think what would happen if the serpent's powerful digestive juices dissolved the condoms before the snake arrived at a zoo in New York, where one of the keepers on Buchreiser's payroll would reanesthetize and disgorge the serpent and bring the cocaine to the local distributor.

To divert himself, Gus Coufos thought of the California biologists, ichthyologists, and herpetologists who had toured the farm recently. How much pleasure it gave him, the son of Greek peasants, whose education ended with grammar school, to have learned men impressed by his knowledge of snakes.

When the anaconda had been stuffed with cocaine, Coufos stitched its mouth and its anus with surgical gut as an extra precaution. Then, with tremendous effort, Coufos stuffed the snake into the large nylon sack. Grunting and sweating, Coufos began dragging the sack slowly back inside, where he would place it into an empty cage to await the arrival of the truck that would take it to the airport.

"You can say, Miles, we deal most in people," Coufos said as Michael sat down.

"So?"

"So. There is a woman. My business people want to find out what she knows about us."

"I see. A test."

"Say it is to build good faith, eh? Everybody gets tests all the time from big boss. Me, also. He likes this. You would be well paid."

"Please go on," Michael said.

"The woman, her name is Nicole de la—something. I cannot say it. Here, look."

Coufos produced an eight-by-ten glossy and handed it to Michael. The woman was dressed in a bush jacket and shorts. He recognized her. She was Nicole de la Houssaye, the Olympic gymnast. She was certainly attractive. But what fascinated him was her expression—she looked at once open and self-contained.

"What is she doing here? Wasn't she missing for a long time?"

"They say she came to cure herself of arthritis."

"Did she?"

"The Indians say so."

"Do you believe someone can cure themselves of arthritis?"

"Nah. She is probably crazy. But the Indians know more than you think. Maybe. Who knows? But we get away from your assign—good faith."

"I don't mind the word assignment, Gus."

Coufos smiled quickly. Then his features became uncommitted.

"We would like you get this woman to trust you."

"Who do I tell her I am?"

"Here is card from new charity to help Indians."

Michael took the card. It read:

> Save World Cultures Foundation
> 23 Fifth Avenue
> New York, New York 10010
> (212) 535-5606
>
> Miles Rudd
> Representative

"What if she phones this number?"

"She will speak to someone who knows all about Indians. This is one of my boss's fronts. Here is pictures and things which tells us what they do. You tell us what you learn; we will pick what we use. She is best friend of Chochobo, chief of the Carrijura Indians. They are farmers of the coca. We want to know every time she meets with him. What they say. Where they go. Tribes have come from all over the

Amazon to come live with the Carrijura. Why? To
fight the white man? How many have come? Where
they get guns? Not only Chochobo. You listen to
anything what happens with Carrijura. Very
important there is Wactu, chief of tribe from Brazil
who has come to visit with Carrijura. What does
Chochobo say to Nicole of him? What do they both
feel for Wactu? I have tape of her. You can look over.
Study her. Then go. That is all for now."

"Are you always this cautious with new people?"

"At beginning only. Do not get mad. It is nothing
per—"

A knock on the door interrupted them.

"Personal," Coufos finished. Then he shouted,
"Come in!"

A white-smocked herpetologist opened the door.
"The tour of scientists from California will be here
in a little while, Mr. Coufos."

"Okay," he said, standing up. "So. We have deal,
Rudd?"

"Deal."

They shook hands.

"Good. Now you come watch tape of this Nicole
woman, and then you watch when I give these
educated idiots a lesson in serum, okay?"

"Delighted."

Michael watched a half-dozen scientists come into
the room. Soon after, a woman entered. At the sight of
her, Michael froze. She was a pert blonde with an

almost aristocratic fragility—above her waist; below it, she had thick legs and a peasant's ass. The halves of two different women in one. The long, tapered fingers of her hands obviously belonged to the aristocratic half of her. His own hands felt skinless, with the nerves laid bare. She had been a biology major in college—Leslie Zahler! Of all the places! He felt a runnel of perspiration course down his spine.

Suddenly he realized that in college he had worn the moustache he had recently shaved off. Also, his hair had been curly then, and brown, instead of straight and black. He let out a great breath, relaxing a bit. He saw now that she'd aged—lines across her forehead, at the corner of her eyes, and bracketing her mouth. Markings of someone who had lasted through something. What? A bad marriage? Sickness?

Despite his dread, Michael couldn't stop his mind from leaping back twenty-two years to Columbia University.

"We shall overco-ummm . . ."

He saw Leslie and himself and a half-dozen others standing on top of the steps of the Student Union Building where a banner flew, proclaiming SDS. At the foot of the steps were thousands of students.

He heard himself shouting, "We ain't gonna study war no more!" Patrol cars were parked half on, half off the sidewalks surrounding the campus, their red beacons playing on the windows of study halls and biology labs. The odor of horse manure and urine mixed with leather from the mounted police rose up to his nostrils. A police helicopter whirled overhead. And there stood Leslie next to him, carrying a placard reading, *"ROTC! Reserves Off The Campus!"*

Suddenly the riot police were thrashing their clubs at them as though in panic to stamp out a fire. He winced, seeing a cop whip a club across the face of a boy wearing glasses. The boy fell to his knees and then went stumbling off, his mouth wide open, apparently in a scream. Sun reflected off the chips of glass in his nose and cheeks. When he saw Leslie again, she had about a three-inch-square bald spot on her head where her hair had been torn out.

Above the chant *"We shall overcome"* came the sound of an ambulance's siren.

Now, Coufos was approaching with the scientists—and that same Leslie—to introduce her as a zoologist.

He managed a "Hi" in a deliberately deep voice.

"For you," Coufos soon began, "who never sees a snake milked . . ."

Seeing Leslie listening raptly to the lecture, he turned his gaze on the Greek, too.

The snake man stuck his arms into a cage holding a fer-de-lance. Michael gasped with the others as the snake sprang at Coufos, sinking its fangs into his arm.

"Nothing to be scared of," Coufos said proudly. "I been bit a hundred and forty times. Immune."

There was a silence followed by enthusiastic

clapping. Despite himself, Michael admired the man's courage and joined in the applause.

He saw Leslie turn to look at him curiously. Then he remembered that his alias was close to the name of an old classmate of theirs. Did she remember? She turned her attention back to Coufos.

"We take only what snake gives by himself when he bites." Coufos directed the mouth of another snake, a bushmaster, over a test glass, and allowed its fangs to puncture a rubber cover. Amber-colored venom dripped into the glass.

"Why must the snake be handled?" a bald biologist asked Coufos. "Why not let the creature bite an object from which the venom can be removed?"

"Holding him is only sure way to get snake to let go his poison in glass with no squeeze the animal."

Leslie turned around and looked at Michael again, and he remembered the scar over his left eye. It had been made by the impact of a policeman's ring on his face during the same riot he had just remembered.

"Most of poison we got here," Coufos was saying, "is made to get stuff to stop blood clots."

He was sure that Leslie was looking at his signet ring now, a gift from his parents. He had worn it all through college. He covered his ring finger with his other hand, then twisted the onyx stone so only the band showed.

"There is two kinds venom, one that most has to do with blood and tissues—he-mo-toxins is called, and two, that has to do with nerves and breathing—neu-ro-tox-ins. Experts like you know every venom is what you say, one of a kind. Like . . ."

Michael thought Leslie was backing herself slowly toward him! It couldn't be. The ring! It must have been the damn ring!

". . . some of you must hear," Coufos said, "of work they do with king cobra venom to take pain away in arthritis or cancer, the kind of cancer that you die for sure. Here we also working with fer-de-lance venom in new ways. Also . . ."

Leslie was only an arm's distance away now.

". . . we find out fer-de-lance venom makes crazy people happy. How come is that? We do not know nothing. Anybody got questions?"

"Haven't I met you before? In New York?" Leslie whispered.

Pushing into the floor with his toes through his shoes, Michael managed a weak smile. "Never been closer to it than Ohio."

"You remind me of someone I knew in college. Sorry, it was a chance in a million."

"It's quite all right."

Michael didn't relax until fifteen minutes later, when Coufos turned the group over to a herpetologist who was going to show them a film of a viper giving birth.

In Coufos's office, the Greek, obviously pleased with

himself, offered Michael some *aguardiente* from a bottle in his desk drawer. This time Rush didn't hesitate.

"So, Rudd, you watch this woman for us. My people would also like you write other report. On your ideas. Like money washing. But more than that, if you have ideas. I show it to some people. The report will be torn up soon as we read it. Do not worry. Here is to you and Nicole—what is her name?"

"De la Houssaye. Here's to bigger things," Michael said, thinking of the boss Coufos took his orders from. Probably Buchreiser was knowledgeable when it came to laundering money. He must have a battery of stockbrokers. Michael would have to come up with something really different to entice such a man.

Chapter Fifteen

Walking was painfully slow. Michael tripped over vines. The undergrowth which pulled at his clothes slowed him. Once he plunged into mud up to his knees. Blue grasshoppers were everywhere, often showers of them. Iguanas and small lizards skittered noisily in dry leaves. Michael was engulfed in haunting sounds: hisses, crackles, peals, whistles, wheezes, honks, brayings.

There were spiderwebs everywhere: veils of gauze. "Damn!" he said to himself. One left irritating and foul-smelling fibers on his face and hands.

As he and the Carrijura guide Xingu walked on, Michael felt trapped *inside* a world, surrounded by a wall which he could run into but not through. With each step he took, he pushed aside the creepers, snapping them as he broke through. Then the wall disappeared, only to reappear again. When at last they reached a sunlit clearing, where vultures like broken umbrellas perched in the trees, he felt he was going *outside*.

At the edge of the clearing stood a strange, confusing sight—a white tree with thick, snowy ꞏranches. White orchids had overgrown it. As he drew nearer, suddenly the flowers leaped into the air and converged in a brilliant cloud that whirled above the jungle. Seconds passed before Michael realized that the white cloud was dozens of white herons and storks flying away en masse.

The air was stagnant, and the slight breeze smelled of the foul breath of the jungle. *What a curious rain,* Michael thought, as they began walking. *Not really rain, but mist. Not falling, but seeming to hang suspended in the air.* Branches plucked at Michael's clothing, twigs whipped across his face. There was the smell of freshly cut wood.

It began raining heavily and they took refuge under the canopy. Xingu told Michael it would be a long time before any drops penetrated the leafy understory of the forest where they sat eating lunch. Michael decided to time it exactly, and looked at his watch. Then he looked at Xingu. In the sepia light the old Indian guide's bones showed startlingly clear through his parchment skin. Liverish gouges underscored his eyes. Here, on the soft carpet of rotted wood and molding leaves that comprised the forest floor, it was surprisingly cool. Michael hadn't done this much walking in years, though, and the humidity made him feel as if his safari shirt, cotton pants, and tennis shoes had melted. Within the forest, the jungle sounds so evident outside seemed to merge with the immensity of the great trees and the brilliant hues of the wild flowers, birds, and butterflies to become one with them, natural and harmonious. Only they, the human intruders, seemed out of place, puny and transitory against their surroundings.

Michael thought of the videotape Coufos had showed him of the recent interview between Nicole de la Houssaye and Mary Mahoney. Because of the TV special, the snake keeper said, journalists from all over the world had been overrunning the Indian village where Nicole lived. She had sought privacy in another village farther down river, in a more remote part of the jungle.

Without warning, there was a sound like a squeaking hinge. His expression quizzical, Michael turned to Xingu.

"Toucan," said the guide.

It was Coufos who had told Michael to send word to Nicole through Xingu. In his message Michael included the business card Gus had had made for him, and a note. She had agreed to let him spend some time with her, doing research and determining what his foundation could do for the Indians. He hoped he could act the role of foundation researcher convincingly. During the six years he had spent in night school—after he had been thrown out of Columbia for political activities—he had taken some elective anthropological courses on Eskimos and other North American Indians. He hoped this would help.

Now rain began to reach them from the treetops 130 feet above. Michael checked his watch—it had taken nine minutes. Xingu stood as a signal to leave. Michael followed the Indian, who carried a bark canoe over his head. He noticed that below his tonsure Xingu's hair was as coarse as a deer's.

Moments later they came out of the heavily canopied jungle and stood by a tributary of the Amazon. Michael was amazed to discover it had stopped raining, even though there was still the sound of water hitting the ground where they had just been. The sun seared his face.

A tiny spoonbill fell from its nest and landed clumsily on a water hyacinth a few yards away. It flapped awkwardly, trying to decide what to do next. Michael and Xingu saw the bird disappear in an explosion of splashes. Moments later, they saw an alligator devouring what remained of the spoonbill. Neither of them had seen the reptile approach. It had come up beneath the bird and snapped it downward into the water. The alligator had lain precisely where they had been wading seconds ago. Michael took a long swallow of water from his canteen.

"Watch near your shoes."

Michael looked down and saw thin, matchlike creatures looping with blind purpose across the muddy bank.

"What are they?" Michael asked.

"Leeches. They live on blood."

"Let's move!"

"Look there," Xingu said, pointing a knobby, arthritic finger at a formation of five parrots that had swept into view. "One does not often see such a sight. Parrots mate for life. The one too many must be a bird who has lost his mate or is yet too young to mate."

Michael rubbed the pale space on the finger of his left hand where his potentially dangerous signet ring had been. Without it he felt less himself, somehow, than he did from the absence of his moustache, or from his dyed and straightened hair.

They had traveled no more than a hundred yards when they saw a clearing in the distance.

"We will soon be there," Xingu said.

Suddenly Michael heard a huge rumbling swelling the jungle. When he looked up, he saw a jaguar crouched on the flat limb of a low tree directly over his head. The cat looked ten feet long from jaws to tip of tail. The reek of the jaguar came up to his nostrils, sharp as the point of an arrow. The cat watched him with green pupils that burned like butane flames.

"Do not move, or he is sure to attack," Xingu said. "You smell his fear."

After a few seconds which felt like many minutes, the jaguar slunk down the tree and loped away with its head and tail down and belly close to the ground. Soon the green jungle absorbed him.

Michael let the breath out of his lungs and began to relax. Water dripped from his face. He inhaled slowly.

"It is brave not to move," Xingu said.

"And wiser," Michael agreed. "Let's go."

"How much farther?" Michael asked after a while.

The Indian said nothing, but looked across the river. Directing his binoculars to where the Carrijura was staring, Michael was startled by an incongruous sight on the opposite bank: Nicole de la Houssaye stood balanced on an improvised high beam carved out of jacaranda wood set before a background of ancient trees as high as skyscrapers. He guessed the beam was no more than four inches wide. She was wearing a leotard and what looked like ballet slippers. Her hair was splayed back from her forehead, as though she had just surfaced from a dive. A young Indian girl sat a few feet away, watching her in awe. Nicole was poised so still that she appeared an extension of the beam.

All at once she did a somersault. Michael marveled at her lack of hesitancy, perfect timing, and surefooted perfection as she completed the exercise on the narrow beam. Then he watched fascinated, seeing concentration etched into Nicole's face. When she did a back somersault, he held his breath, hoping she wouldn't fall off the impossibly narrow beam. Nicole completed the exercise perfectly, with a grin and a kind of impudent grace he guessed was a part of a highly competitive spirit. As Michael and Xingu moved on, the Indian explained that Nicole spent time teaching the young Indian girl every day.

As soon as Michael was settled down outside Nicole's hut, the girl who had been watching her work out brought him a bowl of dark honey.

How can I spy on anyone in this peaceful, innocent place? he thought. *For Ava*, he reminded himself. *For Ava*. When Nicole approached, he noticed how petite she was—maybe a foot shorter than he. And her eyes! Michael was unprepared for them—especially the one fringed with a bluish-gray halo. The effect was arresting, esthetically titillating; somehow the halo gave him the sense there was a focus in that spooky fringe that enabled her to probe into anyone's most hidden core.

Her smile was genuine, despite some indication of restraint and suspicion, and he felt a twinge of disquiet.

"It's nice to meet you, Mr. Rudd," she said. The hand she extended was strong, a surprise in a woman her size.

"You, too, and I certainly enjoyed watching your workout."

Nicole invited him into her hut. It looked like the one on the videotape. There was a straw basket filled with tubers, a hammock, an earthen jar, and, on the hearth, a steaming clay pot from which wafted the delicious scent of—what? Vegetable soup? The bed was a surprise, so strange in these surroundings.

She offered Michael some fruit juice. As she passed him the calabash, he brushed her arm; its firmness surprised him. The juice tasted delicious; it was strange and familiar all at once.

"Where would you like to begin?" she asked.

"There are many things you understand and . . . many questions I need answered. Our foundation is interested in the Carrijura tribe, as my note said. We're thinking of providing a grant for them. Could you tell me why you took up their cause?" He took a pen and notepad from his shirt pocket. "I mean, we both know the world is full of refugees. In my work I hear of hundreds of cases a week. Why especially them?"

"Because here," Nicole said, "there won't be anyone left to be a refugee. These people will cease to exist at all."

"Genocide? How is it happening?"

"Simply by contact with what we call civilization. The Amazon Indian has no resistance to flu, pneumonia, tuberculosis, or even to measles. And once he is sick he often decides the evil is too strong for him, so he just lies in his hammock waiting for death."

Nicole's eyes flashed now with her zeal for the Carrijura. "When an Indian is thrust directly from the Stone Age into the twentieth century, a great tragedy occurs. Amazonia is filled with them— witless, demoralized remnants. Once they were vital and proud; now they've become passive robots of civilization, waiting for decisions to be made for them. But not every tribe just sits back and permits the destruction of its culture. The Mayaruna on the Brazil-Peru border, for instance; their land was penetrated by an oil company in 1972, and they are so desperate they have decided just to die out. They execute every newborn baby."

"God, that's tragic. But it brings us again to something I've heard about in the town—this tribe's chief —what's his name?"

"Chochobo."

"Chochobo, yes, Didn't he lead his tribe deep into this area so they could farm coca?"

"Yes, and with the profits they buy guns. About a month ago Chochobo invited other tribes to join his own to fight the white man. For the first time, tribes that have been fighting each other for thousands of years are joining together. It's a miracle, but it's very dangerous for them."

"So he's trying to change things. But you think it's very bad, that they may all die off? Just how much time do you think they have? Before . . ."

"How much time they have is less important than

the fact that their extermination is succeeding, secretly or by open massacre, directly or indirectly. And now this coca business. I'm more afraid for them than ever."

In her sandals, Nicole's smallest toes, bending with the adjoining ones, were inordinately appealing to him. In the torchlight, the short layered helmet of her hair gave off glowing reflections. *Damn it*, he thought. He was distracted by this woman. But he had to concentrate on finding out what had really happened to Ava. He could allow no distractions.

"Miss de la Houssaye, why do you object to the Indians selling their coca to the white man? After all, they've been farming it for thousands of years anyway. How does that lead to their destruction?"

"Coca is part of their culture, and it's also a food and medicine. To process it into cocaine, which people steal and kill for, is just not the Indian's way."

"No," he said, "but is it any man's way to have nothing, no land? With the dollars from coca they can buy some land, and with a grant from us they could learn agriculture."

Nicole leaped up. "This land can't be owned by individuals! It's not a commodity. It belongs to no one. It's a trust, to be used and passed on. You can no more sell or buy this land than the sea or the air."

"I know some places are sacred to the Indian, but what difference will any of it make if he's gone . . . or dead?"

"Maybe the Indians would be better off buried on sacred ground than living in humiliation and with broken hearts. Look, Mr. Rudd, let's slow down. I haven't even asked if you're hungry. And you've just had a long trip here. How about sharing some supper with me?"

"Does that mean you don't feel like answering any more questions?"

"No, it means I'm hungry," she said, smiling and gauging him.

Michael laughed gently in response.

Chapter Sixteen

"I am not sure I trust Buchreiser," Chochobo said to the Brazilian chief Wactu as the two sat on a fallen tree outside the Carrijura village.

"There are white men worse than that one," Wactu said. Chochobo looked at the chief, who was as large around as a banana tree. He had almost no neck, and he wore stones found in the brains of the piraruci fish in his earlobes, which stretched them almost to his shoulders.

"What can be worse than a man who does trade with you only because he must have your coca? If my people did not have the plant, we would starve before he gave us one seed."

"I will tell you of worse white men. In my land the white men gave gifts of salt and sugar which contained poison. Even our children were given candy which held death. From their planes, clothing was dropped containing the white man's diseases which brought death and pain. My people were even shot down from the air. Those who fought were punished. Eyes were pierced, eyelids stitched up, hot oil poured in their ears. Whole clans—even tribes— have been destroyed. Those who survived were made slaves. Their women made to break taboo and lie with white men. Land stolen. That is why you must keep your land by any means."

"As long as we have the land," Chochobo said, as if speaking also to Nicole, "even to be buried on, our spirits are safe."

"True," Wactu said, rising slowly. They had been talking for a long time. "And the agreement we have made this day will bring our peoples together always and make us stronger."

Chochobo rose, too. Each wished the other a safe journey home.

As Chochobo made his way back to the village, his head was filled with thoughts of Liara, his newest wife—the only one he had chosen for himself. The others had either been gifts or the fruits of marriages prearranged by his father. He imagined Liara's gleaming hair and her eyes like blackberries with tiny flecks of gold. She did not stand tall, but her body, her flat belly, and her hips like a man's, all made her appear tall. She walked gracefully, and her small feet and her hands seemed to move like a flight of butterflies. He hurried his step. How, he wondered, with a cold emptiness in his belly, would he find the words to tell her about the new agreement with Wactu without hurting her?

Liara took one last bite of the maize she had chewed into pap and passed it into the mouth of her infant daughter. The baby's ears were pierced by ornaments of small capybara teeth decorated with feathers. Liara had birthed the child alone, as was the custom. She had tied the cord with her own hand, and she had eaten of the afterbirth to keep off whatever spirits might try to harm her child and to relieve her of any fear that she would never again bear a child.

As she passed more corn into her child's mouth, she became aware of the weight of the bracelet of armadillo teeth Chochobo had given her after last week's hunt. Since that same day, she had not met her daughter's hunger, and she pondered why her breasts were dry. A woman's breasts, the grandmothers said, always know when her children meet with difficulty. But her child was strong and beautiful. Also, Liara was a happy woman. Chochobo was a fine husband and father, a respected leader, and the handsomest man in the village.

As with any handsome man, women came to the hut looking for hairs combed from his head to tuck between their breasts to help win his affection. But Chochobo, she was sure, was faithful to her and his other wives.

Perhaps her milk had dried because of the beautiful white woman Nicole and how she had disturbed her husband. Yet she knew it was Nicole's words that had disturbed her husband, not the white woman's beauty—for, breaking the custom, Chochobo often discussed the future of their people with Nicole. *Maybe,* she thought, *my breasts know about my husband's great troubles, his work to make all things right for our people. Yes, that must be it.*

Chochobo's second wife approached and asked if Liara wished her daughter to have any of her milk for the next meal. Liara was hurt that she could not feed her child from her own body, but she said yes. The woman returned to her separate sleeping area and fire in the hut. All wives were afforded this separateness, as well as their own individual gardens outside. The first wife always retained a prominent position, and enjoyed the right to hang her hammock closest to that of the husband. Usually Liara held little jealousy toward Chochobo's other wives, consoled by the knowledge that she alone had been chosen by him. Today, though, all manner of things annoyed her. Then all at once she recognized she had become *tangu.*

That blood should flow from her now troubled her. With Chochobo returning soon, she would have to move into one of the *tangu* huts at the edge of the village until the influence of the moon passed.

Near her paints and those little bundles of healing roots that every woman kept for the relief of scratches and cuts and stings and burns, Liara took down the sack of absorbent down plucked from milkgrass and of use to women *tangu*. Then she lay down on a tapir hide, back humped, knees slightly spread, resting comfortably and with her scratching stick within reach. The grandmothers told that a woman so posed never will feel discomfort when the moon sits over her, nor will anything impede her flow. She would move into one of the *tangu* huts as soon as she had seen Chochobo.

When he arrived, Liara was grooming her hair with a comb made of twelve piranha teeth bound with thread. He paid his respects to the wives he had been married to longer, as was the custom, and then came into Liara's area. His heart was gladdened and set faster by the sight of her smiling eyes and shining hair.

The tiny rectangular apron she wore suspended from a cord of white beads seemed, in the flickering torchlight, to be moving on her sensuous body in a teasing fashion. The soft, warm air seemed full of secrets. His hand reached out, touching her face, his fingers following along the smooth line of her cheek, letting her know that he saw beauty. He would sooner pain himself than her, but he knew he would eventually have to tell her.

Liara's heart fluttered as if a bird were trapped inside her chest. Together they moved over to the little hammock where their child lay. Looking at Chochobo, Liara saw the child in the man's face.

"Now I must see to your food," she said.

He lifted her chin in order to gaze at her, and brushed her cheek with his palm. She felt as nervous and excited as the first night they had lain together, when he had untied the virgin's cord she had worn around her thighs.

While she prepared his meal, she saw him bend over the baby and cover the little one's mouth with his own. Knowing that he breathed his good nature into the child, the bird inside her breast sang.

After he had finished eating, he went over to the bamboo basket he had brought and took out a pack of talking leaves, the kind the white men scratched a mysterious mark in to tell what a certain person owes.

When he handed her the book, she saw that besides the talking signs it contained pictures of her tribespeople.

"'Indians' they call us," he said, "whatever this strange word means." And they both laughed together at the white man's foolishness.

"It is good to hear you laugh, my love," he said. "This morning, when I traded coca with the white man, I heard much laughter, but it was not the laughter that makes a person feel good."

"How I worry that you must trade the coca with such people," she said.

He sensed his chance to tell her now, tell her what he must do to protect their people from the white men, especially Buchreiser, the cocaine king who lived in the palace. That evil one would kill an entire tribe for money. He could tell her now. But other thoughts crowded his mind, sweet and warm.

"I would deal," he said, "with the spirit of the jaguar and anaconda to save our people. But enough of these sad thoughts. The sale of the coca is over, and it was a good one. Now we must celebrate." He reached out a hand to her body in such a manner that his intent could not be mistaken.

"I . . . I am under the influence of the moon," she said. "And I have behaved badly. I should already have gone to the *tangu* hut."

Chochobo jumped to his feet and her heart quickened. She did not fear punishment—he had never struck her—but she dreaded a reprimand. Instead, she saw he had stood to reach his paint, stored in the rafters above. He began painting her cheeks with the red lines that speak of a husband's affection for his wife.

She took his other hand and kissed his fingers. Chochobo, smiling, drew his finger along the part in her hair—another recognized sign of a man's admiration for his woman.

Then he asked her to go into the forest, and her heart filled with love for him, for his wanting her in privacy.

"But," she said, "you forget what custom says about women under the power of the moon."

"Once custom said a man must, like the four-legged ones, make love to a woman only from the rear."

"But never before—"

"I do not care about 'never before' on such a night."

He stood and waited, his silence more compelling than speech. She intended to pretend fear of abandoning this custom, but whatever one pretends, the grandmothers say, usually occurs. She reached out a hand and he pulled her gently to her feet.

Among all their ancestors, was there ever a man who loved his wife so much more than custom?

Liara motioned to one of the other wives, and the woman came over to rock the child's hammock.

Outside, a bitten moon hung in the clear night sky. The fragrance of night-blooming flowers came on a breeze gentle as a baby's breath. Somewhere in the distance water fell from the sky. He moved his hand over Liara's face, then placed his mouth briefly upon hers.

"Come," he said, adjusting the deerskin of water he had taken from the hut and hung on his waist, as he led her toward the tall trees.

Once in the cool privacy of the forest, she found herself as shy as on that day three seasons past. Then, too, he had brought her to the canopy, and afterward she had known wonder and marvel as the tongue of his mouth had known her, as the tongue of his loin would later know her.

Now, under a *samauma* tree, his whisper had spread her legs and she felt him wash away the absorbent down with the water in the deerskin. Then his hand began washing wherever her body curved, making known to her the depth of his desire, and she responded by touching him where he had grown and risen.

Presently he moved around her and washed her shoulders and back. And then his hands lingered briefly at her breasts, making her aware of their fullness and the hardness of her nipples. When his hands, moving down her belly, came near the aching place between her legs, she shuddered in the night air.

Soon he placed his hand firmly over her short hair. And as her pleasure mounted she understood that holding her here when the moon's power was over her would become the natural thing for them in the future.

When they moved to a dry place, his hands rubbed the water from her glistening skin. Then she felt herself pushed gently down until she lay on her back on the cool, spongy earth.

As his hands moved over her, the fragrance of night blooms intensified, and something deep within her began to throb.

His hand found the throbbing place and he spread her legs and lifted himself upon her and soon emptied his spirit self into her.

Afterward they lay quiet while new life flowed back into him. In time she reached out and touched the warm and sticky part of him, and then he sought her excitement and pleasure as he had his own until she experienced the sweetness approaching pain. And each heart expanded till no distance existed between them.

It was not until the following morning that Chochobo told Liara the news he had been carrying with him like a great stone. Then she knew what had dried up her flowing milk.

"I must take a new wife. She is the daughter of the powerful *cacique* Wactu from a place called Brazil, with as many warriors as hairs on your head. I do not want this woman, for I am a happy man. But if I refuse his gift I will lose his friendship, as is the custom of his tribe. And if the white man does not honor the land we buy with the money from our coca, we will need all the warriors of this chief. Do you understand?"

"How old is she?"

"A child of fourteen."

"Fourteen is already a woman. A female is a woman as soon as she comes under the influence of the moon. Is she pretty?"

"Not as pretty as you."

"She is pretty."

He cupped her face in his hand. "I do what I do for our child, for all the children of our people. We must survive. Please tell me you understand."

She understood that he had broken a custom of their tribe last night, and made her feel more loved than at any time of her life. But he would not break the custom of another man's tribe.

"I understand," she said, biting back her pain.

Chapter Seventeen

"Miles, could you reach me some of that coffee from the hearth?" Nicole asked. They sat opposite each other on the wicker chairs in her hut.

He stood and had taken a few paces when the sudden presence of a stranger jarred his heart. He saw a giant of a man dressed in a crisp shirt with epaulets and razor-creased twill pants, his slick black hair parted perfectly, looking surprised and dangerous. Christ! It was his own reflection in the full-length mirror.

"Are you all right?"

"What! Oh, fine, yes. Just remembered something." Realizing he was lying to her again, he shrank a bit inside.

When he returned and handed her the cup of coffee, he marveled at how the torchlight was captured in the sheen of her russet hair, and how it made the bluish-gray fringe of her brown eye appear hazel.

Night had fallen, and Michael let the tocking of frogs and the chirring of insects outside distract him from thoughts of Ava, helping to quiet his still-strong rage over her death.

"You've said you're close to the chief here, Chochobo. He doesn't sound like the type to be dealing with whites at all."

"If you mean the whites that he sells his coca leaves to, you're right."

"Are you saying he doesn't trust them?"

"They're vicious, criminal. Would you? But I don't really want to talk about Chochobo, if you don't mind."

"I'd like to meet him sometime. My people will want to know about the Carrijura tribal leader."

"Maybe . . . sometime." Her evasiveness made him wonder if she suspected what was behind his prying questions.

She took their empty cups to the hearth. The firelight glowing through her skirt silhouetted her legs.

"Here, let me help you," he offered, standing.

How healthy and strong she appeared, he thought, remembering her account of her arthritis cure on the tape.

Suddenly she grabbed his arm. Raising the edge of her other hand to his lips, she motioned to him to be silent. When she took her hand away, she leaned

toward him and whispered, "I heard someone outside." Then she said loudly, "I don't feel like talking
anymore, if you don't mind."

She began to move as stealthily as Xingu to the
doorway of the hut, grasping a knife from her skirt
pocket.

Michael followed, his right hand balled into a fist.
The flickering light of the torches on the roof beams
caused the hanging calabashes and gourds to cast
jagged shadows on the walls. As the other fist
clenched, he bit back a sudden, terrible sense of
finality.

Despite Michael's size, Nicole thought he'd be little
help against enemy Indians accustomed to fighting
in the jungle in the dark. There had been fear in his
voice. Wishing she had another knife for him, she, too,
began to feel afraid.

Michael became aware of the roaring of his own
racing blood and the beastly grunts and cries that
came with no warning or pattern from the surrounding darkness. The hut groaned almost like a person:
wood and palm fronds and hardened mud expanding
and contracting. Coffee residue rose bitter in his
throat.

In the eerie light Nicole was surprised and relieved
to see that his face held an expression of singular
determination.

Suddenly the explosion of a downpour filled the
hut. More than the darkness, more than Michael's

being weaponless and unfamiliar with fighting in the jungle—or anywhere else, as far as she knew—this silencing and blinding rain, she sensed, would help her enemies. A small, quavering sigh escaped her.

Without warning, something immovable hammered against the big toe of Michael's right foot. Reaching deep inside himself to keep from screaming and jumping, he saw he had stubbed his toe against an earthenware jug. Swallowing hard, he managed to keep moving.

At the entrance Nicole made signals to Michael. They would continue, and when she raised three fingers they'd dash out together.

Michael braced himself.

At the designated signal, both charged. The torrential rain smashed into their faces and blinded them. Nicole raised an arm over her brow and spun about with widened eyes. Michael felt as if he were looking through tears. Through the downpour of water, they could each see there was no one outside.

"What did you hear?" Michael asked after they had dried themselves by the fire and each had taken a long swallow of fermented liquor. The rain had stopped as quickly as it had begun.

"I heard a false tucca bird out there. They sing only at dawn."

"Then who do you think it was?"

"An Indian."

"Why would a hostile Indian be out there?"

"Spying. I have enemies. Because I'm so close to these Indians."

"But I thought all Indians were so honorable and had such great integrity?"

"Most do, but you can find a few spies in any society, I guess, no matter how honest."

Michael winced, then remembered Coufos. Whoever was spying on them must have been sent by the Greek. He would have to be even more careful.

"Who are your enemies?" he asked.

"For one, that bastard Buchreiser, who lives like a king on other people's blood."

Michael felt as if he had been jarred awake. Afraid his reaction might be revealing too much, he poured himself some of the fruit juice and hid his face behind the cup.

"Buchreiser?"

"Don't tell me you haven't heard of Buchreiser— the snowman, the White Jaguar, the world's largest dealer of cocaine!"

"Well ... I have heard of him." He shifted his trembling left leg and it quieted. "Doesn't he also have something to do with the snake farm?"

"It's one of the fronts for his smuggling."

"I've heard some gossip. What do you know about him?"

"I know he kills anyone who gets in his way. You

asked me before about other white women around here. I had a friend once who learned too much—Ava—and . . ." She reached with a shaking hand for his drinking jar and downed the dregs. Despite his forced expression, Michael was afraid she might see his pain.

"Ava was a very special person. *Lagniappe.*"

"*L-lagniappe?*" he managed to say.

"It's a Cajun word. In New Orleans, where I come from, if the oyster man gives you fourteen oysters and charges you for a dozen, we call it *lagniappe.* That's what Ava was: a little something ext—"

He felt his heart jump. Ava. Before Nicole's eyes filled, her sudden girlish expression connected with a young part of himself he thought he had lost long ago. He had wondered if he would ever find it again. He studied her face, searching for more, but she was closed off. He sensed she was reining herself in.

"I'm sorry you feel so bad," he said, really meaning it.

She didn't answer. She took a handkerchief from the pocket of her shirt and dabbed at her eyes.

"I think," he began, "you're a very special per—" Suddenly remembering that Nicole had used the same phrase to describe Ava made something inside him crack open. If he wasn't careful he would cry and tell the truth, and Nicole would know he was Ava's brother, and his entire plan would evaporate like drops of water on a jungle leaf touched by the high noon-day sun.

Part II

Chapter Eighteen

Coufos had often been to the palace but now—as in all the other times he had come within sight of the awesome structure—he felt like the uneducated son of a peasant he was. Hell, he could never even begin to organize the simplest maintenance of such grandeur. Buchreiser's private world in the middle of the jungle had enough room to sleep and feed a hundred people.

The futuristic architecture made the snake man even more uncomfortable. He had seen mansions—even plantations—belonging to many rich South Americans, but all this geometric glass and concrete reminded him of Buchreiser himself: handsome, but hard and cold. Cold as snake turds. The Greek shivered and patted the 7.65mm Pistola Savage tucked into his waistband. Its presence wasn't the least bit reassuring. Somehow Buchreiser made Coufos aware of all his shortcomings, and the Greek never felt as vulnerable as he did in his boss's presence.

From the Land Rover he saw Buchreiser's guards standing atop the palace walls. Automatic rifles were slung over their shoulders, rifles he knew could fire a thirty-round clip in three seconds.

At the main gate a guard stopped him.

"I have appointment with Mr. Buchreiser. Gus Coufos."

"I have to call to confirm."

After all these years, Coufos thought, *and still he thinks of me a stranger. Always the guards put me through this, even when they know me. Never mind, soon I will be able to retire like a king in my hometown on Crete.*

"Please step out of the car. I must search you."

Coufos looked quickly around—the guard had returned.

The Greek swung himself out of the Rover and stood spread-eagled against the car while the guard frisked him and removed his pistol. "You can pick this up on the way out. Mr. Buchreiser may be a little late. He said to wait."

When the Greek climbed back into the driver's seat, he felt even more vulnerable without his pistol.

As he drew nearer to the palace, he saw the bottled glass windows through the security grille and was reminded of some monster's bulging eyes from the myths of his people, and portholes from his years as a young man at sea. Although it was bright daylight and the palace was on solid ground, he realized just the sight of it was even more frightening than being lost in the fog at sea—because of its owner, and because of what went on inside. Perhaps the most fearsome thing about the palace to Coufos was that despite its being in the middle of the jungle, there was hardly a blade of grass or an insect on the grounds—as though Buchreiser's building had conquered nature herself.

Karl Buchreiser strode briskly across the elaborate parquet floors of his private library and study. He threw open the great door to his suite of rooms and stepped into the corridor.

Moving quickly along the central hall, he passed the reception room, the music room, the banquet hall, the exercise room, till finally he came to his office.

Two women passed him: a middle-aged redhead and a blonde in her twenties. He recognized the older one as the overseer of the corps of prostitutes he employed for guests and his high-ranking staff.

The women couldn't keep from staring at his broad, rangy shoulders and his surgeon's hands. He was tall, in his late thirties, with blonde hair as shiny as silk ribbons, a long nose, and thin but sculpted lips. Even his eyebrows looked groomed. He was wearing a hard gray sharkskin suit. His shirt matched the sky blue of his eyes, and his tie appeared to have been cut from a bolt of jeweler's wine velvet. His navy calfskin shoes gleamed.

Buchreiser took out a key, opened the doors to the office, and locked them behind him. All the office walls were bare and stark white. The furniture, though expensive, was coldly modern. The room gave no hint of ever having been lived in. He pressed a button on the intercom and gave permission for Coufos to be allowed inside.

"So you like this Rudd, eh?" Buchreiser said to Coufos from behind his white marble desk. To Buchreiser's right stood Escobar, one of his top aides, a Colombian with a short potatolike body and graying wavy hair. The man's irises were so black they appeared to merge with the pupils.

Coufos already liked Rudd more than he ever liked Escobar. Something about the way Escobar tried too hard to look him straight in the eye every time bothered him. And his Zapata moustache somehow did not fit with the vested suits and wing-tipped shoes. He was trying to be somebody he was not, and it showed.

"I have good feelings."

Coufos sat on a chair made of slung leather and chrome, looking at a jacaranda coffee table which held a sterling bowl filled with passionfruits and bananas. Somehow the fruit was not appetizing; it seemed more like a display than a gesture of hospitality. Escobar had colorless polish on his nails. Coufos disliked any man who had his fingers painted like a woman's.

Coufos went on. "I told him we have plenty money-washing ideas, tell us something we do not have. Is very good what he wrote, no?"

"It is called laundering," said Escobar, and Coufos resented the amusement around both men's lips.

"What matters is not how you call it, wash or laundry," Coufos said, "but if when you are finished it is clean."

"That is true," Buchreiser said. "And why do you think Rudd's plan is so good?"

"I am not so sure I understand the plan so much, but like I said—"

"Yes, I know," said Buchreiser, "but I do not run my business on feelings."

Soon, Coufos thought, *I will not have to take this German's shit.* Soon in Greece he would have enough money to have a different woman every night for the rest of his life. Greek women with faces like Helen of Troy and buttocks like Aphrodite of Cyrene. And what did anyone in this part of the world know of food? He could almost smell the sharp aroma of calamata olives in brine mingled with the scent of mezethra and kaseri cheese. . . .

"Escobar, you read Rudd's plan—what do you

think? I do not mean his so-called new twists to laundering, which we are already doing. I mean this." He picked up Michael's report. "Quote. 'Every Friday at four-ten New York time, the Federal Reserve releases the figures on the U.S. money supply. If someone knew these figures beforehand, he could make unlimited amounts of money. He could buy fixed-interest securities like bonds, when supply is down, because interest rates would fall, driving bond prices up. Always. Meaning one hundred thousand times out of one hundred thousand times. One could also profit by selling dollars at the different foreign exchange rates, because a lower money supply always makes the dollar worth less. Unlike buying common stocks, where a sizable investment will drive the cost of a stock up, creating interest in the investor's identity, someone could invest a billion dollars and not make a ripple in the bond or foreign-exchange markets. I have an associate (a mathematical genius with a heavy coke habit) who can tap into the Federal Reserve computer and give us these figures before they are released.' Unquote. Well, Escobar, what do you think?"

Both men continued to look at Coufos as Escobar spoke. It gave the Greek the impression that they were looking into a TV camera behind him.

"I think it is better than the coke business. Why has he not done it himself?"

"He says later in the report that he and his computer man do not have much capital. They would have to tap often, giving them more exposure. I like this report. It is well organized. Professional. And he is careful. Everything Rudd recommends places safety first, volume later. I like that kind of thinking."

"With all due respect," said Escobar, "I do not think we know enough about him. What if he is with the government?"

"What if I had been too worried about you being with the government? The organization would have lost a good man."

The ensuing silence made Coufos nervous, but he was pleased that Escobar had been put in his place.

"Have you got Rudd doing what I ordered, Coufos?" Buchreiser said.

"Yes. He is trying to find out what that Nicole knows about Chochobo and the other Indians. Why so many Indians come here from so many places. What Chochobo thinks of Wactu."

"I want one of our Indians set up in her camp, to find out how and what Rudd is doing with her. I want to know if the river is rising one inch more than it is supposed to when he is there. Arrange it, Coufos. And when Rudd is through with his assignment with the gymnast, I want a full report." He smiled coldly. "If he does well, I have an absolutely foolproof way to test him."

Coufos and Escobar eyed each other, full of nervous memories. They were used to Buchreiser's tests and the pleasure he took in devising and giving them.

"If he does not, you know what to do. That is all for now."

"One minute," Alma Ramirez called to Buchreiser in the whiskeyed, smoky tones of a woman in a night-club at 2 A.M.

Alma was sitting at her mirrored dressing table brushing her hair with one hand and holding a cigarette in the other when Buchreiser gave his familiar knock. She gave her hair, which was like polished ebony, one last stroke, put down the brush, and stabbed out her cigarette in a pre-Columbian pot she used as an ashtray. Checking her makeup, she decided to sponge some mauve shadow above her piquant green eyes, whose slant suggested a touch of Oriental blood. Actually, she was a pale-skinned mulatto with straight hair.

Alma rose from her Lucite chair, her eyes fixed on her reflection. Even in her layered, oyster-white satin dressing gown, her full figure was apparent. It was nearly the same body that had won her the Miss Bogotá title seven years before, when she was nineteen.

Despite her emeralds and her Incan jewelry, she still had a street-urchin look about her.

I must avoid letting him see my eyes, she thought,

seeing how large her pupils had become from the line of coke she had snorted only moments ago. She hadn't expected Karl. When normal, her green eyes shone so they seemed to be radiating an inner energy. With the added effect of the cocaine, her eyes glowed with an almost phosphorescent intensity.

Alma opened the door and rushed into his arms so Buchreiser couldn't see her eyes. But he lifted her face in his hand and looked purposefully at them. He broke away and slammed the door so hard the window behind the wrought-iron grille pinged frighteningly.

"I have told you—" he began.

"I was depressed and—"

"You agreed!"

"I am sorry."

"I cannot—I will not have it. Do you know what the people I deal with would think if they knew you were an addict?"

When he had first entered the apartment, the sight of him, of his very cruel mouth, had made her remember his meanness, and she had felt her skin tighten. A moment later, all she had become aware of was the warmth of his body. And now all she felt was hate for him.

"To you," she shouted, "if someone has one or two lines a week they are an addict."

"If all you had was one or two we would not be discussing it."

Buchreiser had not brushed back the forelock coming down over his eyes, and his eyes had turned the shade that made him look like a mean stallion cornered in its stall: his head down and his mane shagged forward between his eyes, his eyes wild and shrewd at the same time.

He stomped across the glazed tiles till he reached the window overlooking her garden, where an artificial stream ribboned through orchids and bromeliads, bubbling over a waterfall to a hundred-foot pool where lily pads and water blossoms floated.

Alma knew how he hated the jungle. Here, right in the middle of it, he allowed no greenery or flowers. Just a few random tufts of rebellious grass thrust through the concrete. (Alma did not count her garden, which he had granted her reluctantly.) And the bug killers—those enormous electric grids with purple lights which he had placed everywhere—succeeded in keeping out the birds along with the insects. She knew what was oppressive to him about the jungle. The latent violence of its poisonous green flesh and the sheer weight of it made his skin crawl and sweat and shiver. But he had to be here at least part of the year. The other times were divided between his homes in Zurich and Berlin.

"I told you," he said slowly and deliberately, "I will not have you taking that garbage. If I find out who you are getting it from, he will be eating his own balls for dinner."

She had no energy to argue with him. It always took all she had, and she never won. She was grateful she was not expected to answer. In the sunlight coming through the window, even the blond down on his earlobes showed. His whole body was dense with hair. Since people with Negro blood were generally less hairy than whites, she thought, this proved which people had come farthest from the monkeys in the trees.

Suddenly he stepped away from the window, looking more worried than angry. His gaze was piercing and, somehow, outside time. She watched him go to the coffee table and take a cigarette from a crystal box.

When he treated her like this—like a child who annoyed him—she could not help feeling that her color was the reason. Most Brazilian men were compulsively drawn to dark-skinned women. Many envious white women were known to call themselves *mesticis*—those with at least some strain of a darker race in their blood—to enhance their appeal for white men. But black blood, useful as it was erotically, was a social stigma not to be forgiven in a marital prospect. She knew the Germans were more prejudiced against blacks than Brazilians, so she concluded he could not tolerate her Negro blood. She had tried hard to want other men. She was only twenty-six. But other men were not Karl.

He approached, and when she could reach out and

feel him he put his cigarette between her lips. His touch was like a kiss.

"Sorry I could not see you last night," he said. "Business. Did you sleep well?"

"How can I sleep well when you are not with me?"

"Yes," he said. He was pleased to have a woman so in love with him, but annoyed at the reciprocal expectations such a strong feeling brought. Still, there was something about the woman. She was conquered, but she had not surrendered. She was bought and paid for, but still, somehow, a part of her remained elusive. He did not feel her respect.

So near him now, Alma felt as if she was trying to run two ways at once. She felt herself retreating from him, yet she was drawn toward him and sensed he knew it.

"I get frightened sometimes," she blurted. "But when you are with me," she said, unable to help herself, "as long as you are holding me . . ."

She felt his hands go around her. She wished he would never let her go. At the same time, he made her feel dirty about her black blood, and she was ashamed and angry at herself for allowing him this influence. She wished she had never met him, never been touched by his cold, cruel whiteness.

His hands moving over her body both aroused and repulsed her. She should have found a black man with an easygoing nature, she thought, a man filled with laughter and gaiety and natural sexuality, who would give her children and the peace that would enable her to endure. She lifted her head and looked into his eyes as his hot hands slipped inside her gown, and she saw there was a war going on inside him, too. She sensed that at his core he felt as susceptible as a boy. She was shot full of hope and joy at that moment, and wanted to tell him that if the door to his soul were to be replaced by a pane of glass, he had nothing to fear from her.

In the next instant, a hard film seemed to freeze hard his ice-blue eyes.

Everything that divided them charged for an instant and widened the space between them. But desire and habit had already brought them to a place from which neither could bear to retreat.

He put his thin lips on her full ones. Their breath was short and hot. Slowly she surrendered.

Chapter Nineteen

"I don't feel like talking now," Nicole said.

Michael nodded his understanding. He rose and went to the hearth for a whiskey bottle and an earthenware cup.

"This'll make you feel better," he offered, pouring the sludgy, yellow-white liquid.

As she reached for it, he was so close to her he could see the soft fur of her lash. She took a big swallow.

"Are you all right now?"

"I'm okay."

She saw that transparent peels of sunburned skin had shriveled on his nose. Oddly, the fact that he was not an outdoorsman was appealing. Despite that attraction, she felt a sense that something significantly essential to her in a man was lacking in him, and she was glad.

"I'd like to get on to something else," she said.

"Sure," he replied. He felt he could burst with the pressure of his deception.

Ava's friend, he thought. If he couldn't trust this woman who had been his sister's friend and who cared so unselfishly for the Indians, there was no one else he could trust. In the firelight, her clean scalp glistened in the part of her hair. The tiny droplets at her temples melted whatever hard edge he had determined to hold.

"I . . ." he began. "My name isn't Miles Rudd. I'm Ava's brother, Michael."

At first, Nicole could not assimilate his words. She gazed into his eyes for what seemed like hours. Slowly, imperceptibly, her face began to change. Wonder suffused her features.

"You're Michael?" she said.

He nodded. "I'm sorry I lied to you."

"But you don't look like the picture Ava showed me."

The idea that his sister had shown Nicole his picture made him tearful again. "My hair is part of the disguise, too."

"How do I know you're not lying now?"

"I used to be active in the SDS at Columbia. I manage people's portfolios. We were born in Brooklyn, New York."

"Anyone could have found that out." *Is he dangerous*? she thought.

"I paid for Ava to go to college," he went on. "Our parents owned a candy store on Avenue M called the Three Corners."

"That would have been real difficult for you to find out," she said, hearing her own sarcasm and anger. She checked herself—Buchreiser might have sent him.

He frowned, searching for a memory that would convince her, anxious to win her forgiveness.

"There was a boy when Ava was sixteen, maybe seventeen. Brian Zalvo. He died of leukemia. It was her first love and she never quite got over him."

Nicole sighed, relaxing a little. She remembered Ava telling her about Brian; she had said she hadn't mentioned him for at least ten years. Aware that her mouth was open, Nicole closed it.

"I'm really sorry," he said.

"Why? Why lie to me?"

He told her. His conviction that Ava had been murdered. His plan for revenge. Coufos. Buchreiser. Everything. He didn't allow her a moment to speak.

Finally he asked, "Who killed her? Do you know?" He could feel the hairs on his arm lift as he waited for her answer. A vein bulged in his neck.

"The Indians called him 'the man with the rain-colored eyes.'"

"Eduardo Estevez?"

"That's him. The one who was killed by a snake at the place where Ava worked."

"Seven times he was bitten. A person wouldn't stand still for all those bites unless it was—"

"—no accident."

"Exactly. What else do you know?"

"People say Coufos had Estevez killed. There was a lot of talk in town after his death. Xingu told me. Probably he wasn't supposed to kill Ava, just frighten her off, they say. It's too dangerous killing Amer—"

Nicole jumped at a sudden exploding sound. Looking down, she saw Michael had smashed a cup on the floor. Then she looked up and saw his teeth bared.

"I could peel his skin like an apple, and even God would call it justice!" he shouted. "Coufos is a Buchreiser lackey. Buchreiser is my real enemy!"

The look in his eyes was terrible. There was no room for anything except hate. She stared frozenly at the glittering mad eyes, at the rage she saw there, afraid for him.

After a time he said, "Sorry."

"Look, I understand how you feel about Ava, but don't you think this is something the police should handle?"

"They're either convinced it was suicide or too corrupt to care."

"That's true. That was naive of me. But there's always the American embassy."

"Sure. And Batman and Robin. No. This is something I've got to do myself."

"I want to help you," she said, surprising herself, realizing she had decided to trust him.

"It's too dangerous."

"More dangerous for a gymnast than a money manager? Don't forget . . . Ava was my dearest friend."

"Thank you," he said gratefully.

She made him another drink. As he cupped the gourd, she noticed his hands. Hands were important to her, and his were like the rest of him: long, large, strong, but with good shape and refinement that overcame any suggestion of brutishness. She realized she was looking for a wedding ring on his finger, and she was annoyed with herself.

Outside, the storm erupted again, reminding Nicole of her tears. Ava. Ava's brother. How upset he had been over lying to her. She smiled tenderly.

Suddenly she became aware of the hot, thick, tropical air mingled with the distinct but not unpleasant male scent of him. Something brushed the core of her like a feather. She recognized the feeling. It puzzled her that this stranger could be the catalyst for it.

A charged silence filled the room. They both sensed that something had happened between them. In a little while Michael implored her with his eyes to look at him. When she did, he saw that there was a new level of intimacy between them.

Chapter Twenty

"Take some coca," Chochobo said to Meewahn, reaching down among the branches which were covered with leathery elliptical leaves. He clipped one of the tiny clusters of yellow flowers and placed it in her hair.

Her eyes, unlike any he had gazed into in a non-white human, were the sky blue he had seen once in an albino jaguar just before he hurled his lance at it.

"Thank you, my chief . . . my husband," she said, smiling with delight.

Meewahn's hair contained the reddish tint he had only seen in Nicole's hair, and never among the women of his own or neighboring tribes. She also wore her hair much longer than was the custom of his tribe. The sight of her rare-colored hair growing so abundantly and reaching down to her firm young glistening buttocks stirred Chochobo.

"What happens to the coca here, my husband?"

"Come, I will show you," he said, taking her little arm and leading her away from the terraces of plants down to one of several huge unwalled thatch-roofed huts. Thinking of Nicole, he remembered the white man Xingu had said was visiting her. A man who was always writing words on paper. And handsome. Was he a brother? A lover? If he had been sent to spy on her by the foulness who lived in the palace, he would kill him personally.

Inside, the workers greeted Chochobo and Meewahn with the traditional nod reserved for a chief and his wife, but some of them breathed heavily. He knew they had been busy hiding their white man's toys: wristwatches, radios, tape recorders, calculators, cube games. He grew sad. They could afford these toys—even afford to buy their food in cans and jars like the white man. But Chochobo feared that if these new ways were allowed, the old skills of hunting and fishing would be forgotten. Then, if the new ways were lost to them, his people would be helpless. He thought of Buchreiser—how he would love to have the Carrijura people at his mercy!

"You said you would teach me about the coca," Meewahn whispered.

"In a moment," he answered as he walked over to a young man lifting a bucket of soggy leaves into a gauze strainer. The young man wore a gold cross around his neck. When Chochobo approached, the tribesman's eyes registered the realization he had forgotten to hide the crucifix.

"Once," Chochobo began, "I asked a missionary, 'Will your God punish a man who does not know him and his religion?' 'No,' said the missionary. I said, 'Then why do you want to teach me of him?'"

The young man unclasped the chain from his neck and threw it to the ground.

When Chochobo returned to Meewahn, she was watching a worker add chemicals from a mason jar into a huge black pan filled with pulverized leaves.

"What is he doing?" she asked.

"He will place the crushed leaves and the chemicals over the fire and make it into a paste which the white man pays more for than the leaves."

"Someday I would like to learn just how to do this thing," she said.

"Women do not learn this."

Meewahn sensed from his tone that she had displeased him—perhaps she was asking too many questions too soon.

"Is there anything you wish to do now?" she asked coyly.

Chochobo looked down. He recalled the way she had responded to his touch. Too eagerly, perhaps. A woman may enjoy herself, but should still remember herself as the submissive one.

"I wish to go home," he said.

Moments later their hut came into view and

Meewahn gave out a small cry, pretending to have stepped on something sharp.

While Chochobo examined the ball of her foot, she reminded him with her eyes of the pleasure her young body had given him. When he did not respond, she wriggled her body so her hair fell back over her shoulders and her finely shaped firm breasts were visible. She saw a glimmer in Chochobo's eyes and a vein began to throb in his neck.

Chochobo grew aroused more by her immodesty and her certainty that she was a joy to behold than by her nakedness.

When he lifted her to her feet, he said, "Let us continue home now to bed."

"Whatever my husband wishes," she demurred. Then recalling his earlier displeasure, she added, "If you will forgive a young girl, perhaps the hut holds too many child cries to suit my chief. For now, my husband, perhaps a cool bed of leaves under the great trees would be more soothing?"

He nodded.

When they were inside the forest, he looked down at Meewahn. Here, where only narrow shafts of light penetrated, her hair showed in places red, brown, black, and even yellow. And he was certain he would never find anything usual about this girl-woman.

Meewahn lay down on the fragrant leaves, eyes gazing unblinkingly into his.

Soon she felt a strong leg flung over her slender

one. Then a hardness like bone. She closed her eyes to hide the power of her womanhood behind her smile. Let the great chief think he subdues a child, she thought, and not the other way around.

"I have made your favorite things to eat," Liara said to Chochobo while lifting the clay lid off the steeping turtle soup. The bird again fluttered in her breast in response to his presence.

"I . . . I am sorry, I should have told you. I have already eaten. Perhaps later."

The bird grew so heavy so quickly when it fell from her breast that she almost fell with it.

"You look strange, Liara. I did not mean to disappoint you so. Here, let me help you sit."

The familiarity of his touch both comforted and angered her. She was surprised at the intensity of her anger and afraid its force might cause Chochobo to become aware of it. To show jealousy was one thing; to be jealous is to care. But anger was another; it showed only weakness of spirit. To show a man he has made you less because of something he has done was unbearably disgraceful.

"Does she feed you as well as me?" She could not believe she was asking the question. She already knew the answer.

"She does nothing as well as you."

He would not lie to Liara even to save her pain, because he thought too much of himself and respected

her too greatly to do so. Still, he felt a muted shame
for what he was omitting rather than lying about. For
even though it was true that Meewahn did not do
anything as well as Liara, there was an excitement
in him when he was with the young new one. This
came, he knew, from more than just her novelty. She
was as untamable as a piranha, with the spirit of a
jaguar.

"Not yet, she does not, you mean," Liara said. She
felt as if she were two women: one who was angry and
hurt, and one who watched her shameful behavior
incredulously.

"Not yet?"

"She does not do anything as well as I do *yet*, is what
you mean."

"Now you tell me what I mean. Soon you will tell
me what I feel and then what I think."

"I am sorry."

"No, you are not. You say the words, but the way
you say them tells me you are not sorry at all."

A part of her listened and agreed with him, but
another part rose up and denied the truth.

"Why should I not be sorry?" she said, hearing the
taunt and not being able to hold it back. "Are you not
the man who overcomes even custom for his love? So
why should I have expected that you would ignore the
custom of taking a gift from her father, who is not
from our tribe and not even from our own land?"

"Because you forgot to say that I accepted

Meewahn because of what her father's warriors can mean for us."

Hearing the other woman's name spring from his mouth made the part that was truly sorry disappear before the powerful part that spoke.

"What sacrifices you make for us all, o wonderful chief, in Meewahn's bed!"

Liara's words repeated in her mind, startling and frightening her.

"I will not be attacked when I do no wrong. Change your talk or talk to the wind."

"I am truly sorry, Chochobo. Sorry and shamed by my words. Although it does not excuse me, a part of me is mad and hurt, and therefore angry, that . . . that you and I are not as special as once we were."

He stood and came to her then and cupped her face in his hand as he had always done, and it melted her. When she gave him the greatest test—to look into his eyes for his heart—she saw openness and love.

"Come," he said after a time. "We will have some *chicha*."

The word "we" was so sweet it made her eyes water. It was the custom for a husband to say "I" and "we" only when he spoke of a brother, a son, a friend—a male did not use the term "we" when referring to himself and a woman.

Even as Liara ladled out the soup, though, the part of her that had spoken so angrily earlier said to her, Beware, you blind fool, if ever the shameless girl bears him a boy child, for he will give more of his heart to her.

Because she had already been consumed in the blaze of her thoughts, Liara did not feel the heat from the soup in the bowl she carried to Chochobo.

Chapter Twenty-One

"What else do you know about Buchreiser?" Michael asked Nicole as they sat in her hut drinking fermented bananas. He had been with her for ten days.

"People say he grosses about five hundred million dollars a year and that he exports twenty-five tons or more of cocaine to the States. He's more powerful than the President of Colombia or any military man. His payroll includes generals, customs officials, cabinet ministers, police, and thousands of peasants. People say there's even an army of bodyguards, headed by a former SS colonel. He's chairman of the board of Colombia's largest business. Not even the coffee business produces as much money or uses as many people as the cocaine industry."

"How did Ava ever wind up on his payroll?"

"Of course she didn't know the snake farm was a

front for smuggling coke. She believed snake venom was going to be the new wonder drug for many diseases. She wanted to help and be a part of it."

"Why did Ava want to live in such an out-of-the-way place? Sorry, I didn't mean you—"

"It's okay. I think I can answer for both of us. Out of the way of what? Human life? Nature? The Amazon is not out of the way of these things. It is the way *of* them."

In the firelight the hollow place above her upper lip was as soft and delicate as a flower petal. How refreshing she was from the world he had left, where caution so often passed for wisdom.

"What was so fascinating to Ava and you about this place? No, I can understand the fascination. But why do you stay here now?" Now, he realized, meant now that she was cured of arthritis.

"I don't know. Why do you stay in a place like New York where the race goes only to the swiftest?"

"Not everybody there is in the race. Not everyone is trying to win it."

Nicole thought about what Ava had told her about Michael—his being thrown out of college, and then their father's death. He had had to run the business for their mother till she died. Then he had to work days to send Ava to college, and go to school nights himself. She remembered what Ava had said about the effect all this had on him.

She was sure now what the missing ingredient in him was: he had stopped dreaming. She wanted to talk to him about it, even though she knew he was filled with vengeance.

"Do you mean," she asked, "New York is like a kind of swim meet where all you have to do to remain eligible is tread water?"

"That's exactly what I mean. And you—I still don't understand why you stay here."

"I guess I'm kind of treading water, too," she said quietly. "Maybe you'll understand better if I explain why I came here in the first place."

"Please."

"I wanted to see if Indian medicines could help me." Nicole hesitated. She had to clear her throat before she continued. "Also, when my friends found out I was ill, they began to avoid me. Obviously they didn't know how to relate to me any longer."

"How awful that must have been."

"It was. That was another reason for coming to the jungle. In a place like the Amazon Basin, sickness is everywhere. People here view sickness as the natural order of things. They're less afraid of it than we Westerners. I'm here because I couldn't stand to be pitied. And I'm not an egomaniac—I just wanted to be remembered at my best." She frowned. "The truth is I'm really afraid to go home."

"How do you mean?"

"There's so much cultural pressure I'd have to deal with that it would get in my way. People aren't as real."

He wondered if Ava had shared Nicole's fear of going back to civilization.

"I have a message," came a voice from the entrance of the hut. It was Xingu.

"What is it?" Nicole asked.

The Indian handed her a slip of paper. She looked at it and handed it to Michael, who lit a match to read it.

Dear Miles:

I will be in Puerto Porqueño tomorrow. Have a little time to discuss the Indians then. Meet you at the Hotel Macaw at noon.

John Hemmings

"Who gave this to you, Xingu?" Michael asked.

"Indian."

"Did he say who gave him the message?"

"I did not ask. This Indian does not speak truth."

"Thank you, Xingu," Nicole said. The Indian disappeared as quietly as he had arrived.

"Coufos?" Nicole asked.

"Coufos."

The black rage was back. "We've got to make a plan," he said. "If we ever get caught, you've got to act as though you don't know who I really am."

"That won't be hard." She smiled wryly.

"After this is over, I'd like to straighten that out."

She liked this side of him, when she could see enthusiasm in his eyes, and an allowance, maybe even an invitation, for her to see deep inside him. But then, she had also thought she had seen those things in other men, only to be disillusioned by them. Maybe she needed to know him better. Maybe Michael should know her better, too. Suddenly she felt sleepy.

"I'd like to go to bed now," she said. "I can't keep my eyes open."

"I can see that," he said, although he was taken aback by her abruptness. "Good night, Nicole."

She fell asleep in moments, allaying his fears that she had used sleepiness as an excuse to get away from him. He lay in his hammock, anticipating that he would be awake a long while with thoughts of all they had spoken about. But soon the mixture of the long day, tension, and the homemade whiskey made him fall asleep, too.

A little after 2 A.M. he awoke, startled by a sound of someone walking outside the hut. He rushed outside and clanged his head against the metal pot hanging from the roof beam. The clamor woke Nicole.

"You okay?" she asked sleepily.

"Sorry, I heard someone outside."

She tensed, listening for the quality of the footsteps.

"It's all right," she said. "It's probably just an Indian walking down to the river to bathe and warm up. The river's always about eighty-five degrees." She drifted back to sleep.

But he was wide awake. He lay watching the girl in Nicole's face in sleep, conscious that they were sharing the same air and remembering how her breasts had shown full, weighty, their nipples erect through her rain-soaked blouse.

Suddenly she opened her eyes and turned toward him, causing the torchlight to reflect at a different angle on her face. She looked like another woman: older, wiser, severely and naturally beautiful instead of pretty. He wondered how many women there were inside her.

He went over to her, his heart pounding. He lifted up her hand, turned it over, and kissed the palm.

She smiled and began unbuttoning her blouse, an act that delightfully confirmed his guess that she would be as unselfconsciously honest in lovemaking as in everything else.

He held her so hard he was almost hurting.

He helped her off with her blouse, uncovering erect strawberry nipples. With each garment he removed, he realized how much her clothing had diminished her. Muscles that would ripple and swell on a man's body were unobtrusively smooth and round on hers, so the impression was one of a perfectly distributed and coordinated strength. It was the kind of woman's body that was both senual and powerful, and suddenly other women's bodies seemed paltry by comparison. As he expected, she wore her nakedness with dignity and grace. Without clothes she seemed larger.

Her hand traveled down slowly. She undid all his buttons and his zipper.

They lay down together, their bare feet brushing. Either he'd gotten shorter or she longer, he thought, smiling. He looked down at the surprisingly wide, high fan of pubic hair, a badge of fecundity, in contrast to her softness. With his eyes closed, he could still remember how her breasts had looked under the rain-drenched blouse. Then he felt her bush like damp wool brush against him. The speed of her arousal intensified his own. He sought her everywhere: in the sweet salt beneath her arms, in her swollen nipples, in the heat between her legs. She took the fingers of one of his hands one by one into her mouth.

He had the sensation that when he touched her, her body grew boundless in the process—from impulse, to act—and that she had willed it so.

As she stroked his cock, she opened her eyes, and then he wasn't sure they had been closed. She opened her legs to him and guided him into her. Her name, starting as a word in his swollen throat, became a grunt.

Soon she began to make tiny tentacular contractions as he thrusted, and he had to stop to keep from coming.

"No, don't stop," she whispered.

"But you—"

"Shhh." And she moved her hips under him then, slowly in circles, all the while constricting.

When she felt him start to shudder, she smiled—for she knew she would now meet his most unselfconscious self.

As their bodies cooled, they lay silently—he exquisitely sated, she blissful.

When they joined together a second time, the distinction between lovemaking and sex was even greater. He discovered that the texture of her skin changed. Softest of all were her breasts. Her body, he found, was not one color, but a subtle collage of shades and tints—browner along the arms, paler surrounding both breasts, pinker on her face, her thighs lighter than her lower legs, which were lighter than her feet.

She sent her hands looking for a softness, a vulnerability, some opening in him that could be penetrated to his core. Realizing that what she sought was too idealistic, she settled for the possible. She found his downy earlobes endearing, as well as the dimples at the base of his spine, the soft crook of his elbow, the hollow below his Adam's apple. Because his buttocks were the opposite of his hard, dominating, insistent penis, she was more playful with them. "Don't hurry," she said when once he had begun to.

After a time she rolled over and swayed above him. He had the feeling that the inside of her was continuous with his own skin, so that he was at once entering and being entered. When he felt her thighs go stiff and heard the primitive sound that escaped her throat, he was afraid of being left alone again and ascended blindly with her, not caring where they fell, as long as it was together.

Later, when the rain had stopped, Nicole rose to brew a pot of coffee. He sat gazing at her, aware of some unfamiliar center overturning deep inside him. His mind was filled with thoughts difficult to bear. What was he supposed to report back to Coufos now? "No, Coufos, she's as far from a spy for Chochobo as you can get. She doesn't have anything to do with coca, and their little battles. How do I know? Well, actually I don't *know*, I just would bet anything. . . . What do you mean I didn't do my job. Of course I'm not in love with her."

"Do you want some coffee?"

All at once a great downpour fell, and he couldn't make himself heard over the din, so he just nodded.

All he could think of was having lost the man with the rain-colored eyes to Buchreiser.

Buchreiser.

Chapter Twenty-Two

Karl Buchreiser locked the door behind him. He often came here to think or just to relax. No one else was allowed in the room. At first glance the rug in this great salon looked abstractly Oriental in design. Upon closer observation one could see that the design was neither abstract nor Oriental; it was a military map showing just how far Hitler's plan to rule the world had succeeded before the Russian counter-attack.

Buchreiser's eyes swept the room as if taking in a lover's features. He moved to the writing table that had once belonged on the Führer's special train. On the table were silver-framed photographs of his father in his black leather SS greatcoat and smart peaked cap on the Russian front in 1941. How strong and elegant and brave his father had looked in that glorious uniform! Buchreiser picked up another photograph showing his father wearing the Knight's Cross. He ran his hand slowly over the photograph showing his father lecturing to SS cadets at the Adolf Hitler School. The colonel was wearing his Knight's Cross embellished with oak leaves and swords. When Buchreiser picked up the photograph showing his father as part of the Leibstandarte honor guard, the pride he felt made his eyes sting. Why, in his father's day, a man would not even be considered for admission to the Leibstandarte if he had had a single tooth filled! And only approximately a third of those who volunteered for the SS were deemed acceptable; the balance had to settle for the Wehrmacht.

How criminal that such a man should have his mind destroyed by the filthy lies about the SS after the war! The whole of the Waffen-SS were declared guilty until proven innocent of war crimes. Even to this day, the most elite fighting force in all history, even greater than the Roman Praetorian Guard or Napoleon's Imperial Guard were denied the same military recognition awarded even to the British troops involved in the Falklands operation or the Israeli Defense Forces—Jews!

The many lessons of the Waffen-SS training for all postwar armies were also denied. So-called SS atrocities such as happened at Le Parades and Oradour were placed ahead of the many acts of chivalry performed by SS individuals and units; the fact that Allied troops were guilty of similar atrocities, including the shooting of prisoners and reprisals on the civilian population of Germany, was ignored. Finally, the SS was blamed for what went on in the concentration camps, when the truth was that fighting men like his father ached for battle, and privately considered these behind-the-lines assignments not worthy of their training.

He would be sure to send the New Nation Party an even larger contribution this month, to rid the world of Jews—who had snaked their way back into power—and other non-Aryan subhumans.

Buchreiser continued to move slowly, savoring the room's treasures. He stopped to browse at one wall of rare military books. He paused at an oak pedestal on which rested a glass case displaying his father's coveted SS dagger—a special mark of distinction given only to graduates of the two SS officer training schools. He thought of the tests of courage SS officers had to undertake once they had received their daggers. Buchreiser swelled with pride, thinking of his father digging a foxhole in front of an advancing tank before it reached him, or removing the pin from a grenade balancing on top of his steel helmet and standing perfectly still while it exploded.

Buchreiser halted at another display case containing his father's SS signet ring, worn only by those men holding SS numbers below ten thousand.

Soon he reached the place where a coat of arms hung on the wall. For his favorites, Himmler had devised an Arthurian round table for which he held court in his Wewelsburg castle, and for each of these men a coat of arms was devised using runes from German and Nordic mythology. What a soldier his father had been, so honored by one of Hilter's inner circle!

Now he stopped to admire an oil of an SS Panzer division approaching the Arc de Triomphe, and then to read a framed parchment on which was inscribed the SS oath.

As he spoke the words aloud, he was both proud and jealous of his father.

I swear to thee, Adolf Hitler,
As Führer and Chancellor of the German Reich
Loyalty and bravery.
I vow to thee and to the superiors whom thou
Shall appoint
Obedience unto the death
So help me God.

As he spoke, Buchreiser felt himself thrust back to a time he had questioned his father about years ago, a moment he had often read about. Once again he imagined himself there. . . .

At 2200 hours on November 9, 1936, in Hitler's presence at the Nazi shrine before the Feldernhalle in Munich. Karl felt himself surrounded by countless SS candidates, splendid young men, serious of visage, exemplary in bearing and turnout. The elite. There were twinges all along his spine when thousands of voices repeated the oath in chorus, by flickering torchlight. The oath was like a prayer. Then he could actually see the great ship that was to carry him and his comrades off to glory on some distant battlefield; he could smell that wonderfully blended scent of ocean, tobacco, new paint, soap, shoe polish, beer, and rifle oil; he could hear the lapping of the waves and the creaking of the ship, and soon that great horn whose sound carried with it the whole history of departure to battle, longing, pride, and—may the Führer forgive him—even a little fear. When the entire shipload broke into a chorus of "Keep the Flag Flying Overhead," tears fell from his eyes.

Buchreiser wiped his eyes again and raised himself to his full height as if to ward off his yearning. If only the war had lasted. The V-2 and V-4 rockets would have won it for them.

He left the room, thinking of the only thing that had sometimes made him forget his unrealized dream to have served in the Waffen-SS: Alma.

As Buchreiser strode toward Alma's apartments, he was thinking of how the trafficking of cocaine was very much like a war. The drug enforcement agencies were the enemy, the informers the spies, the bodyguards the noncommissioned officers, the profits the victories. The greatest of the spoils of this war was the money to finance the New Nation Party around the world, which would someday put into the hands of the sons of the SS and other noble Aryans a weapon to avenge the demeaning end glorious men like his father had met.

Suddenly something blocked the light in the archway abreast of him. To avoid whatever it was, Buchreiser jumped back. He saw a man in a white uniform, his mouth open in a great O, gums curled back from his teeth, eyes gleaming madly, charging at him with a knife in his hand. Buchreiser braced himself. He would wait until the last possible instant. When the man came close enough to touch, Buchreiser jumped aside, at the same time grabbing the knife wielder's wrist. Transferring his weight to the ball of his left foot, he flipped the attacker onto his back. The knife flew from the man's hand. In a single swift motion, Buchreiser dove and retrieved the knife and held the blade poised against his assailant's throat.

"Why?" he spat out between gasps for air.

"Y-You, your cocaine," the man snarled, "made my daughter a *puta*, then into one of your mules. Now she has overdosed."

A whistle blast echoed through the corridors and was followed by the thunder of large men running. The bodyguards arrived, but Buchreiser waved them off.

"What are these clothes you wear?"

"I help cook your meals, you butcher."

First the enemy demeaned men like his father, causing them to commit suicide or, worse, lose their minds. Now, instead of honoring his son for his victories over all the drug enforcement agencies and, even more, his competition, they called him a pimp and a butcher.

"Go on and kill me!" the cook shouted defiantly. "I am already dead."

"No, you are not," Buchreiser said as he slit his assailant's throat, "but you soon will be."

From the neck of his victim, deep red blood jetted rhythmically. For a moment Buchreiser did nothing, as if in deep contemplation, then he turned slowly and deliberately.

His glare made the two bodyguards take a step backward.

"Who is responsible for this area?"

"I—I am, sir," said the one closest to him.

The son of the SS colonel had only to look into the eyes of the other bodyguard for the man to raise his 9mm P-38 automatic and fire. A deafening noise filled the corridor. The bodyguard who was at fault slumped dead onto the tile floor next to the assassin.

"I am worried about you, Karl," Alma said as he sipped the Scotch she had fixed for him. He had showered and changed into a lightweight bleached blue bush jacket and matching slacks. His outfit gave his stark blue eyes an especially vivid hue. Or maybe it was having killed a man that lent them this brilliant shade that was not quite real. Oh, sweet Jesus, what partner of the devil had she had the misfortune to fall in love with?

"I will not be caught again without a gun," he said. *Today*, he thought, *when I need to drown in the black river of her hair, she has it wound into a coiled snake atop her head.* But he saw now that ends were escaping. It made her throat look very slender and vulnerable.

"Please do not get angry, but why should you stay in a business where you need to carry a gun? You have enough money to—"

"Enough? Do not ever tell me when you think I have enough of anything! For a former *chinche* I saved from the streets, you have become quite presumptuous."

A *chinche* was a bedbug. He had promised never again to bring up that she had spent years of her pubescence and early adolescence as a member of a *camada*—a loose-knit group of gamins who slept together for warmth and protection in cities like Bogotá. *He is probably still upset from the assassination attempt*, she thought. This was the worst of all. She knew that she made excuses for him, excuses she would never believe, except for her relentless desire to do so. Still, she could not stop herself.

"I am sorry," he said. "There are many things today that burden me."

"I understand. Can I get you another Scotch?"

"Please. And please close the drapes over that window. I cannot bear to see the view just now."

How could she possibly be in love with a man who hated a beautiful view of nature, who loved marble only because of its coldness? Once, she would have called someone like Karl a white devil. How she could stand a good toot right now! Before she had met him, she had not even taken aspirin. She drew the drapes.

"Better?"

"Much."

The killing had quickened his blood, and the sight of her long, vulnerable neck had warmed it. The last time, she had ignited into such excitement she had bitten her own shoulder.

He has only to look at me like that, she thought with weariness and eagerness. *If only once he ever said he needed me.*

"I do not want an argument tonight, Alma."

If only he could say please. The way he said it, it was an order: I forbid you, and I will not allow myself to argue tonight. But at least he is telling me he wants me so much he cannot stand for anything to come between us. But he only wants to use me.

He came up and kissed her neck. The act made her blood thicken, and a warm wave passed over her. She remembered how she had sighed last time when he had withdrawn, and she drove out all her thoughts and moved her body to wherever his hands sought her. So what if she would never feel cherished with

Karl? She had never felt cherished by anyone else. At least, at times, he could make her forget that. Forget everything.

"Has Rudd reported anything yet on the gymnast?" Buchreiser asked Escobar hours later in his private office.

"Coufos met with him only last night," the Colombian said, caressing his moustache with his manicured fingers. "Rudd claims he needs more time. When Coufos asked him what if he had to make a bet right now, he said he did not gamble."

Buchreiser smiled. "I like that."

"I do not know why we just do not get rid of this de la Houssaye girl."

"That is because you do not listen. I do not get rid of her because she is internationally known and there would be an army of reporters around here. Now, what about the Indian we set up in her camp?"

"He has not heard anything suspicious, but he thinks Rudd may be fucking her."

"That is the first thing I have heard about him that was not professional. The more I look at his proposal about the Federal Reserve, the more I like it. Arrange for him to come here. I want to meet him."

"It is too dangerous. I do not trust him. We have not finished testing him. You cannot—"

"Do not ever again tell me what I can or cannot do!"

"I . . . I understand."

"Good. I told you once I have an absolutely fool-proof way to test Rudd."

"May I ask what that is?"

"No. But you will find out soon. You are going to be the proctor for his final examination."

Chapter Twenty-Three

From the river grew limbs and aerial roots of submerged trees. Ahead, on a sandbar, Coufos saw a pale caiman five feet long, its jaws agape. At the approach of the Greek's boat, the alligator got up on its short legs and ran, carrying its body clear of the ground, almost as though it were not a body at all but a log, and plunged into the current. With a swish of its powerful armored tail, it disappeared in a swirl of bubbles.

Drawing nearer to Monkey Island, Coufos cut off the dugout's motor. He would paddle to the opposite shore, away from the abandoned tourist lodge. He had sent word to Wactu and Meewahn to meet him inside the island's single, deserted shack. The shack was almost overrun by jungle growth and thus known to few. *What a stroke of genius*, he thought. Buchreiser had made the Brazilian chief give his daughter as a wife to Chochobo so she could spy for the organization. And Chochobo, thinking all the time Wactu would help him fight against the organization! The snake man felt the corners of his mouth lift in a smile.

Now, alone on the great river, Coufos heard the sound of his paddle in the water as though he were another person. At times the river and the jungle were like the presences of powerful gods. He felt unprotected, an intruder. Holy Zeus, how had he come to be in such a place? For money—what else? Soon he would have all the drachmas he needed to retire to his beautiful homeland.

Despite his fear, Coufos felt a certain attraction to this thousand-acre Island of the Monkeys, knowing that a Greek-American from Florida had bought it during the early fifties. The Greek had brought thousands of male and female yellow-footed monkeys here, planning to sell their babies to research labs and zoos. *He got screwed,* thought Coufos. The Colombian government had stopped him from exporting them. Stuffing themselves with fruits and bananas over the years, the monkeys grew in numbers, and now there were about fifty thousand. What a food paradise for snakes—especially vipers.

The canoe nosed into the muddy shore and Gus stepped out, pulling the dugout after him. His jungle boots slithered in the clay at the bank. At least back near the lodge there was a gray sand beach. What would he not give to take in once more the blinding talcum-colored beaches of home! Ah, soon.

As he made his way through the brush to the shack, he cursed the oozing mud where lizards had left their tail-dragging marks. Despite GI Vietnam surplus jungle boots, which were made from leather and canvas with Vibram soles, his feet and shoes were never completely dry here. The best he could hope for was to dry them partially between cloudbursts. Coufos pulled down his hat brim against the sun, untied his bandanna, and wiped his face.

Surrounding him was a solid sound wall of monkey drumming mixed with insect droning. Distant birds cackled deep in the trees. Once he caught the sudden slither of a snake. In an especially dense place the bright blood color of an orchid seemed like a heart beating inside a tree's ribs.

By the time he could see the shack, the sky began to shimmer like a weakening fluorescent tube.

Coufos slipped quickly into his poncho and broke into a run, frightening thousands of parrots that exploded from the trees. The rain descended at once, as if it had at last broken through a dam of clouds. The booming downpour crackled. Twigs, ripped leaves, and branches littered the forest floor. If he didn't get out of it soon, the stampede of water would lash the clothing off his back and split his boots open.

By the time he reached the shack, it looked larger and friendlier than he remembered. Although it was not much bigger than a woodshed back home, it would not have done even for a chicken house because of its loosely slatted boards. These clapboards had once been white, but were so weathered now that the shack looked as if it were being turned back into a tree.

He burst through the door and stood panting against a hammock made of green vines.

Wactu and his daughter did not speak, so the only sound was the rain sizzling on the windows like grease on a griddle. Even over the breathless feeling, which he hated, he was aroused by the sight of the girl's hair reaching to the swell of her buttocks. He knew Wactu believed it taboo for any daughter of his to lie with a white man. The chief would kill them both. Coufos wrenched his gaze away. It was so hot he could smell old paint on the windowsill.

When he had caught his breath, he apologized in their language for possibly having frightened them. Reaching into the folds of his poncho, he took out a flask of ouzo and offered it. Each refused, and he took a swallow himself, but no more than that, because as the great Aristotle had said, "A wet stick does not make a good fire."

"How you been, great chief?"

"You did not ask me here to find out how I am."

Muscle tension rippled along the Indian's jawline. Wactu, a great block of a man, was the color of uncooked liver and gave off an underground smell of earth and roots and compost. His constantly blood-shot, yellowy eyes had no lashes, which made him look as if he were outraged by everything said to him. Coufos could picture the chief diligently dipping arrows in poison or shrinking a human head.

"I know you do not like dealing with whites," Coufos said. He found it difficult to look at the man instead of the girl; her eyes were on him all the time— Coufos knew this without looking at her. His mind was divided between her and Wactu, between a girl who probably carried ringworm in her bare feet, and the business he was there for. The rain and heat and jungle droppings clung to him like resin. "But we all do what we have to do."

There were no chairs. This unnerved the Greek. In his country one did not converse about such things for long without sitting. Still, he was comforted by knowing how quickly Buchreiser would turn against Wactu when the Indian was no longer needed.

The sound of a tree crashing suddenly in the jungle made the chief avert his gaze just long enough for Coufos to glance over at Meewahn. She gave him a quick smile with her eyes while managing to keep her lips daringly pouted—a Juno of a girl!

"Have you learned, Meewahn," Coufos asked, "how Chochobo's people make coca paste?"

The girl looked at her father for permission to speak. Coufos did not see the movement by which the chief gave his approval.

Meewahn watched the strange-looking man. She had never lain with a white man, and probably she had done well not to. At times the hungry look of a pale one repelled her; something in their tense expression, the fixed eyes, the slightly parted mouth suggested to her a pent-up fierceness, a withdrawn power that frightened her. If ever she did lie with a white man, it would not be with someone as hairy as this one. Besides the hair on his arms and peeking out from his bandanna, there were even dark tutfs sprouting like tuber roots from his ears!

Still, she thought, most men, even white men, were probably the same where they felt the most joy, and giving them their pleasure did not take very long anyway. It was like a nap she lay down to give to someone else, and most times the nap she gave them made them sweet and generous. This man had great wealth and power beyond even her father, probably beyond anyone except the yellow-haired chief in the palace. *Look at the stone he wears in his ring—it glows like fire.* She was curious about what he was thinking behind his narrowed eyes and monkey mouth. Did he want her? If her father turned away, she might smile at the white man again. Why not? It cost nothing.

"Long, slender tubes," Meewahn began, "of rolled and almost dried leaves are half filled with small lumps of the white resin of these other kinds of leaves—I have brought some of each. The tube is then lighted and the burning end put into the still-glowing pile of cecropia ashes. By blowing hard on the tube, the smoke gets into the ashes and gives them a very strong flavor, which is then mixed with finely mashed up coca."

Coufos wondered if the taunting creature speaking to him dreamed, and if so, of what? Would she not be pleased by a plate of moussaka or lamb with green beans? Was she not admiring his diamond ring now? He decided he would even risk ringworm to once have those reddish-brown feet crossed over his back. The ugly old chief would never have to know.

"And how," Coufos asked, "is Chochobo's way to make paste different from how it is done in Brazil?"

The chief's head seemed even more turtlelike now, and a bubble of spit had formed on his lower lip.

"In Brazil the coca leaves," Meewahn answered, "are just roasted on an oven and afterward ground into a fine green powder in a large round wooden mortar. Sometimes a little tapioca is added to make the paste stick together better. But it is nothing like Chochobo's way."

A diamond ring for a brown Diana, Coufos thought. Of course not this ring, which everyone could tell was his. He realized the rain had stopped outside. Suddenly the shack seemed filled to bursting with silence. Coufos's looked over at Wactu; a vein in his forehead looked like a worm in the chief's flesh, ready to squeeze through his skin.

"I do not believe," the chief said in a new and more

threatening tone, "that you white men needed my daughter to learn this. There are many tribes close to Puerto Porqueño who also make the paste our way, just as there are many who make it as Chochobo's people do." Another vein rimmed Wactu's eyes like a livid thread.

Coufos's bowels churned. He had heard of one of Wactu's methods of killing a man: first pulling out his tongue, then cutting his belly open, and afterward pulling his guts out with a stick and feeding them to rats in front of the man's eyes. When he spoke, it was in a tone he had not heard himself use since he played with his nephews and nieces in Crete. He had not known that that voice remained in his throat—packed away with the memories of his family.

"What you say is true, great chief, but often there are tricks." He did not want to insult the chief by calling him one who performed tricks, but there was no word for techniques in his language. "There are different ways certain tribes and clans know, even in some families, that are special, better ways than others. To make beer, to grow corn, to make a loin-cloth."

Coufos watched the chief pondering. The taste of his own blood was in Coufos's throat.

Finally Wactu said, "This is true."

The Greek, hearing the shift in the chief's tone even more than his answer, continued, "There is a sweet drink of the white man—Coca-Cola—which, though it is not important for our talk, once contained the coca. The drink is much prized and many try to copy it. These copiers would pay a fortune, they would sacrifice much people—*anything*—to learn the special way the Coca-Cola is made. And even though this has been going on for a very old man's lifetime, no one has yet learned the secret."

"I understand," the chief said in a way that was tantamount to an apology. Indians didn't apologize.

As the Greek soothed and then complimented the chief, he also took greater liberty with the length of his gazes on Meewahn. Perhaps, when inevitably it became necessary to get rid of Chochobo—the Indian would find out sooner or later that Buchreiser would not protect his people from being killed—he would then buy her. How could such a black pig produce so bewitching a daughter? Or perhaps after Buchreiser had Wactu and his many warriors destroy Chochobo, and he in turn destroyed Wactu, he would simply ask Buchreiser for this girl. That German Turk! Perhaps even better, he would just damn well take his due himself!

Suddenly Coufos saw himself adjust Meewahn's naked body underneath him, deciding upon which of the two openings below her reddish-brown pelt he would enter first. And then all at once he was in a gleaming white house filled with the stringed music of *santuris* on a green hill overlooking an expanse of sea to the south, and to the north trees—dark carob

and silvery olive, orange, fig, lemon, and pome-
granate. The first tender flowers of the yellow gorse
were already showing among its thorns, and there
was a wonderful mixture of scents: of sea and thyme;
of lemon blossom, honeysuckle, and wild violets;
and of his favorite—dew on olives. Somewhere in the
house, someone—a woman, of course, they were in
every room—was roasting salted pumpkin seeds and
slicing great chunks of freshly made halvah. Soon,
when the night closed the flowers, he would listen
with one ear to the sea and with the other to the song
of the nightingale. And all that he had to do for
Buchreiser in the jungle to get the drachmas to
return home on his terms would be worth it.

Chapter Twenty-Four

Liara washed her hair with the skins of the fruit which made suds when soaked in water and squeezed between the fingers. She would love Chochobo the same, she knew, even if his hair did not shine, but a man's love carries more conditions than a woman's. As she dried her hair with a bark cloth she had soaked, beaten with flat stones, and dried until it became very soft and white, she looked over at Chochobo's third wife, Eena. The woman was feeding Liara's daughter from her breast, as her own were still dry. If this trouble between her and Chochobo continued for long, her child might take more of Eena's milky spirit into her belly than her own.

When she had finished drying and combing out her hair, she went to the hut of the woman shaman called Lino, taking the earthenware beer jar she had made as payment.

Outside, she thought she had rarely seen such a retiring sun: red becoming violet, the dark sky swallowing up the shape of things as if the river had burst its banks to cover the earth. No wonder it was the custom for cures to take place at dusk.

The inside of Lino's hut smelled pungently of burning herbs and other potions. Despite knowing that Lino was a good woman, Liara had never gotten used to the initial shock of seeing her. It was jarring seeing the old woman's completely hairless head and pubic area. The contracting coillike designs on her face and around her breasts and crotch in pigment made from white clay were worse. They seemed in the flickering torchlight to glow and move, as if a snake were moving across her body.

"Here," the old woman grunted, pointing a twiglike finger at a hammock.

Liara lay down. The walls were lined with bark to insulate the hut from outside noise. A harpy eagle sat in a conical cage of peeled poles which were rubbed with white clay. The bird received its share of all the village's game in exchange for its feathers, which had magic healing power.

"First," the shaman said, "we will treat you for jaguar spirits that may be drying your milk and shaming you with this jealousy of your husband's newest wife."

It was the treatment after this one that Liara was afraid of.

Soon her nose stung from the acrid scent of burning tobacco. The old woman sat by the hammock, holding a harpy eagle feather in one hand and a large round clay pipe in the other. Liara closed her eyes when she felt the medicine smoke blown over her body. Soon she could feel the strong, dry, bonelike hands of the old woman massaging the sickness away.

When the shaman stopped massaging, Liara was grateful she had received treatment, but she was fearful of what was to come.

"On your feet," the shaman commanded. The feather in her hand had been replaced by a rattle. Liara's knees locked when she saw what was in the other hand: stinging ants, numbed by having been left in water overnight, were caught in the mesh lining of a huge flattened cloth hand, its wrappings woven from strips of fiber and adorned with macaw and royal hawk feathers. She wondered if Chochobo would suffer as much for her as she was about to for him.

"This will teach you how to hold pain without showing it," the shaman said—but it was more chant than speech. "Pain of body, or the pain of mind, which is your jealousy." The hairless woman shook her rattle and blew tobacco smoke on the ants. "You may not scream or dance or cry when I place your arm in the cloth. For how you show your pain is how you shall show your jealousy to your husband."

Liara braced herself as the old woman wrapped her hand in the fiber cloth, all the while repeating Chochobo's name under her breath.

When it was over, the old woman placed a poultice of coca leaves on Liara's arm to draw out the infection and relieve the pain. Despite the pain, which had made her legs bend on their own, the bird had returned to her breast and even fluttered its wings tentatively. The burden of steamlike jealousy inside her had been dispelled. She stumbled back to her hut, weak but encouraged. In a little while Chochobo was expected for dinner and she would be able to feel like herself again, free of jealousy. Maybe she would get some of her strength back with a rest. Then, if she hurried, she might trap enough frogs to make him a special treat for dinner.

The truth is, Chochobo thought, as he approached his hut, *I do feel strongly for Meewahn. So far, the feeling is made mostly of sex, but why should I not want a woman who is my wife?* Did his urge for Meewahn diminish his love of Liara? Certainly not. He was weary. Jealousy was a shameful enough taboo—but followed by Liara's anger! His patience was nearly gone. He had told Liara once that if she did not change her way she would talk to the wind. He would not tell her again. Still, he was deeply pained by the hurt she must be feeling.

"I have been hungry for frogs," Chochobo said as he sat by Liara's hearth. He had tried to force enthusiasm into his voice as a sign of his eagerness for a new beginning with her.

"I am glad you are pleased," she said. *When was he last so enthused about food?* she thought. *Maybe it is the excitement he feels in Meewahn's hammock spilling over onto my hearth.* Then she remembered the stinging ants.

She served him the frog meat, careful to keep the swollen arm as much out of sight as possible.

"A meal like no other," Chochobo said.

"Thank you," she said, and thought: *He comes to me for cooking because Meewahn knows little of food and does not care to learn.* Why had she suffered so, to be thinking like this so soon? She tried to soothe herself with other thoughts but could not. She had no doubt that Chochobo had first accepted the gift of Meewahn as a wife for the welfare of the tribe, but she had seen the way he looked at Meewahn. He was much moved by the girl's beauty and fire. Nothing she could do or say would change that fact. She believed that in time he would be able to look past the foreigner's beauty and become aware of her shrewdness and cunning, her lying, vanity, and laziness—traits Liara knew would kill Chochobo's desire for any woman.

She looked up and drew great succor from how zestfully he ate her food.

"Would you like a quid of coca after your supper?" she asked him.

The question had always been a cue to each that they were going to make love.

"I . . . I would, but I must meet her and her father, who have spent the day visiting a sick relative in their country. It is the custom to welcome a father-in-law home."

"I do not need to be reminded of custom again! Sorry . . . I—I am sorry." But she was not sorry at all. Why were the stinging ants failing her?

He would not speak of her disrespectful tone; perhaps it would pass, yet his own anger would not leave him.

"How is the child?" he asked in an attempt to

change his mood. Whatever had happened between them, so that he heard himself speaking to her as though they were not far from strangers?

"She is fine, and grows." If only she could see love in his eyes, the pain in her heart—even greater pain than in her arm—would be bearable. She sat waiting till he raisèd his eyes.

I will not let her see my anger, and it will soon be pushed away by my love for her, he thought.

She watched him avoid her eyes—her highest test of his true feeling for her—and all the pain in her heart and arm exploded.

"Afraid I might see in your eyes how you love her now!" she spat out.

"I love you, but I will not take much more of this shameful jealousy."

"And I will not take your putting Meewahn over me any longer!"

Chochobo jumped to his feet. "Talk to the wind!"

He whirled and stamped out of the hut.

After a while, her shoulders slumped, a moan broke out of the bird who had fallen in her breast, and she bent to the ground.

Chapter Twenty-Five

Michael unbuckled his seat belt as the plane, coming out of its bank, climbed higher over the night air of Puerto Porqueño. How strange to be the only passenger in a plane.

When Michael had come back to Puerto Porqueño at Coufos's summons, he found that the Greek had left instructions: a plane would be waiting at the airport to take him to the palace.

The sudden image of Nicole shedding her clothes with such sweet deftness made him shut his eyes. Remembering a tremor that ran through her like a wild undertow made his mouth go dry. Each time he had entered her, he shared her sense of being filled up. Unlike any of the women he'd known who had tried to change him, Nicole seemed to want nothing but to deepen the qualities he already possessed. He believed this was because she was so self-reliant and healthy. She could afford to look for and find the best in him. He believed she would always see his best—not just when he showed it, but even when he wavered.

The steady droning of the jet engines had lessened, and the plane was descending.

"We are almost there, señor," came the pilot's voice from the cockpit. "It is best to tighten your seat belt."

Michael looked out but could see nothing. It was one thing to talk about the jungle and another to realize that only this flimsy assemblage of aluminum and straining engines kept him safe from the largest unexplored area of land on the surface of the earth. He rubbed his wrist where he had worn the watch he had lost yesterday. It was not the absence of the watch that bothered him; it had only been a cheap Bulova he used for traveling. It was the terror he minded, the terror of the unfathomably large mass of unmapped jungle below, the mighty river with its endless, intricate network of thousands upon thousands of islands, tributaries, inlets, and bays. The mocking emptiness all around him made all Western civilization seem merely a momentary aberration in history. The Amazon was a great, unfeeling void that he might get lost in, along with his wristwatch—or be killed in, like Ava.

"There is the landing field," the pilot said.

Michael could see tiny specks of light. Soon the plane was skimming over the treetops. The full moon threw off enough light so Michael could see other planes on the ground. He recognized a Learjet. There were two helicopters, a green and white jet about the size of a 727, and two others that looked like Beechcrafts.

Just then the palace acreage came into view. The moonlight shone like mother-of-pearl, and the structure itself looked like a great monument in the surrounding unbroken ocean of wild foliage.

The plane landed with a series of jarring bumps. When Michael stepped outside, the air was stagnant, and the slight breeze carried the miasma of the jungle in its foul breath.

As he stepped off the plane, he was frisked by a man built like a body builder carrying an automatic rifle across his back. Without saying a word, the muscled man led him to a jeep and they sped off.

Up close, the entrance to the palace was even more forbidding. Great searchlights, like those on prison walls, constantly surveyed the iron-grilled main gate, armed at the top with sharp spear-pointed rods. Windows were no more than slits, mean lookouts that gave nothing away.

Michael was impressed by the two-story-high entry hall. He was struck immediately by dual impressions of wealth and stark asceticism. Everything, from soaring arches to table lamps, was designed in the geometric lines of high tech, constructed of concrete, glass, and brushed metals. The resulting impression was of cold, soulless, virile power.

The muscular bodyguard led Michael down a glazed tile corridor, past marble stairways and rooms with doors twice his height, to a windowless, coffin-like antechamber where he was told to wait.

The smell of chlorine seeped into Michael's nostrils, and he became aware of the tightness of his muscles. He yearned for the swim he usually took every morning at his health club.

The bodyguard came back and led Michael to a grottolike gymnasium, the likes of which he had seen only once—in an exclusive health spa in Palm Springs. It was hard to grasp that what lay before him was but a single example of property belonging to one man. Perhaps fifteen or so men in their twenties and early thirties were exercising: running around the track, doing sit-ups on slantboards, lifting weights on the Nautilus machines, pedaling stationary bicycles, and working rowing machines. Others swam in the huge pool or sat in the hot tubs and whirlpools, their bulky muscles glistening. Inside glass-enclosed courts which Michael presumed to be air-conditioned, still others played squash. Michael guessed the men were, like his guide, bodyguards.

"Rudd!"

Michael turned round and saw Coufos with a short

man whose conservative suit and British-looking shoes were at odds with his unruly graying hair and bandito moustache.

"I will leave you to them," the bodyguard said and was gone.

"Miles, you meet Escobar. Escobar is Buchreiser's right-arm man."

Michael shook Escobar's hand. His grip was surprisingly warm for a man with so wary a look. The man's face was at once cold and sensual.

"I have heard many good things about you, Rudd. I hope I will not be disappointed."

"I certainly hope not."

"Come," Escobar said, "let us see if Mr. Buchreiser is ready for us."

Michael followed the two men, wondering whether either of them, or Buchreiser himself, was responsible for Ava's death. They led him to the rear of the spa where two bodyguards stood outside a door. The guards lowered their rifles and moved aside as Escobar knocked on the door.

"Come in."

They entered. Before Michael could concentrate on a blond man whose body was wired to a heart-rate monitor, and the man who stood over him with a stethoscope, his attention was riveted by the room. Everything was entirely furnished in Lucite: desks, desk accessories, bar, bar stools, wall clock, even the telephone—it was transparent, and its bared wires made him feel as if his true identity were also visible. The terrazzo floor was the color of wet white paint. The effect was like opening a door into a room in the century to come.

He was scrutinizing the tall, muscular body of Buchreiser—not an ounce of friendly fat on him—while the German looked back at him with opaque eyes. The blue eyes didn't seem to reflect any mood. They appeared new and raw, untouched by experience.

"A perfect heart," the man with the stethoscope said, detaching Buchreiser from the monitor.

"Good. Get Mr. Rudd a drink, Gus."

Michael was suddenly acutely aware again that he was an imposter to these cocaine dealers and murderers, in a fortress patrolled by an army of well-trained bodyguards. He had to reach deep down inside himself for the proper tone of voice. "I don't drink during business discussions, thanks."

Buchreiser rose, shooed the doctor out, and grinned as hard a grin as Michael had ever seen. It was an expression the German would be able to keep even under torture. He realized Buchreiser had not shaken his hand.

"Sit. Please," Buchreiser said.

Despite the request, Michael knew from the tone that it was a command. The Lucite chair was cool and hard.

"I do not believe in civilities and small talk, Rudd.

It wastes time and clouds issues. I am told you are fucking the de la Houssaye woman."

Michael sharply squelched an impulse to smash his fists into Buchreiser's face. "If the Indian you have spying on me told you that, his fantasies are getting in his way. I can assure you I've never experienced a shortage of women in my life. I don't need to mix sex with business. Not, understand, that I wouldn't have sex with her if I thought it would help me to learn what I went there for."

"Well said," said Buchreiser.

Michael watched as the German glanced at Escobar. The Colombian's whole face sagged as if pulled down by the weight of his moustache. Coufos beamed.

"Say what is on your mind, Escobar," said Buchreiser.

"I do not trust him. His answers are quick and well oiled, but they have no substance when you examine the—"

"Like your answers when you first come," Coufos cut in. "Only you use grease, not oil."

"Silence!" Buchreiser shouted.

Michael saw the Greek look at the floor. The Colombian bit his moustache.

"When can I meet your computer wizard?" Buchreiser asked.

"You can't. If you know who he is, you don't need me."

Buchreiser smiled. Then, in a new, almost patronizing tone, he said, "I like your report, Rudd. It is bright, orderly, clean, efficient. So are your ideas. But I never allow a man to join my organization unless he has proved himself. Not only under fire, but on the front lines as well. And that goes for everyone from a bodyguard to a man on your level. You must be tested. Of course, every possible precaution will be taken. The plan, as you will soon hear, is a good one. Still, the unexpected is always somewhat of a factor. If you succeed, in the future you will be rewarded with more money than many of even your own rich countrymen earn. If you fail, you will not get so much as a decent burial. How ambitious are you?"

"Not so ambitious that I won't ask what the plan is, exactly."

"Of course. Just what I would have said in your place. Now, if my Colombian friend has mastered his temper, perhaps he will explain what must be done."

Michael turned from Buchreiser's cool flat eyes to Escobar's hot round ones.

"The duplicate-bag switch," Escobar said, as though he were beginning a sales pitch he had made many times, "is designed not to protect the goods but to protect the carrier. The cocaine is packed in Madeira wood, chosen for its high specific gravity." He unzipped a suitcase, reached down, and pulled out a statue of the Virgin Mary. "When a Madeira statue is hollowed out, it does not *feel* hollow." He handed the statue to Rudd, who, surprised by the weight, nodded and returned it.

Escobar looked at his watch, went to the door, and opened it. A petite woman in a halter and slacks entered, carrying a suitcase. Clearly young, she looked willful, dangerous perhaps. *Wanton*, thought Michael.

"Mr. Rudd, this is Maria, otherwise known as Snowdrop. She is the best mule we have got, and you will be working with her."

"Hello, Maria." Michael extended a hand. Maria regarded the gesture with disbelief, then held hers out hesitantly and shook.

"You will have two suitcases exactly identical, right?" said Escobar.

"Right," said Michael.

"The statue with the cocaine will be packed in one case by me, to look like a souvenir."

Michael nodded.

"Now the suitcases have to open, like this"—he drew his arms inward—" at a right angle. No zippers. And it has got to stand up—she has to be able to open it away from her—so that when it is opened and the inspector is going through it, Snowdrop cannot see what he is doing. The top is between them. Okay?"

Michael nodded.

"Okay. Now, in one of the suitcases she puts all her clothes, her shoes, anything that fits, and a few things that will identify her. And *she* packs it. All right?"

"I understand," said Michael.

"Now, the other suitcase, the duplicate, is where the load goes. And *you* have to pack it. Her fingerprints cannot be anywhere near the duplicate bag. *You* pack it, and you pack it with a lot of women's clothes all a larger size, like a fourteen. What size are you, Snowdrop, about a seven?"

"Six," she said, giving Michael a sidelong glance that was a curious mixture of seduction and amusement.

"Good. So all the clothes in with the load are size fourteen. Shoes to match. Makeup, everything. Looks like a woman's suitcase, same as any other. Everything much too large. No fingerprints. Absolutely clean. And none of it hers. She never even touches this particular bag. *Comprende?*" he said to Michael.

"*Comprende*," Michael replied.

"All right. You board the same plane, but you do not sit together. Both bags are checked aboard. They are identical except for a scuff mark on one of them. That is the loaded one. When you get off the plane, Maria picks up the loaded bag and carries it through customs. That is the first time she has touched it. Rudd, you are delayed. Maria opens the loaded bag. She does this away from her—undoes the clasps and pulls the top up toward her. She cannot see what the customs man is doing."

"I know, I understand," Snowdrop said.

"Right." Escobar turned to Michael. "The lid of the suitcase is between Maria and the customs man. She is short, and the counters are usually high at customs, so that helps. While the agent is examining the contents of the suitcase, she fools with the rest of her stuff—whatever else she is carrying. Maria, you do not look at what he is doing. Rudd, if that bag goes through, you just pick up her real bag and carry it through yourself, understand?"

"Yes."

"Maria, if the agents crack the statue, *if* they nail you—"

"I never seen no bag before in my life," Maria said. "This is not my bag. That must be mine over there all by itself on the carousel."

"Perfect!" exclaimed Escobar. "Because that *is* your bag. Rudd has left it there. No possible way they can connect the one they have got with you. No fingerprints, no personal belongings, nothing. You got the wrong bag, you moved in on somebody else's hustle. No record, no nothing. You walk away."

Michael's nervous stomach was rumbling so loud he was afraid the others could hear, so he cleared his throat and spoke.

"Sounds good. Foolproof, in fact."

"Yes, it is," said Escobar. "María, you can go now."

"Thank you, señor."

Coufos let the woman out.

In the silence which followed, Buchreiser stared coldly at the Greek, who was studying his finger-nails. Finally Coufos became aware of the silence and looked up. Seeing the German, he muttered in chagrin, "Uh, yes, very brill—very good plan, Escobar."

"Yes," Buchreiser said, and turned toward Michael.

"Normally, Mr. Rudd, a carrier has to be propped up, which means confident, unafraid, not suspicious looking. This plan even takes your fear into account. The only things it does not make allowances for are panic and the fact that you just may very well not be who you say you are. Let me remind you that if we find out on this trial run or at any time in the future that you are a spy or a traitor, you will be given over to a tribe of Indians which is still very active in cannibalism. In front of your eyes they will draw twigs for delicacies: the first swallow of your heart's blood, the first bite of your liver, the mash they will make of your eyes, the right to smoke your tongue, which will be used as a kind of beef jerky on long hunts. And after your marrow has been sucked clean, the prize of your long bones, which they favor for flutes. They will torture you in ways you could not imagine in your worst nightmares. Finally, they will cook you alive while old women painted black and red dance around you carrying newly made vases for your blood and entrails.

"Mothers will smear their nipples with your blood so that even babies can have a taste of it. Your body, cut into quarters, will be roasted on a barbecue, and the old men will lick the grease running along the sticks. Your head will be shrunken, your hair made into a belt, your teeth into a necklace, your lips into a bracelet. Your fat will be collected and stored in kettles with other human fat for seasoning their food. I think you get the idea, do you not, Rudd?"

Michael was barely able to mutter yes while he kept his jaw clamped to trap the sour bile that had risen into this throat. "When does all this take place?" he finally managed.

"First thing in the morning," Buchreiser replied.

Part III

Chapter Twenty-Six

"You look troubled, Chochobo."

They were inside Nicole's hut. One night had already passed since Michael had left, and this night was nearly over.

"You have always been able to see trouble being worn on my face, my friend. I feel somehow things are worse with Buchreiser."

Conspicuously absent were those tappings in her breast she was used to experiencing in Chochobo's presence that made her nipples change size and texture slightly, and the butterfly wings brushing the inside of her thighs. Although she was worried about the Indian, she felt herself surrendering instead to the morning that was gradually making itself known: to the changing light, to the way the shadowy shapes outside were magically turning into a hut, a tree. The wolf whistles of screaming pia birds were like nightingale songs. *How differently*, she told herself, *love makes you see the world!*

"What do you mean about Buchreiser?" she asked.

"I do not know. A feeling."

"Buchreiser isn't your only trouble, is he? I sense there's something else."

"You sense right. Why I cannot be like other men with their wives I do not know."

So that was it. "Because you are better than most other men."

"If that means I must suffer more, how does it help me to be better?"

"You speak as though you have the power to change, to be something other than what you are."

"Now I know I sound as foolish to you as to myself."

"What is it, Chochobo?"

"Liara. I am angry at her for her jealousy of Meewahn, but I also miss how it once was with us."

"And how are things with you and Meewahn?"

"She is like a wonderful thirst I cannot drink enough to quench."

"It seems to me the thirst that can be satisfied is more wonderful than the one that can't be."

"You have always been against the custom of many wives."

"I am against any custom devised by men which only benefits men. And if I remember well, you have lived with Liara for a long time as though your other wives barely existed. I don't mean to insult you, but you abandon the custom when it suits your purposes, and you try to enforce it when your needs change."

"I do not wish to talk of this any longer." The brown of his eye had turned darker.

"You mean you won't."

"Does our friendship now give you the right to tell me what I mean to say?"

"I'm sorry."

"But tell me, please, what has brought such a shine to your eyes and a color to your cheeks? It is Rudd?"

"You know him?" For a second she thought: *Chochobo sent an Indian to spy on Michael and me.* Then, ashamed of her distrust, she dismissed the thought.

"I know of him," Chochobo said. "From Xingu, and others."

"And?"

"I only know of him. You know him."

Suddenly she thought of Michael. When he listened to her, he drew his legs up and crossed his feet, making her feel his attention was total, somehow, because in that position he looked very young. As she thought of him there was that prickling, tingling sensation along her arms and thighs and belly.

"I love him, Chochobo."

"I am happy for you."

"How sad I am, my friend, that you can't be happy along with me."

"I have had my share."

"You speak as if you don't expect to be happy again."

"It is said that every time you cut down the jungle, it fights its way back. But what comes back is not what was there before."

"The jungle is not a human being. A married man from my country hurt me so badly once I did not want to live, and I'm sure that's part of why I got sick. But here I am, feeling newer and better than ever."

"I did not say I have stopped trying to be happy. To get answers, to find my way, I have fasted for two days now, to prepare for the *ayahuasca*."

Nicole drew in her breath with surprise. She knew the *ayahuasca* was not taken casually. The drug was used to induce visions, telepathic states, metaphysical contemplation, and transmigration—but only by *caciques* and shamans, and then only toward the goal of solving great problems.

"If I had known you were so troubled, I would have come to you."

"And I would have asked you to come. The trouble crept up behind me and arrived all at once."

"I understand."

"Understand, too, that I must leave you now. To go into the jungle to drink the *ayahuasca*."

"Be careful," she said. *God*, she thought. *Men have lost their sanity under the influence of that drug.*

"Remain happy, my friend."

Chapter Twenty-Seven

After Chochobo left Nicole, he went to the holy hut used only for making ready a *cacique* or a shaman to drink of the *ayahuasca*—the wine of visions.

Inside the hut, Lino, the hairless female shaman, met him. He knew there was no speaking in this place where the walls were black from fruit stain. She gave him the juice of the *bamba* root to drink, which made his belly pour out of his mouth. Then she led him to lie on his side, and made water go up into his backside with a turtle bladder tied to a reed nozzle, and his belly poured out from his other end. Then he was given cool refreshing water, which he drank quickly.

Soon he would be ready for the magic fluid that would help him to know what troubled him about Buchreiser, and what could be done about Liara's jealousy. But also his legs felt weak with fear. He had seen shamans shake on the ground, their eyes rolling up in their head, and then die for having taken too much of the *ayahuasca* poison. But he was a Carrijura chief and would not shame himself and his tribe by showing his fear.

A tribesman came into the hut and gave him a small clay pot filled with the *ayahuasca*. They wished him good visions and that he would be safe in the jungle.

When he got to the jungle, it was dark and he heard the *chieu, chieu, chieu*, the call of the night bird of bad omen. The call, if it didn't end, was a sign of death. The bird stopped, and he began to breathe again.

After he made a fire, he opened the pot and poured some *ayahuasca* into his gourd. He swallowed the potion; it had little taste, like boiled green corn. He heard an owl mock him in the dark, and then a sound like *ummm* began in his ears. His skin felt like alligator hide as he touched it with his fingers. He was hot and then cold and then hot again. Water broke from his skin, and he felt that his stomach would pour from his mouth. He knew well what too much *ayahuasca* could do, but he must drink more.

He began to chant:

> *Spirit of the jungle*
> *Reveal to me by* ayahuasca.
> *Give me the stealth of the boa,*

Sight of the night owl,
Hearing of the deer,
Endurance of the tapir,
Grace and strength of the jaguar,
Knowledge of the moon.

He drank the potion. He closed his eyes and the colors began: greens and blues and reds brighter than any bird in mating colors. He knew his blood in a way he had not before, and could follow it as it passed through his body. He opened his eyes and felt he had left his body and was watching himself from outside. He could not tell how far one of his arms was from the other, or how long it would take for the two to touch. He could see things in the dark that no man should see.

Shapes with colors that hurt his eyes moved around him, shapes of great four-legged ones which became snakes that hung from trees. He was with a cricket on a stem, rubbing his legs against the box of his body, heard a small lizard lapping water from a leaf overhead. He felt himself inside a snake and screamed, but no one could hear him. An orchid fell slowly from the treetops onto him, knocking him into a blackness so dark and still he thought it must be death.

Still, he knew nothing more, understood nothing more.

He knew that more than two swallows of the *aya-*

huasca could bring danger, even death. But without the answers he needed from it, he was in another danger, and part of him felt he was dead.

Lifting the gourd, he paused, remembering that he must chant of what he wanted to see.

> *Spirit of the vine*
> *I seek your guidance now*
> *To translate the past into the future,*
> *To understand what I should do with*
> *Liara and Meewahn,*
> *To understand what troubles me anew*
> *About the man in the palace.*
> *Reveal a spirit,*
> *The secrets that I need.*

Then he drank every drop of what was left of the *ayahuasca*.

Soon the whole jungle rushed down into the part of him that had been made dead by the questions he needed the *ayahuasca* to help him answer. He was swallowed up by his own emptiness and then sent flying up into the sky, where he saw his dead father, and his father's father, and their fathers before them, whose faces he knew though he had never seen them. "Do not look for the answers in us," their faces said, though their mouths were still. "Look for them in yourself."

And then he was a light in the sky that was falling,

and he was also watching the light that was Chochobo falling. The light that was him, and was also lighting him from above, blinded him. He felt and also saw Meewahn come to him and kiss him with great skill and warmth, and he felt for the first time with her the skill more than the warmth. It was not warmth but fire. Meewahn was skill and fire.

He fell to the earth and broke into as many pieces as there were hairs on his head. And when the pieces came together he understood how everything he did with his body—turned, stretched, shook—began in his head. He saw Meewahn and her father, Wactu. Wactu spoke to him of war with the white man, but he had no anger in his throat. They said he went to their home in Brazil, which takes two days, but they returned the next morning. They lied. He saw Meewahn and Wactu with Buchreiser. He opened his eyes to shut off the pain of what he had seen, but there was only darkness to stop him from seeing anything else.

When next he opened his eyes, his head was light and his body hurt, but he felt strong and sure. He knew a rain had just stopped because he was wet. There had never been so bright a day. The arms of the sun reached down and filled the jungle with color and sweet smell. And he heard the flute-like call of the tinamon bird.

Back in the village he went to the hearth of Liara.

The beginnings of little bird's feet at the corners of her mouth and eyes were like signs of all the time they had spent together. He took her to walk by the river with him. There was fear in her eyes, so he spoke quickly.

"I need your warmth, Liara," he said.

Water came to her eyes.

"And if you were jealous, jealousy cannot be an evil thing, because you could not do an evil thing. It was just a human thing."

Her cheeks were wet when she spoke. "But to be jealous is to go against custom."

"I would sooner go against custom than against you."

And when she came into his arms his cheeks also became wet.

As they walked back to the village, her hand in his, he was also thinking: *I will tell those chiefs that are not with Meewahn's father it is time to fight against Buchreiser. It is time for us to make the coca into cocaine ourselves.*

Chapter Twenty-Eight

"If the coke business was put in that list of the five hundred largest corporations," Escobar said to Michael, "it would be number seven in sales, between IBM and AT&T. About thirty-two billion *norte-americano* dollars.

"Now watch," Escobar continued, walking to the bathroom sink in Michael's room and filling a tumbler with water. "This is one of the easiest ways to test coke." He pulled out a clear polyethylene bag. "You notice the stuff is triple wrapped, to keep moisture out, so it does not dissolve?"

"I noticed."

"Good." Escobar shaved a piece of the "rock" with a single-edge razor blade and dropped it into the glass. "Crystals of pure snow dropped into the water will dissolve before they reach the bottom of the glass. The impurities will remain. What do you think of this stuff?"

"Looks great to me."

Escobar twitched his moustache, as if to acknow-ledge his agreement. "Now we do the burn test." After shaving off more crystals, he placed them on a piece of cigarette-package foil taken from his pocket and heated from beneath with a lighter. "If the coke is pure, it will bubble and have a light brown film. A mix will turn black and leave lumps, as you can see it is doing right now."

"Interesting."

"I am glad you are being entertained."

"What don't you like about me?"

"I never said I did not like you. I just do not trust quickly."

"So why are you teaching me anything at all before I prove myself?"

"Because you will be dead soon enough wherever you try to hide, if you are not who you say you are, and Mr. Buchreiser does not like to waste any time."

For the fifth time since Ava's death, Michael failed to experience his usual exhilaration and sense of escape during a plane takeoff. Instead, he battled against the feeling of deep despair as the wheels retracted and the flaps slid into the wings.

He took the wad of gum out of his mouth and got rid of it; he would just risk his ears being plugged up from the pressurized flight. An excruciating ball of tension centered at the base of his skull. For distraction, he concentrated on the delicately molded profile of Snowdrop a few rows ahead. Bit it didn't work. If only he could stop his lungs from feeling as if one deep breath would burst them. Or if he could end his cottony thirst. What if he couldn't go through with the smuggling? And what if he did and got caught by customs? Would they believe he had only done it to gain the trust of Buchreiser, so he might find his sister's murderer? How many years could he get on that cocaine charge?

Oh, Ava. I can remember the color of your eyes, but not their real expression.

Something warm and tender and familiar touched his shoulder—Ava? The Avianca flight attendant said something about a cocktail before lunch. He rubbed his stinging eyes and wrenched himself back into the world of the Flight 172 from Bogotá to JFK.

"I'll have a martini, please."

When the flight attendant returned and handed him his drink, he sipped the cocktail, thinking about how quickly he and Snowdrop had passed through customs at Bogotá. He had been surprised, but Escobar had told him last night that the Colombian authorities were on the organization's payroll. The customs inspectors in New York wouldn't be so easy.

The base of his neck pained unmercifully, but

eating and drinking had unclogged his ears, and he was grateful for the mildly comforting sound of the normal tourist voices around him.

How, on such a day, could the middle-aged couple next to him be arguing whether to take a taxi straight home or stop to visit the woman's mother at her apartment in Howard Beach, near JFK?

Michael and Snowdrop stood on opposite sides of the carousel, looking for their bags. New York custom officers seemed to be everywhere. *This is only the set of a Hitchcock movie*, he thought. *In another moment, the director will shout, "Break!" and all the actors will scatter for lunch.*

Then an officer appeared, holding a German shepherd. The dog pulled the officer to a pile of luggage and began sniffing.

When Michael saw the dog sniffing at one of the suitcases belonging to Snowdrop or himself, he tried to assure himself that what Escobar had said was true. The inside of the plastic bag containing the cocaine had been washed with peroxide and then dried off and placed inside two more bags, so the dogs would only smell the peroxide.

But it didn't work for him. He attempted to use Nicole's technique to control his stomach muscles—to exhale as much as possible so that his body would automatically respond by inhaling — but he was too frightened. If he started hyperventilating, he would surely give himself away. He looked around. Making sure no one was looking at him, he jammed his fist hard into his diaphragm.

Just then the dog walked away from the luggage, and Michael started to breathe again.

He started to approach the bag to see if it had a scuff mark when the matching piece bounced off the conveyer onto the carousel. What he saw next froze him solid. There, between a Louis Vuitton and a Gucci carryall, was a third case identical to their matching cases!

When he had regained some of his composure, he snapped a sidelong glance at Snowdrop, breaking a rule Escobar had repeated countless times. The beautiful professional mule did not respond, although he was sure she knew his eyes were on her.

He spotted the suitcase with the scuff mark. He was just about to grab it when he realized he couldn't, because it would leave him without an alibi. When would Snowdrop see the damn scuff!

Suddenly a man in a brown business suit carrying an attaché case reached over and picked up the scuffed case.

Michael turned to the man and opened his mouth to speak, realized he couldn't, and shut his mouth.

As the businessman began to approach customs, Michael prayed for a miracle, the design of which was a mystery to him. He looked around for an exit to run to and saw there were armed officers everywhere. He must have been crazy to think he could outwit both the U.S. government and the biggest cocaine smuggler in the world.

His breathing had become tortured gasps, and he could feel blood pounding in his head and in the pit of his stomach. In another second he was sure his locked knees would give way.

He saw what happened next as if from behind a foggy shower in which he was unable to move: Snowdrop grabbed the suitcase, which he noticed had a leather identification tag attached to it, and lifted it from the carousel. Michael heard her say, as though from a great distance, "I think you made a mistake," and she exchanged cases with the man, who appeared more startled by her beauty than by her intrusion.

Snowdrop smiled broadly at the businessman, without a trace of fear or concern, and he bowed mock-gallantly as a signal that she should go ahead of him. Despite his fear, Michael realized Snowdrop's act was one of the most consummately professional gestures he had ever witnessed.

Gradually he became aware that he had been standing frozen for what seemed like minutes. He had to repeat the rest of the plan to himself over and over, because his brain seemed stuck repeating what had just occurred.

Michael picked up the second suitcase. His legs felt as if he had gotten over a bout with the flu.

As he moved along the line, the voices of the other

passengers and the sounds of shuffling feet assaulted his ears. Somehow everything seemed blurry. Then he remembered Nicole telling him fear could dilate the pupils.

"Do you have more than five thousand dollars in cash?" the customs officer asked.

"No," Michael answered.

He was grateful the officer did not know what his usual voice sounded like. The blue-shirted man looked over his passport. Michael noticed his hands were sweating. *For Ava*, he thought. *This is for Ava.*

"Have you acquired any gifts over four hundred dollars in value? Cigarettes or liquor?"

"No." Why was the man examining him so closely? Could he tell his knees were shaking?

Michael tore his eyes from the officer's gun. Up ahead, he could see Snowdrop in a group of blue-shirted men—had something gone wrong?

There was a pause during which the officer looked him up and down. Michael realized he wasn't breathing and was amazed that the act would not come automatically but had to be remembered.

Finally the officer signed his declaration card, handed back his passport, smiled, and said, "Welcome home, sir."

Outside the terminal he blessed the New York air, which reeked of exhaust fumes. He hailed a cab to the nearby New York International Hotel on the airport's outskirts. He needed a cigarette, but a yellow sticker with large black letters on the taxi's glass partition warned that the driver was allergic to tobacco smoke.

At the hotel, he waited in the lobby for only a few moments before Escobar's taxi pulled up outside. Then Snowdrop showed up in a Checker with the man in the brown business suit who'd been carrying an attaché case—the businessman with the matching third suitcase!

Stunned, Michael was led by Escobar to the Checker. Escobar told the driver to take them to the Lower East Side.

"The third suitcase—" Michael began.

"—was Buchreiser's idea of testing how you would act in an unexpected crisis," Escobar said. "Meet Marc Weiss, one of our best. He used to be an actor."

Michael shook hands with Weiss.

"I . . . I could stand a cigarette," Michael said as the taxi pulled away.

Snowdrop handed him a pack.

"We are not through yet," Escobar said evenly.

Chapter Twenty-Nine

It was dusk and drizzling, making the air even more foul. With Weiss, Snowdrop had left the cab in Jackson Heights to visit relatives before her return to Colombia.

As the cab came to the Lower East Side neighborhood known to its junkie inhabitants as Alphabet Town, Escobar explained that the menacing tangle of burned-out buildings, tenements, and garbage-strewn vacant lots was one of the country's hottest drug marketplaces. Michael tried to listen as if he really did come from San Francisco.

As they headed toward the building where Michael was scheduled to complete the transaction, the Colombian told him that the blighted, mostly Hispanic, fourteen-by-four-block "town" was open twenty-four hours a day — for buys of cocaine, heroin, crack, amphetamines, angel dust, and an array of other drugs.

Suddenly three police cars screamed past, their flashing lights turning the rain puddles the color of blood. *If I hailed a cab*, Michael thought, *I could be home safe in my apartment in ten minutes. Away from all this. But they'd find me later. . . .*

"It is not the police you have to worry about," Escobar said. "Because of the cuts in budget, the three hundred cops in the Ninth Precinct are now only a hundred and twenty. Look around."

Michael stole furtive glances at a black man nearby. He wore a contoured silk shirt, velvet trousers, a white felt hat with a brim as wide as a Frisbee, and a cane with sterling-silver brightwork. On his arm was an emaciated pink-sugar blonde in designer jeans and a fishnet blouse. A jewel-encrusted gold and ivory coke spoon dangled from her neck by a gold chain.

"Get your"—*sniff*— "Lucky Seven here, brothers," the black man called, "and all your Christmases'll be white." *Sniff*. "We got good Ivy League"—*sniff*—"and I mean Colombian."

"That is who we worry about," Escobar said. "'Beat artists'—pushers who sell shit that might be talcum powder. If the buyer complains, they will slip an ice pick into his heart. They do not like the competition."

Michael shuddered, then asked, "What's Lucky Seven?"

"A house brand of coke. The big-time dealers organize 'clubs' that change locations every few hours and have as many as forty people as lookouts, runners, and baggers. There are even bouncers who check the needle marks on customers' arms as though they were membership cards."

They had reached East Fourth Street. A dead chicken lay in the gutter next to a copy of *El Diario La Prensa*. The street was crowded with people Michael guessed were waiting to score: blacks, Hispanics, and middle-class whites. Clean-cut young men in linen jackets, and attractive young women in French jeans listened intently to the dealers' pitches.

"Colt forty-five is Jesus bread."

"Poison is mellow today."

"Coke brands?" Michael said.

"Heroin," Escobar said. He asked the cabby to stop in front of a mural on a tenement wall that showed an eagle clutching a hypodermic needle above the legend in red letters: COME FLY WITH ME, FOOL! He checked his watch. "We will wait here till you leave."

"Hey, mac," the driver said. "I ain't exactly crazy about this neighborhood."

Escobar took a hundred-dollar bill from his pocket and handed it to the cabby.

"Jeez, mister."

A pole-thin black pusher dressed in a brocaded white suit approached the cab. Despite his fear, Michael was amazed at how the pusher moved—

never bending his knees or back, but folding at the waist, pivoting from the hips, and strutting like a water crane.

"Seven-Up best today, man."

"We are not buying today," Escobar said, shooing the pusher away.

"What now?" Michael said.

"Now we do what takes up most of our time—we wait. Smuggling *is* waiting. No matter how careful is the preparation, no matter how airtight is the scam, smuggling is waiting."

Michael tried concentrating on a billboard advertising Goya Frozen Flan—anything to make him forget how frightened he was. Wherever he looked were the two most prominent Hispanic colors: Woolworth-paint-set turquoise and flamingo pink. Painted in the colors on a storefront window: JESUS SALVA.

Suddenly a terrible scream from one of the crumbling tenements prickled the hair on Michael's neck and he lurched forward. He glanced quickly over at Escobar, imagining for a moment that the drug man could read his thoughts. The Colombian caressed his moustache, apparently lost in reverie. In his three-piece pinstripe suit, he looked more like an investment banker than a smuggler.

"It is time," Escobar said. "You know what to do."

Michael picked up the suitcase and stepped out.

At the tenement he rang the bell as Escobar had

instructed him. Inside, the doorways were covered with layers of diamond-steel plate. Despite having been warned, when he looked up he was astonished to see the landings were all gone. A safelike container was being lowered in the empty stairwell. He placed the suitcase in the container and it rose slowly. Michael looked behind him. Any number of people outside the front door, just a few feet away, would kill him for a fraction of the value of the coke in the suitcase. He could feel cold sweat running down his neck.

The container came back. Michael removed the suitcase, opened it, and gaped. He had held millions of dollars' worth of stock and bond certificates before, but never this much cash.

He closed the suitcase and left.

Crossing the sidewalk to the cab, he imagined every passerby was staring at him hungrily.

Escobar swung open the door and Michael pushed the suitcase in and fell back onto the seat. Thank God!

"Kennedy," Escobar barked at the driver. The car bucked, then sped away. Michael rolled down the window to force air into his starving lungs.

"Well done," Escobar said, extending his hand. "We have all had to go through this. It will not be the last time for you or me. The boss does a lot of testing."

Michael did not bother to dry his sweating hands. It was over.

When the taxi stopped at a traffic light near a group of all-night Con Ed excavators, Michael saw

Escobar staring at them intently. A man with a hard hat was lowering himself into the hole in the street.

"They look like *garimpieros*," the Colombian muttered, as if to himself. Then he went on, lost in reverie. "My father could not feed us all. He took us to Cristalina, near Brasilia . . . the city of crystals."

Michael listened, fascinated.

"*Garimpieros*. Many thousands. Digging with their hands like moles for diamonds . . . deep, foot-wide wells . . . cave-ins. . . . He lost an eye."

For a moment Michael found it hard to remember the man was his enemy. The cab lurched forward.

"I'm sorry," he offered.

Escobar turned, fury in his eyes, as if surprised to see him. "Sorry? You will be sorry, all right, if your Federal Reserve plan does not work!"

Michael's palms were still perspiring seven and a half hours later when he accepted Buchreiser's congratulatory handshake. The German ordered him to continue checking on Nicole, on her interaction with the Indians, and on their coca labs.

"You have passed your test well. There may be others. Very soon now I would like to put your plan into action."

"Glad to. As soon as my contact returns to New York. I checked. He's out of the country."

Michael would have to find an opportunity to destroy Buchreiser quickly and escape, or he would be caught in his bluff about a genius who had tapped into the Federal Reserve computer. And he had about as much knowledge of foreign exchange trading with laundered cocaine money as he had of atomic reactors.

As he left the palace for Nicole's, a light rain began to fall. Maybe he would make it. He could stall for a short time, say he was waiting for his "computer genius" to return to New York. He could say he needed time to set up an operation complex enough to subvert a foreign exchange.

In spite of Michael's attempt to see his situation in a positive light—after all, he had passed the first test—doubts and fears descended on him as inexorably as the summer drizzle.

When Michael and Xingu set out from Puerto Porqueño to Nicole's village, it was a deep green night. Vampire bats squeaked over the forest.

A few miles outside of her village, Michael stopped and leaned against a prickly tree to rest. Suddenly he felt an excruciating pain on the right side of his neck. He froze in place. Was this voice bellowing through the jungle really his? He felt the slap of Xingu's hand over his mouth. His legs wouldn't budge. They buckled under him. He collapsed on the forest floor, dripping as if a bucket of water had been poured over him. The perspiration trickled into his eyes. He reached for his neck, to see if he had been shot there, but he could not lift his arm. His lungs were pressed flat. One instant Xingu's face was inches away, the next, he saw the Indian as if through the wrong end of a telescope. When he could see Xingu no longer, the ground slid away and he fell backward down, down, down into a place where there was no sun and it was painless, dark, and airless.

Chapter Thirty

Michael opened his eyes to see Nicole by the hearth with her back to him. His head ached and he felt woozy. He managed to pull the mosquito net aside and get his feet swung out and over the mattress. When he tried to rise, his legs gave out and the earth smashed up under him.

Nicole dropped a clay pot and it shattered on the ground.

"*What?*" she said, bending over him.

"I . . . I must've washed my legs today," he said, "'cause I can't seem to do a thing with them."

She burst out laughing. Then she cut her words short and helped him into bed.

"What happened to me?" he said.

"You were bitten by a tarantula about the size of my fist. Tarantula poison is weak, but you're obviously allergic to it. Xingu gave you an herb that acts like an injection of adrenaline, or else you might not be here. One of the old women prepared a tea you'll have to drink for the rest of the week. That was what just dropped on the floor. She says you'll probably feel weak and dehydrated for a few days, maybe have diarrhea and a recurring headache, but you'll be fine."

"How's Xingu?"

"He's fine."

"Good. Thank you for taking care of me." He saw that her eyes were filled with relief.

"Drink what's left of the tea in this cup. I'll go get some more."

He took a sip from the cup she held. The tea had a minty taste. Its scent was vaguely familiar. "I missed you," he said.

"How could you miss me when you've been sleeping for almost twenty-four hours?"

"Trust me, I missed you."

She smiled. "Me, too. But the tea can't wait, really. I'll be back as soon as I ask the old woman to prepare some more."

He knew that scent from somewhere. Of course—patchouli! The tea smelled of that fragrant oil popular with both men and women who were supporters of the peace movement in the sixties.

The aroma sent his thoughts back to a halfway

house in Manhattan. He sat next to Ava. It was his first visit. Seventeen . . . eighteen years ago.

"Why the 'ludes, Ava?"

"Oh, I got to feeling that no woman escapes servility. That men long ago learned to domesticate us like hunting dogs and racehorses. I began to take on a new role. I learned to fuck men the way they used to fuck me."

He winced from her pain.

Her usually soft voice was harsh. "I soon saw that it wasn't worth the trouble. I always wound up being the one to get fucked anyway. I'm not a lesbian, and I'm not crazy about fingering myself. So I stopped all of it. Or you could say I started taking drugs instead of it."

Nicole interrupted his thoughts. "Michael?"

He turned and saw her approaching, carrying a ceramic bowl.

"Fresh tea. Here, take some."

The scent of the patchouli-smelling tea brought him back once again to the halfway house, and he saw the peace-sign pendant on Ava's fragile neck, saw the hopelessness in her eyes. Something deep inside him opened so wide that the grief finally broke through. He welcomed the pain which took away his guilt for not having been able to mourn properly for Ava.

Nicole held him and cried for him, for Ava, for herself.

After a while Michael said, "I'd like to listen to her tape about snakes."

"I understand," she said, drying her tears.

Soon Ava's voice filled the hut.

". . . I first got the idea for using snake venom for pain one day when I saw an Indian dipping an arrow in fer-de-lance venom. He allowed me to watch. I had a small cut on one of my fingers, and as I touched the arrow, venom got into the wound. My finger felt numb and the hurt from my cut was gone."

"Pretty smart lady," Michael said to Nicole and felt diminished for not having understood Ava's interest in herpetology.

They held hands, listening to the tape.

When the tape ended, Michael felt guilty for those acts of the past which had displeased his sister, even those he believed justified.

"I'd like to see the book you two were writing, if you don't mind," he said.

"I don't. There are mostly notes, though."

Soon Michael held a loose-leaf binder. He read the dedication: "When one loves the Indians of the Amazon, one loves people nearly as God loves them. You know the worst about them—not a pretty pose or a sentiment artfully assumed."

Nicole watched Michael. She knew that in hearing Ava's tapes and reading her notes, he sought to feel more of the pain of his loss. The pain was telling him he was alive again, and, along with wanting to learn more about Ava, he needed to prolong his own sense of life.

"The theme of the book," she said, "is that the Indians can be saved by the resources that they already have in the forest if the forest is not taken away from them. Here, let me read to you." She took the loose-leaf. "Quote. 'First some facts about the resources we hope you will find eye-opening. Seventy percent of the three thousand plants identified by the U.S. National Cancer Institute as having anticancer properties are rain-forest species. . . .'"

"Incredible," Michael said, and Nicole went on.

"'Tetrodortoxin, derived from various species of frog, is an anesthetic one hundred sixty thousand times as strong as cocaine.'"

"Pretty terrific what you two did here."

"It's mostly Ava's work. Here, let me read you something else. 'Generations of Amazonian Indians in Paraguay have used the leaves of the stevia plant as a sweetener. Now Japanese researchers have analyzed it and found a chemical that, according to the Japanese Minstry of Health, is calorie-free, harmless to humans, and three hundred times sweeter than sugar.'"

"Millions, *billions* of dollars growing on trees," Michael said.

"And there's much more, Michael," said Nicole.

"There's a tree here called copaiba, I think it's pronounced. Anyway, it has a sap that can power a diesel truck. From another tree you can get an oil almost identical to olive oil. The list is unbelievable. Michael, you know about making money. Couldn't you help the Indians?"

"I could certainly try."

She beamed, then came over and put her arms around him.

"Easy, please." He felt a wave of weakness.

"Sorry, I'll heat up the tea."

"Anything happen with the Indians while I was away? With the coca? Wactu?"

"Chochobo. He took a hallucinogen and discovered he's truly in love with one of his wives."

"Sounds like he's got a logistical problem," Michael said wryly.

They laughed together, but gradually Nicole's mood darkened. "I'm worried about Chochobo. He figures that Buchreiser arranged for a Brazilian Indian chief to give him his latest wife so she could spy on him. Anyway, he's desperate."

Michael took in a slow, deep breath, listening.

"He's planning to make the coca into cocaine instead of paste right here."

"Does he know how?"

"One of the Indians who had some education from the missionaries knows. He's been to Peru, where they have coke labs."

"He'd better be careful," Michael said. "Buchreiser's not going to like that." He wondered if Coufos knew Nicole had been talking to Chochobo again.

"I hope Buchreiser doesn't press me too soon about the computer scheme. I'm getting so much closer to what I really want."

"Are you going on with your plans of revenge?"

"I never gave them up."

The joy had gone from her face.

"Once," he said, "you even offered to help me."

"I offered to help because I thought you wanted to bring Buchreiser to justice."

"That's what I do want."

"Justice is civilized. Vengeance is not."

"I know you're afraid that I have some kind of pathological hatred for Buchreiser. Because of what drugs did to Ava once, that kind of person has disgusted me for a long time. I hate drug people like I once hated the establishment, when I was a kid in the SDS and the Weathermen. Then when Buchreiser had her killed . . ."

Nicole stood in the entrance looking at him. At first her look seemed to express disappointment and annoyance. There was caring and tenderness in it, too, and it was entirely devoid of pity. Her look showed that she was deeply accepting of him as a man struggling with problems and temptations larger than himself.

What Michael received from Nicole at that moment

was not maternal or sentimental feeling, but respect and liking. It was a kind of liking he had never experienced before with a woman.

He knew then how deeply he had come to love her and how deeply she had come to love him.

"C'mon," she said, "let's try those legs again."

Outside, she led him to a bower that was riotous with glaring red flowers whose perfume was strong enough to be popular at a cut-rate drugstore. He was grateful that the scent overpowered the heavy odor of jungle decay.

"Are you okay?" she asked.

"Fine," he said. "What was that?"

Michael turned. He had heard something moving in the brush behind him. When he looked back at Nicole, he saw she had drawn her knife. Who else would be sneaking up on them but Coufos's Indian spy? Remembering what they had just talked about, he grabbed the knife away from Nicole.

"Wait here," he said.

As frightened by the murderous look on Michael's face as by the threat of who was in the brush, Nicole followed.

Suddenly a scream sent birds darting under the canopy of leaves. Michael and Nicole ran toward the sound. Xingu stepped over an Indian sprawled under a bush with an arrow in his back.

Nicole looked away, but not before she saw a terrible glow of satisfaction on Michael's face.

"Good work," Michael said.

"To kill is never good. But he tried to kill me. And he was watching you."

"You'd better bury the body. God, I hope Buchreiser doesn't miss him before I do what I have to do."

Choose to do, Nicole thought, filled with doubts about their relationship.

Chapter Thirty-One

"Did you know, Karl, that before we used it, cyanide gas had been used in certain American execution chambers for fifteen years."

Deputy Commandant Keller refused a pastry and instead poured a cup of caraway tea from a sterling pot.

"No, I did not know," said Buchreiser with forced enthusiasm. He would have liked to tell Keller exactly how big a fool he was to be living in the past, but the old colonel was the largest annual contributor to the cause—after himself.

Keller took a cigarette from a slim gold case and lit it with a German lighter rarely seen these days. It used a wick like the kind Zippo made famous, which you could light even in a hurricane. The case was eighteen-karat gold, and the SS runes with which it had once been decorated had been removed.

By the light of the flame, the camp deputy commandant's age blemishes looked like rust spots on ivory. The colonel inhaled, then moved slowly across the study. Even at seventy-three, Buchreiser thought, Keller was still a tall, straight figure. His clear, slate-blue eyes and sharp, almost classic profile were reminiscent of an SS poster.

"Who else, Karl, but men like your father and myself know what horrible things we had to watch in following our orders?"

Buchreiser bit back an impulse to slap the old hypocrite for mentioning himself in company with a true soldier like his father. He knew how, near the end of the war, Keller had prepared for his flight to Buenos Aires with jewels and money he had collected from the *Juden*—thousands upon thousands of Deutchmarks he had sent to his secret Swiss account, money taken in bribes from prisoners to keep them or someone in their family alive; and they were all sent to the ovens anyhow, once their last *pfennig* had been taken. Not to mention the gold from prisoner's teeth or the clothing off their backs.

"*Befehl ist befehl*. An order is an order. *Nicht wahr?*" Buchreiser asked.

"Of course. Who else would understand but your father and me and men like us how we had to watch every day and night, every hour, the burning of the bodies, the removal of their teeth, the cutting of their hair. The ghastly, interminable business. Standing for hours in the horrible stench while the mass graves were being opened and the bodies dragged out and burned." The colonel crushed out his cigarette in a sterling ashtray. "*Ach*. Enough of this talk. Please put some Bruckner on the gramophone, Karl."

"Certainly, Herr Deputy Commandant."

After the music had been playing for a time, Keller said, "I am thinking of the Fatherland's greatest moment of triumph."

"The surrender of the French, of course."

"*Jawohl*. How sweet for Hitler to have the swine surrender, not only in the same railroad car of our humiliation in the Great War, but at the exact spot in Compiègne it had occupied in 1918. Oh, Karl, it was almost over at Dunkirk, where the Wehrmacht had five hundred thousand Englishers trapped, but that idiot Göring convinced the Führer the Luftwaffe should be allowed to get some of the credit or the generals of the army would be hard to control. How could the Führer, with his military genius, have made such a stupid, inexplicable mistake?"

This was an old game for Buchreiser, and he began it wearily. "And what of his other mistakes? Had the Führer concentrated on defeating Britain, our victory would have been certain."

"True, but even more fundamental was the error in splitting his forces between the double objectives of the Caucasus and Stalingrad."

"If you will permit me to say, Deputy Commandant, even more inexcusable was Hitler's reluctance to impose total mobilization on our people so

that with munitions factories crying out for man-
power, idle *hausfraus* were still employing a half
million servants to dust their homes and polish their
furniture. Drink, Colonel? I know how this upsets
you."

"Thank you, no. Even while the Wehrmacht was
being defeated, the cream of the German Army—the
SS—was busy with the infernal *Juden.*" The colonel's
face grew taut and highly colored. Wasting boxcars
and ammunition was, to him, treason. "I heard at the
time from an officer who had just returned from
Berlin that Goebbels, that club-footed dwarf, wasted
an entire division to make a spectacular film about
Prussia's victory over Napoleon. Please turn off that
record, Karl."

"Of course." *Always the same,* Buchreiser thought.
*Turn it on, he thinks of the war, then asks the music
to be turned off.*

"I tell you what I tell you next, Karl, because I know
you are your father's son."

"Thank you," Buchreiser said, then tried to force
curiosity into his next statement. "Tell me, please."

"A friend," the colonel began in a conspiratorial
tone, "from SS training camp, who was on Hitler's
personal staff, told me what had been responsible for
the change in our beloved Führer."

"I implore you to tell me," Buchreiser said. The
colonel did not hear the monotone in which the
younger man's request was made.

"A visiting doctor," the colonel went on excitedly, "had pointed out to the Führer that a medicine he had been taking since 1936—Doctor Koester's Antigas tablets—was principally based on the poisons strychnine and atropine."

"*Gott in Himmel*," Buchreiser said halfheartedly. "He, with the best medical minds in the world at his call, and they let him suffer from a patent medicine!"

"Suffer is not the word. In my briefcase I have my diary, Karl."

The old officer returned to his chair and unzipped the leather case.

As the colonel opened the faded volume, Buchreiser thought he could recite verbatim what the colonel would now read to him.

"Listen to this, what my former bunkmate said, Karl. 'Atropine acts on the nervous system, causing vivid flights of ideas, restlessness, visual and aural hallucinating, and fits of delirium, which might degenerate into violence and frenzy.' Might. A sad joke. *Ach*, I cannot speak more of this, Karl." He lifted a gold watch from his vest pocket. "Perhaps we should be going to the dinner now."

"As you wish." Buchreiser stood, relieved to go, and thinking that if Dremann's speech could persuade Keller, the rest of the former Nazis would be easy.

As John Dremann stepped to the rostrum, the silence was so profound Buchreiser could hear Keller breathing next to him. Calmly, Dremann adjusted the microphone. He looked up slowly, set his shoulders back, and thrust up a clenched-fist salute. The crowd erupted. Buchreiser smiled. Dremann held up the other hand for quiet. The American was in his early forties, short, and slight. His face, shining in the overhead theatrical light, looked carved.

"Friends and enemies."

Buchreiser joined in the boisterous laughter but stopped when he noticed the stern look on Colonel Keller's face.

"I came here to say we are not simply the New Nation Party. Look around. We are French and English and German and American and South African and Italian and Latin American. We are men and we are women. We *are* a new nation. But that is only a name, and it matters little what we call ourselves. It does not matter because we already had a name long before we began. A name important above all others. We are Aryans."

The proud label prompted fervent cheers like those Buchreiser had heard at soccer games. He, too, was proud to be a part of this great movement. Still, the reaction of the old Nazis, particularly Keller, was worrisome. He was especially apprehensive about the old colonel's reaction to the next part of Dremann's speech.

"We must not think of ourselves as the Fourth Reich, but as the new international Aryans."

Buchreiser watched closely as anger transformed Keller's face. With disgust he noticed that further applause was scattered and hesitant. His eyes swept around the vast hall, decorated with more swastikas and red and black streamers than with emblems of the New Nation Party. There were hundreds of individuals representing dozens of countries. Then he began to concentrate only on the ex-Nazis. To his dismay, few were applauding. He looked back at Dremann.

"History teaches us that to divide is to conquer. We must forget our pasts, our partisanship—even our homelands—and become a new nation of Aryans."

Fools! Buchreiser thought as the applause declined further. When he was working with Dremann on his speech, both had agreed it was time to light a fire under the comfortable asses of those who continued to live in the past. Now he wasn't so sure. After all, it was mostly the cash of ex-Nazis like Keller that had given strength to the party.

"I do not underestimate the great contribution our cause has received over the years from the esteemed former members of the National Socialist Party. However, in order to rid the world of its inferiors we will need more numbers, more money, more influence than can be had from one faction."

"We're with you!" a voice called out and was followed by vigorous applause. Buchreiser smiled until he saw that Keller remained angry.

"The enemy will try with every weapon of propaganda that they know of or can invent to divide us. Dividing us must be as impossible as separating courage from the blood of a true Aryan."

The applause and shouts swelled. Buchreiser thought he saw a smile pass over Keller's lips, but he wasn't sure.

"Let no one be fooled. Those who think the struggle should be peaceful and unarmed want to curb our cause. The bystander is guilty. I do not say the gun is the only way. But the purpose of this cause is not debating. And those who fail to advance our inevitable war are criminals."

More applause. To Buchreiser, Keller seemed to be scrutinizing the speaker rather than being caught up in his words.

"In this disordered world of half-breeds and freaks, each contribution will speed our cause and will mean an infinite amount of dignity spared for the Aryan people."

"Well said!" someone shouted.

"Let us not forget that sabotage does not need great numbers to succeed. Entire armies have been paralyzed and total production of arms in a factory suspended by it. The enemy will continue to intervene in imperialistic wars in other parts of the world, thus draining its might and further alienating its people. On the other hand, others with our case in their hearts will come to our aid. That is why our guts should churn as much when we hear the words 'Wop' or 'squarehead' or 'Polack' as 'Kraut' or 'Yankee' or 'Limey.'"

"We're with you!" a voice called in the thunder. Buchreiser smiled, seeing Keller do so. Still, the old Nazi had not brought his hands together once.

"Remember, too, that a people's army does not meet all at once the full strength of the oppressor's army or police. A people's army strikes at individual soldiers and policemen with surprise. One of our comrades has already told us that worldwide unemployment is through the roof and the governments still call it 'mass recession and volatile inflation.' That is shit! It's a goddamned depression!"

Another roar. Buchreiser thought: *A crowd ready to become an army.*

"I believe our people are ready. Our people want their dignity returned now."

"Now!" the crowd chorused with a roar. Buchreiser watched the eager look of combat around him. A chill of pride shivered his back.

"Now the world will run red. Now there will be the gun and the bomb, dynamite and the grenade. Speaking for my faction of the party, America will suffer for its oppression. Washington will soon be burning, and New York will have dead bodies littering its foul streets. In Los Angeles, half-castes will hang from their heels in public parks, and from Detroit the stench of smoking automobiles and flesh will blow from one end of the land to the other. It is hard to keep these words coming, because words are no longer important. This is year one in the Aryan people's calendar, and our victories shall be holidays written in the blood of America and the rest of the world."

The cheers and applause were so deafening, the crowd seemed to Buchreiser to have doubled. Keller, the old Nazi, was clearly absorbed in Dremann's world now.

"History teaches us we cannot be killed, only our bodies destroyed. In the spirit of that glorious lesson I proclaim to the world that we Aryans are invincible."

The voice of the crowd could be heard halfway across the Amazon. Buchreiser found himself on his feet. He looked down to see Keller's reaction, and his heart expanded in his chest when he saw the colonel standing next to him.

And the old Nazi was banging his hands together.

Chapter Thirty-Two

Alma felt the sweat dripping under her arms—another dress ruined. She ran cool water into a tub the color of dark chocolate. Most of her time now was spent soaking to alleviate the constant sweating brought on by her addiction to cocaine.

Karl is going to throw me out. He wants me out of his life. It was in his walk, his tone, his eyes. She had heard from Enrique, one of Karl's bodyguards who sold her the coke, that a dozen or more private planes from all over the world had been landing on the airstrip since early afternoon, which meant Karl had organized another fund-raising affair for the new Nazis.

While the tub was filling, Alma went to the mirror over her makeup table and stared. Wrinkles at the edges of her eyes. *Five good years* left. *Maybe eight, if I stay out of the sun.*

He would throw her out. Today. Tomorrow. A month from today. It was over. She could do nothing to save herself. She could not leave first, either. She had no place to go, no way to make a living, and she needed at least a thousand dollars a week to pay for her habit. Eventually she would run out of jewelry to sell, or Karl might get even more suspicious.

Suddenly her mind whisked her back to her girlhood. She and her sister Elena were begging outside a restaurant in Bogotá. She was about seven and Elena was nine. As usual, it was raining and cold. Fifty-five degrees maybe. Alma shivered, remembering. People from the warmer cities do not know how cool Bogotá can get. Nine thousand feet up. She and Elena had begged all morning on the buses without success, and their bellies growled with hunger. Their heads had been shaved by the police, ostensibly for reasons of hygiene, but also so they could spot them more easily. Not that it mattered much to them, because most of their hair had fallen out from scurvy anyway.

Elena said she could still remember Mama, but Alma had not even a small thought left of her. If they could get something to eat, they would join the other children of the roost, maybe get high on gasoline fumes.

"Come, little ones," a giant of a man said. "I am the owner and will be your *padrastro*."

Their "stepfather" brought them into a back room

in the restaurant and unzipped his fly and took out his thing that looked like a giant brown caterpillar. "Suck this, *niñas*, and I will give you food."

Now, remembering how the man's penis had tasted of salt and talcum, his sperm of iodine, the revulsion rose from Alma's stomach to her throat. She ran to the toilet and threw up what remained of the single piece of toast she had eaten.

After she rinsed her mouth and shut off the water in the tub, she sat for a while, thinking how Elena had forced her to bathe in the icy water of a city fountain, how each evening they returned to a piece of canvas stretched over a wooden frame, underneath a city street overpass.

Now, as she began to think of what had happened ten years later, her body trembled.

No! She could not allow herself to remember that day when she had been brought by the police to the morgue in downtown Bogotá to identify Elena. But she could not stop the image of her nineteen-year-old sister, her breasts and vagina carved out by a madman's knife—an image that had haunted her at least part of every day since. Shaking uncontrollably with terror, she yearned for her coke. But the fear of losing Karl because of her habit was greater. Karl, who had taken her from the streets and fed and dressed her like a princess.

A cough rose in her chest and grew so intense it threatened to split her collarbone. She raised herself, threw back the toilet seat, hawked up some phlegm, and spat. Her phlegm was the ebony of a cokehead's. How long before it became red?

I must end the habit. I must.

Besides her health, she was losing Karl. Until last year he had not missed a night sleeping with her unless he was out of the country. And he could not sleep without first making love to her—or whatever their savage joining could be called. Now, however, they usually quarrelled instead, and he fell asleep without touching her. Lately, sex for her could not compete with the eroticism of her pipe, but still she missed his wanting her.

How many nights had she watched him stride briskly toward the bathroom. Tight buttocks, dimpled. No hip fat, no paunch. She did not want to lose him, that beautiful creature. But she wondered how she could love a man who made love without mussing his hair?

She wanted to end up with a comforting hand cupping her face. She needed caresses, soft music, curtains swaying in the breeze, a kind voice murmuring sweetness in her ear.

In the stark overhead light of the bathroom mirror, Alma studied her face.

She touched her cheek appraisingly. Despite the ghost of a new line around the left corner of her mouth, her skin still had the firm but yielding texture men found compelling. But how long could such skin last?

Tonight when he came to her he would be filled with ardor. But its source would be only the sense of power and success he got from his Nazi fund-raising affairs. Why did she torture herself with him? *Because I have never met such an extraordinary man.* Sure, he was deceptive, wholly unpredictable, and frighteningly hidden. But never had she met so handsome a man with such intelligence and intensity, a man of such exceptional discipline. Certainly a very clever man, surely a fearless man, and one of great impulse and intuition. Karl was quite possibly mad. He was in full control in public, yet was subject to private fits. A man other men followed even when they doubted—even disagreed—with him. *A man,* she thought, *uncertain of nothing, especially his own overwhelming ambition and sense of personal destiny.* She needed him. Besides, how could she support her habit with no skills—except the ones Elena had had?

Now she was sweating so profusely she was bathed in it. Every nerve end was twitching, yearning for coke.

Alma pulled off her dress, ready for the relief of the cool water in the tub, when she caught sight of her body in the full-length mirror. She gasped when she saw her makeup was barely covering the malnutrition sores on her body. A gulping sob burst from her.

"What is the use? I cannot stop, and I am going to lose him anyway."

Then, as if her words had relieved her of a great burden, she began to move with familiar deftness. Her eyes glittered, and she was unaware that her nostrils were flaring.

She kept her glass pipe disassembled and hidden in a huge jar of blue bath crystals. The coke she kept in her douche bag, where Karl would never look.

She got out a chunk of coke, filed some off, and placed the granules in the pipe. Then she filled it with clear rum, lowered herself into the tub, and lit a butane lighter under the glass bowl of the pipe.

Just the thought of what was coming made Alma's sinuses clog. She laid her head back gently onto the tub and inhaled the bittersweet vapor. Within seconds she was hit by an orgasmic jolt. At that moment Karl burst into her rooms.

For the first time Alma was grateful the rush would not last more than a few seconds. She reached a hand out of the tub and locked the door.

"Fix yourself a drink, darling," she shouted. "I'll be just a few minutes."

Holding onto the porcelain rail, she lifted herself from the tub and spilled the rum and granules from the pipe into the toilet. Running the tub water so Karl could not hear, she pressed the flush lever. Good. All she had to do now was take apart the pipe and put it safely back with the bath salts.

In the other room, Karl chose Scotch, though he preferred brandy. Brandy would only make his already pounding heart beat faster. He placed the gift-wrapped Bulgari box inside the drawer of a Louis XV writing desk. Was it only what he was feeling toward Alma, he wondered, or was the three million dollars raised for the cause today contributing to the speed with which his blood flowed, too? He put down the Scotch, opened the drawer, and looked inside the Bulgari box again.

Alma released the water, stepped onto the gold- and brown-flecked bath mat, and dried herself. Suddenly her fear of being caught stoned by Karl was quieted by an outpouring of ideas that were old techniques. She would give him her winsome smile, her girlish laugh, her deliberately carefree gestures designed to emphasize her many varieties of mood; her profile set in a way to emphasize her right jawline, the better one, her studied look of attention—all the powers of bewitchment she had learned as a beggar, which had been honed to a keen edge as she grew into a young woman on the streets of Bogotá. She scorned her talents for charming men, but what else could she do now to keep Karl from finding out about her pipe?

Opening the door slightly, she called out in her huskiest voice, "Why not shut off the lights, darling, and light the special candles by the bed?"

Maybe, Karl said to himself. Maybe it would be interesting to have her before he gave her the surprise.

From the bathroom closet, Alma chose a white silk robe that would conceal her body sores. Once in bed, he would not notice, with the lights off. Flicking the light switch, she stepped out of the bathroom.

When Karl saw how her rich, black hair reflected the flickering glimmers of the candles—strands of it seemed almost alive—and the wonderful shift of bone and flesh under her dressing gown, he was astonished to feel his fingertips flexing in anticipation of touching her once more.

He lit a cigarette and handed it to her.

The little display of consideration heartened Alma.

"Come here, please," he said, patting the bed.

Although he had said a rare "please," there had been a sudden familiar note of callousness in his voice that she hated. Perhaps it was just her guilt about the cocaine. In the soft light his perfect teeth held her attention. If she could see the shape of his teeth so plainly, he might see her body sores.

She went over to the jacaranda nightstand. Never lifting her gaze from him, she blew out the candle. In the darkness, before the candle was extinguished, she could see how the muscles had tensed along his jawline. He wanted her again as he once had: scarcely in control.

She has the kind of mobile face that provides her no protection from her feelings, he thought. *It betrays her every time.* Was she not aware, before she made it dark, of the small tic at the edge of her left eye, the tremor along her bottom lip, how she's trying to keep from unclogging her stuffed sinuses?

The image of the set of his mouth was still in her mind when he began to remove her gown. Pulling her down to his cock, he winced as she licked away the drop that had appeared at its slit.

She was grateful for his wince, but he still had not kissed her. She thought she smelled the faint odor of Vaseline.

A very good idea before she gets her present, he thought as her tongue probed.

Suddenly, and with more roughness than he had ever shown in bed, he yanked her up onto her knees, curled forward, and thrust a cold Vaselined finger into her ass. Knowing that what was to follow was the loneliest and most degrading part of sex for her, she tried to relax her sphincter muscles.

When he finished with her, he lit a cigarette, and in the light of the flame she saw something on his face she had never seen before.

Without warning he grasped her hand and dragged her into the living room.

"What?" she asked in a tone she recognized as very young. Her beggar's voice.

He went to the drawer in the Louis XV table and handed her the Bulgari package.

"Open it, you cokehead!" he shouted. "Open it now!"

"I ... I am trying to stop, Karl, believe me. If you would only help. I—"

"Open it."

Her hands were trembling too hard.

He grabbed the package and tore off the gift wrap.

"Here," he said, handing back the square box. "Open the lid."

Timidly she obeyed. When she saw what was inside, she dropped the box and a scream came from that side of her that was capable, she knew, of madness. There, on the plush carpet, lay the bloody testicle of a man.

"Enrique's other one," he said, sneering, "is stuffed in his mouth, as I promised you it would be if I found out who supplied your poison."

"Who has been spying on me?"

"You couldn't even hide it from my lieutenant, Escobar, much less from me. You have twenty-four hours to get your things together and get your black ass out of here."

Chapter Thirty-Three

"You said last night that you would show me more of a man's ways, Father," Chochobo's twelve-year-old son said.

Chochobo, as chief, was leading a party of hunters back to their village. The boy strode next to him.

Chochobo looked down with pride at the youth, whose fiercely painted face was at odds with his still-scrawny knees.

"First, my son, you must learn to thank the spirits of the forest for their generosity."

"But how can I thank the spirits when I have not killed a single deer?"

"Thank them for the success of your brothers, which is your success."

Chochobo's thoughts turned again to Nicole. She had warned him yesterday that Buchreiser would take revenge if he found out about his tribe making cocaine and not paste. In his mind, he swept out these thoughts with a tree branch, and he dreamed contentedly instead. Soon, over the feast fires, much meat would simmer in leaf pouches sputtering on the roasting sticks. And small groups of old women would keep watch over this food, ready to throw sticks at village dogs or any youths who came forward to playfully snatch a piece. He smiled.

"Please tell me more, Father," the boy begged as the village came into sight.

The chief put his arm around the boy. "Remember first what the grandfathers say—"

"That a boy should take bows and arrows everywhere he goes, even when he goes out to wet the grass. They also tell of the boy who saved himself and his mother with a boy's bow and a child's arrows."

"You guessed correctly what I held in my thoughts this time. But guessing is not a warrior's work. It belongs to a shaman. Which is it you wish to become?"

"I'm sorry, Father. I wish to become a warrior."

Recognizing the boy's hurt pride, Chochobo made use of the informal, easy-talk custom permitted between a *cacique* and his son, but nothing like sympathy entered his speech. "Yesterday when we went to find the four-legged ones, I saw that when you were in the open you neither crouched nor covered yourself. You did not watch for the protecting trees and plants, and you let your shadow loom on the open ground. You do not pay heed to fresh deer droppings on the trail, or who kicks a pebble out of a nest, or if small birds fly over singing."

The boy studied the ground.

"Perhaps, Father, I am not ready for the hunt." His voice faltered.

"No boy sees himself ready for the hunt. The hunt makes him ready." He patted the boy's head playfully, then slapped his buttocks. "Run off now, and be a boy with your friends. You will be a man soon enough."

After the boy had gone, Chochobo turned around to the band of hunters, congratulated them, and said he would linger for a while before he entered his hut. He watched with pride as the warriors passed him with their bloody spears and the bodies of nine deer carried on lean-tos.

Then, despite his hunger, he sat under a tree watching his son join a group of boys who were running footraces and wrestling by the edge of the forest. As he watched the young, strong bodies, he said aloud, *"There is the hope of the Carrijura, Nicole. The cocaine will help our people to keep the land. But the land will be no good to them if they forget the ways of the hunt and, like the white man, have to depend on money to buy food."*

After a short while he continued on to his hut.

Liara proudly brought Chochobo warm water, and when he had washed the blood of deer off his feet, she dusted his toes with powder. She was grateful he had greeted his other wives and children quickly and come to her hearth. She watched him wash off other signs of the hunt, and when he stood clean, she lifted hot stones from the fire into the cooking pouch, enough to start warming the soup. While he waited for the soup, she brought him a gourd of honey, and as she handed him the honey, he saw the scars on her arm from the stinging ants. He kissed the scars.

A bird that once again fluttered in her breast, since Chochobo had thrown his newest wife and father-in-law out of the village, soared now. She no longer felt divided into two women—one filled with the hurt and anger of jealousy, another who watched her behavior, shamed—but one complete woman, with many feelings and voices.

He cupped her face in his huge hand as he had done so often before and said, "I have told you some of what I learned from taking the *ayahuasca*." He took some honey with his finger and licked it thoughtfully, remembering his conversation with Nicole about this wife and the Brazilian one. "At first it is true, I accepted the girl as wife for the sake of our people. But then she became as a thirst that could not be satisfied. This I felt, though I saw her laziness and her disloyal nature. But with you, my thirst is quenched like no other, and leaves me with a warm heart and tender thoughts."

She no longer had to give him the highest test—to look into his eyes for his heart—because she knew truth and his love lived there.

"I, too, have done wrong, my husband. I spoke often of Meewahn to you and others, and defended her faults."

"That is to be admired in you."

"No, it is not. For I spoke in the manner of a woman who wishes to make her husband think her generous in giving a rival a just hearing. That is why I could not control my jealousy—I did not let it live, so it grew larger than myself. That is what dried my breasts, and why my milky spirit now flows once again into the belly of our daughter."

Chochobo stood slowly and deliberately. He went over to a basket woven of palm fronds and removed some coca leaves from it. Then he wet the leaves with his saliva and, breaking custom, placed a poultice on the one of her arms that was scarred from the stinging ants.

"We are one now," he said, breaking custom again by using the plural pronoun.

She reached up into the rafters and took down some coca leaves. "Would you like a quid after your supper?"

He smiled at the cue.

Chochobo awoke before dawn, and before any of the others in the hut. He kissed Liara, who slept with a smile on her lips, and then watched his infant daughter playing with her toy of frog skulls on a liana string. He was ashamed that thoughts still came to him of Meewahn—of her long, many-colored hair that fell to her glistening backside, and of her fire. But he also knew he would never again wish to act on his thoughts or the desire in his loins for her. He chewed one coca leaf to rouse himself awake and walked out into the sunshine. How peacefully his people slept, their bellies filled with deer soup and meat!

He strolled to the edge of the forest where the young boys had already begun their training games to be warriors. Watching them, he thought, *Maybe I am a foolish* cacique *to make my people fight against the yellow-haired chief. Maybe we should give up our land and find another place to live.*

The sun beat down, and he sought a tree for shelter. As he sat, with the distant sound of the boys shouting as a background, he became aware of his breathing and was filled with a new feeling. The grandfathers and shamans said that a man aware of his breath could become aware of the breath of the whole forest because its breath had become his own. Such a man could feel in his veins the life of a tree, could feel the fruit ripening on the tree; his feet could take hold in the earth like the roots of the tree; and in his ears he could listen to the water being drawn up the roots to give life to the tree's leaves. But these things, these wise men said, could only happen if a man lived on the land of his grandfathers.

This thought filled Chochobo with a sense of union —man, earth, sky, river—and he knew he was right to guide his people to stay and fight, and die, if necessary, on their own land.

He stood then and began to walk, filled with the excitement of his discovery.

He walked down to the riverbank, where the mud cooled his feet. For how long had his grandfathers looked at this river, canoed on its surface, eaten of its fish? Stooping down to scoop up a handful of water to drink, he stopped the motion in midswing and stood, swerving around. A white man, the size of a Carri-jura and almost the same color, wide in his shoulders as the opening of a hut, with an upper lip like a frog, was leading toward him a group of Wactu's warriors holding rifles. Turning quickly about, he saw Wactu approaching with another group of his tribesmen, also carrying rifles.

He felt an impulse to flee, but there was no escaping the bullets.

He could make them earn his death. But to lead them a chase, he would have to turn away from them and run, and finally receive their bullets in his back. He could not do that, not Chochobo, son of his father.

He waited for them, arms at his side, his face composed. With honor and good spirit he would watch his destiny unfold to the end.

It was truly over now.

Watching him, the armed men halted, then came on cautiously. Chochobo looked up at the roiling clouds. He tried to feel keenly the wetness that would soon fall from the sky, to feel it more deeply than he ever had.

The rain fell hard all at once. It would not last long, but its enormous drops filled the air, making it tremble with life.

Chapter Thirty-Four

As the *piragua* beached near Wactu's village, Coufos took a last swig of *aguardiente* and turned to Wactu, who sat in the rear of the dugout. The black pig was as silent as an obsidian statue—not a clue to the surprise he had promised. *Maybe*, thought Coufos, *since I led the black turtle-head to Chochobo, he has decided to make me a present of Meewahn.* Longingly, the snake man thought of his recent night with the girl and how she had made his organ stiff by rubbing it with warm honey.

The Greek stepped into the muddy river water. At eye level the ancient, wizened bark of the numberless trees seemed to know what surprise awaited him. *Fool*, he chided himself, *the jungle makes you see what is not.*

There was the usual greeting party. Men naked

except for woven penis shields. Bare breasts of all shapes and sizes. Painted faces and bodies, spears, blowguns. Drumbeats in the distance. Meewahn was nowhere.

Suddenly Wactu was gone. *Probably the fat swine is eating,* Coufos thought. He let himself be led to a hut by a group of spear-carrying warriors, where a shaman wearing a full caiman skin directed old women in the sorting of roots shaped like fetuses, dried frogs and fish bladders, earthenware jars of deer penises and piranha eyes. The Greek realized no one had looked up when he stepped inside the hut. *Who understands their savage minds?* he thought.

Suddenly the shaman turned, and there was the simultaneous sound of rattled gourds. His body was razor sharp. His yellowy eyes were like Wactu's— bloodshot balls with no lashes.

"You have broken the taboo."

Coufos felt his stomach knot up. "Taboo?"

"You have had *patou* with the daughter of our chief."

He opened his palm, which held the ring he had given Meewahn.

The Cretan's forearms stung with tiny prickings, and his tongue swelled in his throat.

"Sh-She is the one who began—"

"Do not shame Meewahn worse than she has been shamed!" came the shaman's booming answer. "She has received her punishment."

The white man imagined his tongue being pulled

out, then his belly cut open with a grass knife and his guts being fed to rats with a stick.

"Out!" The shaman pointed to the opening through which Coufos had entered.

Outside, beyond the cadre of armed warriors, was a river of dark faces with sharpened teeth.

Great Mother of God, why had he let his ambition take him to this hell!

His knees gave way, and he felt himself lifted and dragged by rough, animal-hide hands and arms.

When the dragging stopped, he was held upright, facing a blazing sun.

Through his tears he could see some of the Indians drawing twigs for—but it could not be!

Suddenly Wactu and Meewahn appeared. The crowd all around seemed to suck in their breaths as one, cry *Aioao!* and take a step back.

Then he felt himself being dragged closer to the father and daughter. Behind them Coufos saw old women painted black and red carrying vases—dear God, they must be carrying them for some other reason!

Meewahn's hands hung meekly at her sides. He remembered how her palms and soles were paler than the rest of her hands and feet—like a monkey's. For no more than a monkey he had risked ringworm, and now . . .

"Please," he pleaded. "I had no disrespect in my heart."

The high, beetling forehead of Wactu seemed to

expand as he spoke. "You have broken the taboo. You will have a death that suits you."

Wactu and Meewahn turned and walked over to the others. Coufos again felt the leathery hands, this time grabbing him and tearing off his clothes and boots. He felt but did not hear his screams. Once he kicked one of the savages squarely between his legs. Once, he was sure, he had bitten off a piece of a black ear that tasted of split olive pit. Once while twisting his head away from an inhumanly strong grasp, he saw in his right hand a butter-yellow flower. In his desperation to hold on to something, he had torn it from the grass. The flower had green tendrils and whiskery trailing stamens—like the yellow gorse at home.

Coufos was dragged to another clearing. Through the maze of bodies he saw a great circular wooden trough on top of a fire. Behind the trough was a huge barbecue spit. Then he was being pulled, pushed, and kicked up the ladder of the great trough.

Steam scalded his skin. As he felt the hands letting go of him, his mouth opened in a gape of terror and his arms reached to the sky. He began to fall.

Chapter Thirty-Five

"Chochobo is dead!" came a shout from the entrance of Nicole's hut.

Nicole and Michael turned and saw Xingu.

Nicole ran to the old man. "How? Who?"

"The snake man and Wactu. As many bullets as teeth in a piranha."

Nicole began to weep.

The snake man, Michael thought, *was Coufos, and Wactu was Chochobo's newest father-in-law.*

"Buchreiser!" Nicole and Michael said at once.

"The snake man," the Indian said, "was then killed by Wactu."

"Where are you going?" Michael asked, watching Nicole run to the hearth and grab the deerskin and her hunting knife.

"I'm g-going to Ch-Chochobo's village," she said between sobs, "to p-pay my respects."

Michael took her in his arms.

"The entire Amazon will be joining you," Xingu said.

The word passed by mouth and by drum. The word ran across thatched villages, leaped wide rivers, and raced through the jungle as a fire races through dry leaves. By midday it had crossed and recrossed itself many times. Individual Indians and entire tribes from all directions began the largest pilgrimage Amazonia had ever seen. They came on foot and by dugout canoe. They came in various degrees of nakedness or in white man's clothing. They brought their wives and children. Tribes that had been enemies put aside their differences, and walked or paddled side by side.

Michael and Nicole and Xingu arrived at Chochobo's village in the scorching afternoon. They sweated through their shirts and pants, staining their belts with wet black patches.

Outside the dead leader's hut stood a line of Indians emitting a wailing dirge. The line extended for miles. Women had chopped their hair short. Like Xingu, the men had painted their bodies black with genipa juice. Both sexes had used scarring instruments—teeth of dogfish set in scraps of gourd—and rasped their faces, arms, and breasts to bleed in mourning.

As they drew nearer to the hut, Michael caressed Nicole's head. She had cried during the trip, and her eyes were swollen and rimmed with red.

"What are Chochobo's widows doing?" she asked Xingu, pointing.

Michael saw a group of women pulling up all the plantings from the fields adjoining Chochobo's hut.

Xingu said, "After his body is burned, the fields will be replanted. Until the plants grow back all his wives and children will be fed by the village. Chochobo's hut will be burned also, and a new hut built by his friends. Here we are now."

They had reached the entrance of the hut. Inside, the place smelled pungently of burning herbs and other potions. In the middle of the floor was a kind of bier on which Chochobo's body rested. The sight of an old woman shaman was a shock to Michael and Nicole. She was completely hairless—even her pubic area. The contrasting coiled designs on her face and around her breasts and crotch were, Xingu said, in a pigment made from white clay. They seemed to glow and move in the flickering torchlight, as if a snake were moving across her body. She blew medicine smoke and shook a rattle over the body to dispel bad spirits.

Michael wondered why he hadn't heard the rattle outside, until he saw that the walls were lined with bark to insulate the hut from noise. The heat seeped in, though, through the thick walls, and the air seemed to glow in the dark room. A harpy eagle sat in a conical cage.

Nicole waited unitl Michael and Xingu had viewed the body. She almost failed to recognize the waxen face, the head wrapped in macaw feathers, the crepe-paper mouth with its subtle, shadowy pleatings, the entire body covered with white and pink petals of orchids. But an unknown energy was in the air when she leaned close, and when she touched the cold forehead it was as if it gave back to her fingers every troubled thought it had ever contained. Nicole felt tears behind her eyes.

Outside, night had fallen, and the line of mourners carried torches off in the distance till they were pinpricks of yellow light. The nearby torches were haloed in the dampness. The sight electrified Michael. The huts in the village shimmered in the irregular light.

"Now what?" Michael asked Xingu as the three sat on the ground watching the procession.

"Now the elders will come to praise his courage at war, his hunting and fishing skills, his wisdom as a leader."

Soon they sat listening to the eldest Carrijuras. Some spoke behind bonfires which flared suddenly with unearthly colors as they threw powders in the flames to make a point. Others used bone horns to underscore a particularly important passage. Moon shadow painted the walls of the huts dull blue; red bonfire light, reflected from the sky, tinged the roofs. The night was awhirr with moths and myriad flying insects attracted to the fires.

A bear of an elder, with a rasping voice, spoke in praise of Chochobo. When he had finished, Nicole listened to the throb of chanting. Hearing the strong rhythms and stirring sounds, she felt as if she were reaching out and touching the hand of Chochobo. *Maybe,* she thought, *maybe, my friend, what the grandfathers say about the Land of the Dead is true: a place where great chiefs reign as they did on earth, where every tree contains all one needs to eat and drink, and later, Chochobo, later, your chosen wife, Liara. . . .*

After many more elders had spoken, the body of Chochobo was carried out by a half-dozen men and set in his canoe. By the light of torches the canoe was brought to the lagoon, where it was held by a long liana and set ablaze on the water by flaming arrows.

A pulse stirred rhythmically in Michael's temple as the flames whooshed in the night, and he thought of Ava who had not yet had a funeral. He would make up for that on his return to New York.

After the canoe had been burning awhile, it was retrieved by those Indians who had acted as pall-bearers.

"Now," Xingu said to Nicole and Michael, "his ashes will be placed in an urn and set under where his hammock was hung. Because such a great man lived there, Chochobo's hut shall be abandoned and set afire. A fire will be kept burning close to the urn till the next full moon."

A draft of cold air tugged at the torches and the splashing light made leprous spots where it fell. Suddenly a hot drizzle fell. Flames sizzled, and incense and woodsmoke burdened the hot air.

"Xingu!"

They turned and saw a Carrijura brave, out of breath.

"Yes," Xingu said. "Speak."

"The chief Wactu, he has been killed by our people."

"So," Xingu said, a great grin spreading on his face, "it begins."

"What?" Michael said.

"War."

Chapter Thirty-Six

Alma scratched desperately at the carpet in her bedroom, searching for any loose grains of cocaine. Frantically she tore clumps of wool apart, breaking a fingernail in the effort. Finally, accepting that there was none, she sobbed, and her nose gushed thick mucus.

She lifted herself to her feet, weak from her diarrhea, and pulled off her dressing gown, which was soaked through with sweat. Stumbling into the bathroom, she thrust open the door of the medicine cabinet, spilled out the remaining 'ludes from an aspirin bottle, and swallowed them with some water.

She stared at her reflection in the mirror. Could this really be her—this broom-straw-haired creature with eyes as puffy as an old lady? She stood back for a fuller view, leaning against the towel rack. Where she had scratched the maddeningly itchy malnutrition sores, thick scabs resembling leeches had formed. She slammed the cabinet door so hard its mirror shattered and the jars and vials inside crashed into the sink.

Get hold of yourself, woman! There was a spa she had heard of in São Paulo where for a thousand dollars a day they gave you drugs and therapy to make you stop the habit. Maybe she would sell all she had to take the treatment. She became aware of the burning place where the coke had seared the septum of her left nostril. Oh, who was she kidding? She could not stop and she knew it. When were those lousy 'ludes going to work!

She turned the cold-water spigot in the tub and stepped inside, not waiting till it was filled. Even in the chill, sweat streamed from her scalp and face. She sat, teeth chattering, rinsing the stinging salt from her eyes.

She lay back and tried to think of other times and places when she had felt young and strong and gay. But her mind soon reached back to that ugly time in a brothel in Bogotá when the madam had demanded she have sex with another woman because a good customer had insisted. She imagined she could still taste the traces of sweat and jism and urine and douche and blood inside the woman's vagina.

Something like seawater sprang from the back of her throat. She leaned outside the tub, anticipating vomit, but only greenish spittle dribbled out. She began to cough so hard her lungs seemed about to burst. Finally she managed to spit up some phlegm. Red phlegm.

The sight of her blood terrorized her. She knew it marked the beginning of the end for a cokehead.

She would not die. She would sell her furs and jewels.

Leaving her bath, she spied the lamp with the rose-colored shade. When she threw it, the mirrors shattered onto an Oriental vase which spewed its flowers and water all over the rosewood Parsons table. The sight gave her such satisfaction she did not know why she had not done it sooner.

With a piece of smashed vase, she gouged each and every painting in the room, then tore great holes in the pillowcases and sheets.

Drawers were pulled from the black-lacquered Chinese dresser and heaved into whatever mirrors had not been smashed.

Finished, Alma slumped to the floor, out of breath and exhausted. After the money from the sale of her clothes and jewelry was gone, she would have no choice but to go to one of the whorehouses in downtown Bogotá and act as if she were perfectly straight to the madam. Madams did not tolerate cokeheads. How many tricks a day would she have to take on, after the house's cut, to support her habit? Twenty? Forty?

Alma crawled across the carpet to where the contents of her nightstand were strewn. She picked up the .44 revolver Karl had given her last Christmas for protection.

The cold, heavy metal felt sure and right and fitting in her hand as she cocked the hammer.

Chapter Thirty-Seven

"It is too quiet," Xingu said, stopping suddenly.

Nicole turned quickly to look behind her—nothing.

Michael said, "Quiet?" and listened to the din of insects. In the clearing up ahead, he was grateful to see the blue woodsmoke from the morning fires of Nicole's village; they had been traveling home since dawn from Chochobo's funeral, and he was tired.

"There are no birds and monkeys here," Xingu said. "They have been frightened away. There are men near us."

"Very good, old man," came a voice from above. They looked up into the muzzles of three rifles.

Michael became conscious of a pulsing behind his eyes.

Nicole felt as if the canopy were pressing down on her.

All at once, the rifles appeared to be falling out of the trees. Soon three men stood on the ground before them.

"Escobar!" Michael exclaimed. Immediately, he felt Nicole's eyes on him.

"Who is he, Miles?" she asked, pretending to be confused.

"Why are you here?" asked Xingu.

"To take you to a palace in the jungle, old man, so we can find out just what your white Indian girl here knows."

"You spied on me?" she asked Michael, protecting their secret.

He said nothing. Her slap, when it came, hurt him as much as if it had come from genuine anger.

"Come on now, get moving!" Escobar said.

With Nicole and Xingu up ahead, Michael followed with Escobar and the others.

"Who taught the Carrijura how to make coca paste into cocaine?"

Nicole heard the question as if from a great distance, though her interrogator stood over her, where she squirmed from the hardness of the straight-backed chair. She had been interrogated for seven hours, and although she could remember hearing the same questions over and over, they had grown numberless, and she could no longer concentrate. Physical exhaustion, grief for Chochobo, and her fear of being tortured and killed by Buchreiser all disoriented her. Her centering was gone, and random pieces of herself were traveling around, in and out of her body, at a speed too fast to contemplate.

"Pay attention, bitch," the interrogator continued. "How much do they produce? Where do they make it?"

She lifted her head and looked at the man asking the questions. He was big and muscular with surreal scars, one of them so deep it intensified his drooping eye, so his expression was fierce as well as scornful.

"I told you," she managed, though her tongue was so thick from thirst it kept getting in the way of her speech, "I don't know anything."

Standing next to Buchreiser and Escobar, Michael watched the scene through a one-way mirror, wincing as the interrogator slapped Nicole's face. He looked away and bit down an impulse to run into the room and smash the brute into mush. If he didn't control himself, his rage and guilt and disregard for his own safety would cause him to lose whatever slight chance he had of saving her. "Stubborn bitch, isn't she?" he said to his two enemies. He had to be careful or the lack of conviction in his voice would give him away.

"We have broken more stubborn ones than her," Buchreiser retorted.

Escobar nodded.

Buchreiser continued, "I will rip out the tongue of

every Indian in the Amazon till I find every last laboratory and every single worker!"

"If you'll permit me," Michael said to Buchreiser, "she won't be very much good to us if she doesn't get some water and sleep." He held his breath, hoping.

Buchreiser turned to Michael with a combination of anger and determination that made clear to Michael why the man had become the number-one drug smuggler in the world. The German's anger gave way to cunning before he spoke. "You are right, Rudd. Give her what she needs to get her senses back, Escobar. But I want answers. Tonight." For an instant Buchreiser was filled with an overwhelming rage at Alma for her drug habit—for having forced him to get rid of her, the best sexual partner he had ever had. "Tonight, you hear? I do not care if you have to rip her tits off her chest. Bring in every man in the palace to fuck it out of her. Just *do* it!"

"You can go to sleep on it," Escobar declared.

"And you, Rudd, with your beagle face," Buchreiser said. "If you cannot stomach the way we do business, I suggest you go back to Fisherman's Wharf."

"I was just thinking of Coufos, that's all."

"They will pay for that," Buchreiser said. "But there is work to do. Get some rest, both of you. And you, Escobar, report to me when she breaks."

"Yes, sir," Escobar said. He moved to the right side

of the mirror and pressed an intercom button. "Give her some food and water, Renaldo, and let her get some sleep. Then go back to work on the Indian."

The three viewers separated.

Michael took one last look through the mirror, and his spirit lifted when he saw the relief on Nicole's face. His blood froze, though, remembering what tonight held in store for her.

How could he free her with an army of trained armed guards inside and outside the palace?

Nicole had been asleep only a little over an hour when a great cacophony of sounds awakened her. She turned to Xingu, who lay on the cot next to her, his face and body covered with red welts from the interrogator's beating. The Indian sat straight up in bed.

"What's going on?" she said and, hearing herself, added, "What does it mean?"

"Many tribes tell of Chochobo's death."

Her head felt stuffed with thick wads that wouldn't let her think. "But I've never heard anything like it before in the jungle."

"There has never been such a sound before. The giant bark panpipes of the Yagua. The gourd horns— wooden and human—of the Wapishana. The drums made of hollow tree trunk covered with tapir hides of the Witoto."

She sat up.

"Yes," she said, "and the perforated conch shells of the Tupinaımbo. But they live so far downstream from here."

The Indian smiled. "I have counted more tribes than there are children in all our villages. Some have even come from Brazil."

"What do they say?"

"They say that Chochobo's death by Wactu has been avenged. And some say that the meat of the white snake man has filled bellies."

"But why are they so close to the palace? Do they know we are being held here?"

"How can so many men from so many tribes not know this thing?"

Suddenly the door swung open and an armed bodyguard and the interrogator barged in.

"Get up, old man!" commanded the bodyguard.

The interrogator was naked to the waist, and she saw that his one drooping eye was the only part of him that was slack.

Xingu turned to her, a peaceful smile on his lips. "Do not be afraid. You are ready. Death is a debt to be paid today or tomorrow."

She hugged the old scout, tears burning her cheeks.

"Hurry up, Indian," Droopy Eye yelled.

Xingu looked far off then, concentrating on the jungle music. "The land and the sky and the river always remain," he said to Nicole. "And so shall my people. Because they are one with these."

The bodyguard stomped over to Xingu, grabbed the old man, and dragged him to the door.

"Be a good Carrijura," Xingu managed before he was pushed into the hall.

Nicole sat on the cot, numbed, listening to the Indian music outside.

Suddenly she heard a scream from the adjoining room and recognized Xingu's voice. *For him to scream*, she thought, *he must be in excruciating pain.* Her throat ached, and tears made her cheeks wet. She shivered with fear.

Hands clapped over her ears, heart beating in her throat, she waited.

Finally, after a period of time that would forever remain a mystery to her, she listened and heard nothing. She sighed, hoping Xingu had just passed out.

"The old shit is dead," came the interrogator's voice from the corridor. "Let's get rid of him."

Nicole sat unmoving on her cot, completely cried out, beyond any further pain.

She was not aware that the music of new tribes had joined in with the previous ones. If she had been, it wouldn't have made any difference—for the music had ceased to be hopeful.

Michael lay in bed, disturbed by the crazy conglomeration of sounds from the jungle. He got up, grabbed the binoculars lying on the dresser, and looked out the window.

Nothing.

Wait! What was that movement?

An Indian. Another. Dozens. Hundreds. All carrying torches. And all in full body paint—war paint. Maybe, Michael thought, if they set fire to the planes on the landing strip, in the confusion brought on by the ensuing explosions Nicole and he might have a chance.

He hadn't switched on the light, and time in the darkened room was oceanic. To stop his anguished thoughts of Nicole's fate, he tried remembering happier moments. He pictured them together, holding hands, their eyes communicating so totally that language would only get in the way.

The fantastic clamor from the bush seemed to speed up, as if to remind him that his time to save Nicole was growing shorter.

Even if the Indians didn't attack, the threat that they could might be enough to distract Nicole's guard so he could rescue her.

He stepped into the corridor. Cadres of armed men ran past, shouting to each other. Slowness now would be suspicious.

The guard outside the room where Nicole was being held pointed his automatic rifle at Michael. Then he smiled and relaxed. It was the same man who had escorted him from the plane on his first visit.

"I'm Miles Rudd. You remember me. I have orders from Mr. Buchreiser to take the prisoners elsewhere because of what's happening with the Indians."

"Sorry. I only take orders from Mr. Buchreiser or Mr. Escobar."

"They're too busy with what's going on. They want me to take care of it." He held his breath.

"Sorry, Mr. Rudd."

"Okay, then," he said, dropping his shoulders melodramatically. "I'll be seeing you. With Buchreiser next time."

"Sure," the guard shrugged. "Whatever you say." He slung his rifle back over his shoulder.

Michael pretended to walk away, then spun around, charged, and slammed his shoulder into the guard's midsection. The weapon flew into the air, and Michael smashed his fist into the guard's face again and again.

Michael searched his pockets, found a key, and opened the door.

Nicole came into his arms. He put down the rifle and hugged her. Moments later he said, "We've really got to hurry before someone comes. Where's Xingu?"

"He's dead."

"Which is exactly what you are going to be soon, Rudd."

Michael didn't have to look to know it was Buchreiser speaking. Nor did he have to see Escobar. His cloying aftershave preceded him.

Michael reached for the rifle.

"Go ahead," Escobar said. "I would love to shoot her head off."

Michael let his hand drop to his side.

Chapter Thirty-Eight

"Put down the weapon, Miles," Escobar said.

Michael dropped the automatic.

Nicole began to move next to him, her eyes full of sorrow.

"You keep your place, bitch," Escobar said. "Turn around, Rudd."

When he did, the two men were smiling. Buchreiser was holding a pistol.

"Get over there with her," Escobar ordered.

He stepped close to Nicole, who came into his arms.

"Enough!" Buchreiser shouted. "Stand apart. I want the pleasure of shooting you myself."

Nicole thought of Xingu's words: *Do not be afraid. You are ready.*

"You'd do better to try and stop the Indians. They're going to be in here any minute," she said.

Buchreiser threw back his head and roared. "Do not be ridiculous. At this moment there are hundreds of armed men from the capital on their way here in planes. Any Indian left here when they arrive will be dead."

Michael, knowing the Indians would be helpless against planes firing at them from above, thought about rushing his captors. But even if he subdued one, the other would surely kill him and Nicole.

"The planes can't land through fire," Nicole said.

"What fire?" Buchreiser demanded.

"The Indians will soon have your landing strip blazing."

Darkness passed over the drug czar's face, followed by a fierceness that made Nicole and Michael take an unconscious step backward. He glared at Michael, his face full of rage. "Who are you working for?"

As Buchreiser spoke, Michael could hear the Indian sounds all around—they had surrounded the palace. He thought he could identify a trumpet, a drum, a flute. The din of the music resembled human voices and made him shiver with hope.

"I said, who are you working for?" Buchreiser repeated.

"I'm not working for anyone. My name is Rush. You ordered my sister Ava's death." He heard Nicole draw in her breath.

"Ava? I do not know an Ava."

Furious that Buchreiser didn't even remember his sister, Michael made a quick move toward the German.

Buchreiser raised his pistol. "One more step. Just take one more step."

Michael stood still.

Now Nicole became aware of the musical uproar. It was all around them, getting louder and nearer. To her the noise was the combined voices of all the Indians of the jungle—brave, strong, defiant. As she listened, individual voices became monkeys howling and drumming, insects shrilling, snakes hissing, birds screeching, great reptilian tails slamming, and the roaring of big cats—the collective heartbeat of this primitive land. It seemed to her the ferocious yet sensuous pitch building all around was the jungle herself, moving inevitably to reclaim her land, to return to it the trees and flowers and animals the impudent owner of this obscene palace had thought he could keep out. Each musical variation pricked her consciousness. Something moved in her abdomen, and a chill raised goose bumps on her arms. Barely aware, she felt her muscles play along in counterpoint to the music till she felt that the sounds were her sounds, coming from her. She became the music.

Buchreiser heard the notes echoing, bouncing off the walls and ceilings. He would not reveal to the others how unnerving this noise the Indians called music was to him. "Pick up that phone, Escobar, and call security. I want to know just what is happening with those savage bastards outside."

Escobar dialed the phone. After a whispered exchange, he said to Buchreiser, "They say there are thousands out there. The whole jungle is filled with them."

"Have they attacked?" Buchreiser asked.

"Not yet."

"Send up one of our Indians to translate this monkey music."

Michael looked at Nicole, whose expression showed such disdain for her captors he had to glance down.

Listening to the music, Nicole even detected the skull trumpets and whistles of the Mayaruna, the tribe that had decided to kill all its newborns. *If the Mayaruna have joined the others*, she thought, *what tribe in the Amazon hasn't?*

At each interruption of the racket, the sudden silence of the room threatened to crush Buchreiser.

When the Indian arrived, the din outside had grown so close Michael could feel drumbeats through his soles.

"What does the music mean, Michu?" Buchreiser had to shout to be heard over the deafening noise.

Nicole saw that all the light had vanished from this Indian's eyes. The skin of his face was etched with deep scars like knife cuts.

"They say they will all be happy to die so their children can live on this land."

"Never mind that witch-doctor talk," Buchreiser spat out. "How many are there?"

"As many as fish in the river."

"The fools. They must have been planning this a long time."

"The music was already in them," Michu said, "like a machine ready to be turned on. Their music is natural. It has been in them, like something stuck in a bottle. They do not think about music from outside themselves. They feel and it comes out music."

"I did not ask for a goddamn lecture on your music, you pig's ass! When do they plan to attack?"

"They have already begun to fight. With the music," Michu said.

"Fight with music? What ignorance!"

Nicole saw that a strand of Buchreiser's perfectly coiffed hair had straggled loose across his beaded forehead. She saw a hint of triumph in the Indian's eyes.

"Get out!" Buchreiser commanded Michu.

Before he left, Nicole was certain she saw a smile begin at the corners of the Indian's lips.

Buchreiser turned to Nicole and Michael. "Your friends are going to fight guns and planes with music!" he sneered. "Too bad you are going to miss the fun. Go ahead, Escobar." The henchman aimed his pistol at Michael.

A madness glared in Michael's eyes.

"Say good-bye," Buchreiser said.

Michael's blood roared in his ears as he moved

toward Buchreiser. He didn't see Nicole's anguish before the shot exploded.

Michael realized to his amazement that he had not been hit. Instead it was Escobar lying on the floor, half his face shot away.

"That was for torturing Enrique," said the black woman who stood in the doorway with a .44 magnum revolver in her hands. Her bulging eyes glittered madly. She seemed to be in a religious trance.

"Now you, Karl."

At the sound of the next shot, Nicole moved toward Michael, pressing against him. A crack-toothed smile showed briefly on the mad-looking woman's lips before she slumped to the floor. Buchreiser had blown a hole in her chest.

"Filthy whore, I—" Buchreiser said.

Suddenly a great explosion blasted Buchreiser's words and splintered the bottle-glass windows.

Michael didn't know how long his total deafness lasted, for his ears kept buzzing. The acrid smell of burned chemicals filled his nostrils. The light fixture swayed threateningly. He turned to Nicole, who was holding her ears so tightly her knuckles were white. He wanted to tell her the explosions had been caused by the Indians igniting the planes on the airstrip. But before he could, another blast seemed to lift the entire palace right off its foundation.

"Get away from that window!" Buchreiser ordered.

The next blast made even the iron security grilles reverberate.

Michael pulled Nicole away while Buchreiser crunched over the shattered glass and looked out.

"Fucking savages! They have set fire to the whole strip. Now they are attacking the palace."

The Indian music had stopped, and now the air was filled with wild shouts. With the windows broken, the overheated jungle stench overcame the air conditioning. Sweat poured down Buchreiser's cheeks, dripping onto his rumpled tan safari suit and turning it dark.

All at once there came the sound of many machine guns firing.

Buchreiser said, "Get over by this window, you two. I want to enjoy watching you see this."

They clutched hands as they went over to the window. All they felt for each other was conveyed through that contact.

Michael tried frantically to come up with a way to surprise Buchreiser, but could not. Through the window they saw a half-dozen or more machine guns firing into the throng of Indians.

Nicole, watching their bodies being blasted to shreds, began to sob.

Michael marveled at the endless numbers of Indians still running out of the forest toward the palace. What he saw next filled him with futility and despair: The Indians were forming dozens of huge tight circles with their bodies and shooting arrows at the machine guns. He turned his attention back into the room, hoping for an opportunity to grab the German's gun.

"Look at those imbeciles," Buchreiser said with delight. "Arrows against machine guns."

Nicole felt Michael send an aura of warmth from his body to hers that was stronger than any embrace.

"What in hell are the fools going to try now?" Buchreiser said, laughing.

Nicole and Michael saw three large wedges of Indians appear from out of the forest canopy. Nicole recognized them as Mayaruna. One group held great shields; the other, arrows the length of a man, with large fireballs on one end. Still another group carried rifles.

"What are those balls at the end of their arrows?" Michael asked.

"They make them of latex," Nicole said.

"What do they expect rubber to do against machine guns?" Michael said.

"Maybe they will try slingshots next," Buchreiser sneered.

In amazement, the trio saw a huge Mayaruna troop shield the other group, holding the flaming arrows while the warriors carrying rifles fired. Soon hundreds of blazing arrows filled the sky. Many of the Indians holding the shields fell under the fire from the machine guns, and other Indians bearing shields ran out of the forest to replace the fallen ones. Another volley of the fiery missiles soon arced into the sky.

Nicole and Michael were delighted when a ball of burning latex and resin stuck to one of the machine guns. Then another arrow hit the machine gunner, and he burst into flames.

Finally believing what they had seen, Nicole and Michael squeezed hands.

"Damn monkeys!" Buchreiser yelled from where he stood behind them.

When they had watched the fourth machine gunner destroyed, Buchreiser shouted, "Get away from that window! You two will be my hostages against your Indian friends."

Chapter Thirty-Nine

Scattered fires had broken out in the corridors, and bodyguards carrying weapons and ammunition ran about, shouting. The panicked bray of a fire alarm resounded everywhere.

Passing a room, Nicole saw a gun and then heard a loud *whupp!* It took her a moment to realize that she had nearly been hit by a ricochet from one of Buchreiser's own men. She almost lost her breath.

Outside one of the banquet halls, a form took shape, and Nicole froze. Michael saw a figure leap forward and hurtle through the air, and he readied himself.

"Move aside!" Buchreiser shouted from behind them, firing a single shot. The right side of the attacker's face burst open. Nicole could see that the man was an Indian. In Buchreiser's eyes was a demonic look that Michael had never seen before, anywhere.

Blood spurted from the Indian's face and onto his chest. Buchreiser shot him in the face again as he sat on the floor. Then he pushed Nicole and Michael ahead.

Michael pressed Nicole's shocked face against his chest.

"Get moving, you two," Buchreiser commanded. "Up these stairs."

Michael searched for a way to take Buchreiser unaware, without success.

"Seems all these Indians are not your friends," the German snapped as they raced up the stairwell.

"No," Nicole managed to utter through nausea created by the smell of burning human flesh. "I don't know them all. But all of them are your enemies."

Suddenly a form appeared on the stairs above. "Is ... is that you, sir?"

As they drew nearer, Michael and Nicole realized that the voice belonged to a bodyguard. An arrow dangled from his right shoulder; his eyes were glazed by shock.

"I will send someone to help you," Buchreiser said as they passed the man.

Michael looked at Nicole. They knew from the German's tone that he was lying.

"Hurry, now," Buchreiser ordered.

All around was the lurid red-orange gleam of fire. The *whoosh* of flames could be heard in the distance, with the sounds of gunshots peppering the air.

The air was full of acrid smoke. Overhead, a

flaming beam fell in a shower of sparks and ignited a drapery.

"Hurry!" Buchreiser shouted.

Michael tore a pocket from his shirt and handed it to Nicole. Her face looked as if it had been wiped with crankcase oil. Her hair was wet and matted. "Put it over your face."

The smoke filled her lungs, clotting tissue that used to be filled with oxygen, making her dizzy. She tried to shake the picture of the dead Indian from her mind.

Michael whispered, "If I see an opening, I'm going to try again to surprise him."

Michael tore off his other pocket and placed it over his face. The heat was becoming intense. From nearby rooms and corridors they heard intermittent gunfire, shrieks, cries of agony from the wounded and dying. Two flights below, Michael glimpsed a cadre of Buchreiser's bodyguards setting up a machine gun.

At the next landing, Nicole pretended to faint and slumped against the wall.

"Get moving!" Buchreiser shouted.

Michael spun around to the German now. His look told the drug czar that if Nicole wasn't granted a moment's respite, Buchreiser would have to shoot them both right there.

"So we stop," Buchreiser concluded. "A few seconds only."

Michael took Nicole in his arms and held her. He

knew her athlete's body could tolerate great physical stress, and he realized that she was using this as a ploy to help him set the German up.

"Not yet," he whispered. "He's got to be distracted."

"You're right," she said. "Let's go."

"Come on," Buchreiser said. "Get going, now!" And he shoved Michael to his knees.

Anger exploded inside Michael.

With her eyes, Nicole implored him to contain himself. She glanced quickly from Michael to Buchreiser's gun and back to Michael.

As Michael got up and Nicole took his arm, a blazing piece of the ceiling crashed not a foot away.

Michael lunged at Buchreiser, but the German reacted too quickly.

"If you try that again, I will have only one hostage," Buchreiser said. "Now turn around and run ahead of me!" He jabbed his pistol into Michael's lower back.

They ran up yet another flight of stairs made sun-bright by the crackling flames, smoke blinding them and stifling their lungs. They stepped over the charred and bleeding bodies of guards and Indians and crunched through broken glass and the clink of spent cartridges.

"Aghhh!" came a sudden scream from above. The three looked up to see a body dropping toward them. It missed Michael narrowly and made an obscene sound as it slammed onto the next landing down. The victim was a bodyguard with an arrow piercing his chest.

"Move on!" Buchreiser shouted.

Nicole bit back nausea.

Through a window, Michael saw thick palls of smoke rising. *If we don't get out of this fire soon,* he thought, *Buchreiser won't have to kill us.*

Finally Buchreiser let them stop.

Turning away for just a second or two, he took what looked like a credit card from his wallet and began to place it in a slot in the wall.

Michael dove at Buchreiser, slammed into the German's body, and wrenched the gun from his grasp.

"Now!" Michael said to Buchreiser. "Now." His eyes wild with fury, he aimed the pistol at him.

"Be logical," Buchreiser said. "I will make you richer than you ever dreamed."

"You didn't even remember my sister's name!" He saw an image of Ava's decomposed flesh when he had gone to claim her body. He cocked the hammer.

Nicole tensed fiercely, knowing whatever Michael decided for Buchreiser would also decide her future, knowing he must decide. She could barely breathe.

Why can't I kill this bastard? he thought, shaking with rage. *He deserves to be killed.*

Michael felt his hand relax and lower the gun, as if by itself.

Suddenly all the wind gushed out of him. Buchreiser had kicked him in the stomach and was trying to wrest the gun from his hand. Gasping, Michael grappled to hold onto the gun.

Nicole, searching for an opening, moved around the two like a referee. Sensing an opportunity, she dove at Buchreiser. The German's fist met her squarely on the chin. Her face exploded in pain. When she threw herself at Buchreiser again, his powerful hand sent her flying. For a moment she heard the shouts of bodyguards and Indians outside. Then she heard nothing. She sank to the floor, unconscious.

Buchreiser kicked the gun from Michael's hand and it skidded across the room. When Buchreiser pounced toward his weapon, Michael took one long stride and drop-kicked him in the stomach, lifting him clear off the floor.

Instead of slowing Buchreiser down, the dropkick galvanized him. He began shouting sounds without words. He came at Michael, drove him back against the wall, and punched him solidly on the left side of the head.

When Buchreiser spun to lunge for the gun, Michael dove forward and caught an ankle, pulled the foot to his chest, and spun with it. Buchreiser went down and turned with the foot, kicked Michael on the side of the face with his free foot, and tore loose.

Roaring, he came back at Michael and hit him with an overhand right that struck his mouth and knocked it open. His knees went loose.

Just as Michael's head was beginning to clear, he saw Buchreiser coming at him again. This time the German launched himself into the air, coming at him feet first. Michael grabbed the heel of one of Buchreiser's feet and whipped it as high as he could. The first thing that hit the floor was Buchreiser's head. The German got slowly up onto his hands and knees, shaking his head. Once again Michael delivered the dropkick. Buchreiser landed on his back, rolled up, and as he got to his knees, Michael chopped him hard with the edge of his hand—a diagonal blow below the throat. Michael knew from the snapping sound that he had broken Buchreiser's collarbone. The German oozed onto the floor, his eyes glazed over. A thread of spittle hung from his mouth.

Michael watched unbelieving as Buchreiser began to climb back to his feet in slow motion. He was amazed that despite the broken collarbone, the slack, unhinged jaw, Buchreiser could even move. Crouched on his feet now, the German looked like a cornered animal. He was blinking slowly, as though trying to understand his fate.

Michael raised his hand to finish the drug czar. Buchreiser kicked him in the head, pushed open the door behind him, and was gone.

Michael lunged for the door.

"He will not get far," a man's voice said.

Michael was at once astonished and relieved to see that it was a Carrijura Indian leading a dozen others.

Michael found the door locked. Forming a wedge, Michael and the other Indians rammed it open. A great wind blasted the room. Michael ran after Buchreiser.

Soon he could see that the wind was being caused by the rotary blades of a helicopter. Buchreiser was already behind the controls. Michael tore open the door of the copter with his left hand and using all his leverage threw a right-handed chop against the bridge of Buchreiser's nose. Then, feeling the plane lifting off the pad, Michael jumped to the ground.

From his knees Michael saw a shower of arrows fill the air. A ball of burning latex and resin stuck to the body of the copter. Then another. A zapping sound rose over the whirring of the rotary blades as wires beneath the skin of the stricken copter shorted out.

As the chopper continued to lift off the pad, a burning arrow entered the open door of the copter and struck Buchreiser in the neck. Michael saw the German writhe in horror and pain.

Blinding purple sparks leaped up, replaced by red-orange fireballs that grew from the sparks eating along the body of the plane. Another arrow hit the fuselage. In seconds the gas tank blew, driving the main rotor into the sky like a child's toy. Immediately there was a terrible clapping sound. Michael saw pieces of Buchreiser's blackened body fly up and spin against the orange glare in the sky.

Only a plume of black smoke remained where the copter had been.

Epilogue

Michael placed the bouquet of Amazon lilies gently on Ava's grave. He stood and looked at her stone again, and at his mother's and father's, as if this visit might somehow ease the realization that his whole family was gone. He was unaware of the frigid New York March breeze.

Reaching for Nicole's hand, he led her quietly from the cemetery to his car.

"I don't want to go back to the city yet," he said. She nodded.

He drove to a cliff outside Port Jefferson that overlooked Long Island Sound. He touched the button that lowered the windows and, staring over the water, said in a faraway voice, "I never dreamed there'd come a time when I'd never be with Ava again."

Nicole touched his hand, looking deeply into his eyes.

"You know, I think I resented her, in a way," Michael said. "And I had, for a long, long time. I suppose it was guilt that sent me to the Amazon as much as anything else. She was such a mirror of what I'd been, maybe a better part of myself that I'd turned my back on. I felt like that part was gone with her then."

"I understand." She patted his arm. "Come on, let's take a walk."

They made their way gingerly down a path on the cliff face, and they strolled along the shore. Nicole was reminded of the summers she had spent as a little girl in the Grand Isle wetlands off Louisiana. She loved the smells of sea creatures, grasses, and sea mulch, of the saltwater with its hint of iodine. She could still picture her favorite childhood spot: a sandy bank along the water's edge where sea lavender bloomed. As she slipped through the grass, she could hear the tiny high-pitched scuttling of herds of fleeing crabs.

For a time, they rested quietly on a driftwood pile.

"Better?" she asked softly.

In response, he kissed her. With her, his entire life always seemed to be in progress, not yet shaped.

Nicole felt her lips lift into a soft smile. She watched as the gulls dipped and wheeled for scraps an old woman was tossing for them. Their squawks reminded her of Amazonian horned screamers. Abruptly, her mood shifted. She tried to hide it, but Michael had already sensed something.

"What?"

"Ava. Chochobo. Xingu."

"I know how you feel. Still, the Carrijura did give up selling their coca to the white man."

"Yes, and I wanted that very much. But not at such a cost."

"Of course you didn't."

"There's something else, too."

"What's that?"

"I never realized how much I was hiding out, back in the Amazon."

"You were sick. You couldn't leave."

"Not really. I had been well for nearly a year before I met you. I was just afraid. I'm still a little afraid, even though I have you now. But I never want to hide out again."

She had tried to tell him something like that in Colombia, but he hadn't been able to hear her then. It would never happen again.

"What are your plans?" he asked.

"It's time to go back to New Orleans. I'd like to work with young kids there. Coach, teach, work on the book Ava and I started."

"I wish I could help with the book. And you'll be a terrific teacher. You've already taught me a lot about life. Living life. I'm not a Weatherman anymore, Nicole. And I've always liked New Orleans."

Their hands touched. They sat for a long while, aware of the traces of new life in the sea.

FREE!!
BOOKS BY MAIL
CATALOGUE

BOOKS BY MAIL will share with you our current bestselling books as well as hard to find specialty titles in areas that will match your interests. You will be updated on what's new in books at no cost to you. Just fill in the coupon below and discover the convenience of having books delivered to your home. *PLEASE ADD $1.00 TO COVER THE COST OF POSTAGE & HANDLING.*

BOOKS BY MAIL

320 Steelcase Road E.,
Markham, Ontario L3R 2M1

In the U.S. –
210 5th Ave., 7th Floor
New York, N.Y., 10010

Please send Books By Mail catalogue to:

Name_____
    (please print)

Address_____

City_____

Prov._____ Postal Code _____

(BBM1)